Jodell caught his breath as the kid in the 7 barely slipped by the whirling car, making a nifty adjustment as he darted to the inside. He steered his Pontiac to a spot just below where he seemed to know the other car would be by the time he got there. The driver that was directly behind the 7 wasn't so lucky. He tagged the spinning car hard in the side and the crowd stood and groaned in unison at the viciousness of the impact.

The next lap past, the kid pulled his Pontiac right up on the back of the Ford that was riding in third place. The Ford's driver would have none of it, though. He tried to ease down the track and cut him off. But the kid held his line like a pro and slid on by to take over the spot.

"Can't somebody find out that kid's name?" Jodell asked.

"Let's see." The man shuffled some papers. "Wilder. Rob Wilder. I don't know why you're so worried about him, though. He won't get past them other two boys if we run 'til Monday."

Jodell merely smiled.

"We'll see."

Follow all the action . . .
From the qualifying lap
to the checkered flag!

Rolling Thunder!

Forthcoming from Tor:

Rolling Thunder
STOCK CAR RACING

YOUNG GUNS

Kent Wright
and Don Keith

TOR®

A TOM DOHERTY ASSOCIATES BOOK
NEW YORK

This is a work of fiction. All the characters and events portrayed in this book are either products of the author's imagination or are used fictitiously.

ROLLING THUNDER #5: YOUNG GUNS

Copyright © 2000 by Kent Wright & Don Keith

A Tor Book
Published by Tom Doherty Associates, LLC
175 Fifth Avenue
New York, NY 10010

www.tor.com

Tor® is a registered trademark of Tom Doherty Associates, LLC.

ISBN: 0-812-54506-0

First edition: April 2000

Printed in the United States of America

0 9 8 7 6 5 4 3 2 1

"There are only three true sports: bull fighting, mountain climbing, and automobile racing. Anything else is merely a game."

—Ernest Hemingway

THE KID

*I*t didn't take much to send the old driver reeling back through the years. A particular sound, a distinctive smell, just the right flutter of a checkered flag at the entrance to some fast food place, and he was instantly swept away again. Caught up in the memories of a time when he was the one who crawled behind the wheel and steered one of those boom-throated machines around a racetrack, intent on leaving the rest of them choking on his exhaust.

He never had to look for the reminders. They came floating at him all the time.

The hard part was to drag himself back to the present.

Or to find the desire to even try.

Thunder rumbled in the distance like faraway artillery fire, punctuating the periodic sheet lightning that lit up the western night sky. So long as the rain held off, though, those folks who were gathered in the bleachers that ran along the front stretch of the small racetrack welcomed the wonderful cooling breeze that blew in off the storm front. They cheered lustily at every jagged streak of lightning, every answering grumble of thunder. It had been a brutally hot week already, the final few days of an unusually dry spring, and a threat that a stifling summer likely lurked ahead of them. Farmers had already been praying for a drink of water for their emerging corn or soybeans. But now, despite the need, those who had come to watch the Wednesday night feature at the little racetrack prayed it would hold off for just a few more hours.

"Let them get the race in, Lord," they prayed. "Then send the rain for the crops. If it be Thy will, of course."

It was an unusually large crowd that had gathered, despite the threat of bad weather and it being midweek. Tags on the cars in the gravel parking lot showed visitors from a variety of counties across Tennessee and Alabama. Sure, they were there for the special card of races that would go a long way toward deciding the track champion for the year. But many were there, too, to meet in person a special guest who had stopped by for an autograph session before the actual racing began.

The lines had formed early at the rickety old gates that led into the track. Many still wore their dusty overalls, their factory uniforms with their names stitched over their pockets, their short-sleeved dress shirts and out-of-fashion ties they had worn that day to the bank or car dealership. They clearly came straight to the races from work.

And most of them dutifully queued up to see the

special guest and get an autograph, take a picture with an arm around him or with him holding one of their kids, or simply share a few words with one of the legends of stock car racing.

They noticed that he still looked like an athlete, especially when he stood and moved around the table to stand next to one of them so someone could snap a picture. He was tall, lean, well-muscled; his hand-shake was was sure and solid, and he moved with the ease and grace of a football player (which he had once been) or a dancer (which he most certainly had not). Only a mix of gray in what had once been crow-feather–black hair, the lines on his face, and a slight paunch gave him away. It was not hard for any of the fans to imagine him crawling into a racecar again and effortlessly guiding it for five hundred miles on the hottest of summer days.

And more than one of them remarked to another about the man's eyes. Those deep blue eyes seemed to grab you, capture you, and pull you in with their clear intensity.

The old driver smiled sincerely at every single one of them as they came by, tirelessly posed with them, signed whatever they thrust in front of him. It still amazed him that they would want such a small piece of him, that his scrawled signature on a trading card could bring such delight to anyone. This was his eighth such event in seven different states in the last three days, despite the fact that he had not driven a car in a half-dozen years, had not actually been be-hind the wheel of a car that had won a race in better than eight. Yet they still came, still seemed excited to meet him, still talked animatedly of races and wrecks and wins he had been a part of, including many he himself had long since forgotten.

Whirlwind promotional trips such as this brought back memories for him. Memories of those brutal early times when they would race three or four days in a row, usually at tracks that happened to be hundreds of miles apart. Days with practically no sleep and filled with debilitating work, each one of them a blur of racing, fixing, driving, and racing again.

Things were certainly different now, though. Flying in his own plane, sleeping in luxury hotel rooms provided by his sponsors, and eating in nicer restaurants with cloth napkins and real china plates were all a far cry from the days when the old driver had first been getting himself established in racing. Back then, most of his sleeping had been in the backseat of the car in some parking lot or on the side of the road somewhere. Vienna sausages and soda crackers had been the normal cuisine. The times and the demands of the sport had certainly changed for him. And he would be the first to admit that it had been mostly for the better.

It had been the needs of the sponsors that had made the biggest difference. Back then, a driver simply had to show up at the track where they were going to race, run hard, and win enough money to get to the next race. Nowadays, keeping the sponsor happy was almost as important as winning the races. Maybe more so. That meant endless days on the road, doing the required promotional work, attending the events, shaking the hands of thousands of customers or dealers or brokers or employees while smiling broadly for the money. For many drivers, the race on Sunday was actually their only chance to relax and get away from the pressures of the business side of racing.

Racing had become more and more about sponsorship money, and it took lots of it to mount a chal-

lenge to the other teams that showed up each week. To be competitive, a team had to have cash. It was as necessary as oil and gas and tires. And to keep the money, it was necessary to keep those sponsors happy. Winning certainly helped in that regard. Leading a race got the maximum television time. The winner's circle was the best place to flash the sponsors' logos. But for the driver, there were far more hours spent on stages and platforms, in parking lots and interviews in front of television cameras than he ever passed in the cockpit of the racecar.

Now, as the old racer signed cards and glad-handed the patrons, he occasionally glanced to the west, to where the storm boiled and blustered. He had his plane parked at a strip five miles away and would have to pilot it on to east Tennessee later that night. He didn't relish having to burrow through thunderheads to get home.

But he could also catch a random glimpse of the dusty garage area outside the first turn wall. He could see row upon row of trucks, trailers, and racecars. From the gleaming Late Model stockers to the beat-up old Limited Sportsman cars to a swarm of mini-stocks, there seemed to be racecars lined up everywhere. And people swarmed all around them.

The old driver knew precisely what types would be milling around down there among all the equipment, too. There were the local hotshots with their own sponsor money to play with, their crewmembers in matching uniforms, their cars shined and ready. Then there would be the dirt-poor part-time racers who scrambled for every dime they could get to try to field a competitive car, the money spent for parts instead of paint jobs or polish or uniforms. And then there would be just about every other kind of driver and team in between. Many of them had traveled a hundred or more miles just to race here on this sultry, stormy night.

Had the old driver been able to see more clearly, he might have noticed a particular red car. A young kid, eighteen or nineteen years old at the most, struggled with three or four of his friends to replace the radiator on the battered car in time to run it in one of the late-model heat races. The car was pockmarked with body damage from some previous wars and the makeshift crew had already tried to bang out anything that might get in the way during the race. The number 7, which had been painted on the side of the car, had been almost obliterated in some type of close encounter with the tire of another racecar; someone had hand-lettered it back, so it was almost legible again. Even though it was obviously a challenge to simply get the car into good enough shape to run, they seemed to be doing so with an abundance of enthusiasm.

The young crew attempting to resurrect the red car would have surely brought back more memories for the old driver if he could have seen them. But Jodell Bob Lee was busier than ever, accepting the praise of those who had lined up to meet him, signing his autograph in his sweeping hand. The crowd was excited about meeting one of their heroes, a man who was now the owner of a team on the Winston Cup circuit and a former star driver there. He was in his fortieth year in the game and he still relished every minute of it. But since he had finally parked his own racecar in the early nineties in favor of someone younger, someone with a young man's reflexes, it seemed the demands on his time had only increased. In addition to trying to watch the car he owned run in every race he could, he still did appearances for his sponsors whenever they requested. He suspected there would come a day when they would no longer ask.

Now, here he was, on the last lap of this three-day trip, going above and beyond the call of duty for one of his old friends. He didn't usually stop by small tracks in the middle of nowhere for a Wednesday night feature anymore. Even if he had been so inclined, the pressure of an out-of-control schedule would likely prevent it. But the call had come and he had agreed to do it when he checked his itinerary and saw it was only a quick jag from his preplanned route back home from a luncheon at a manufacturing plant in the Midwest.

He had to laugh when his old friend who had made the request had asked him where he was at the moment.

"Tell you the truth, I don't remember," he had said, then reached into the night table next to the hotel bed and looked at the telephone book cover. "Kansas City. Yep, that's where I am. Kansas City."

But not only was this stop a favor, it also gave him a chance to see a bit of real small-track racing, a rare treat for him nowadays. He suspected that his appearance allowed the owner/operator to squeeze in an extra night of racing at his track with the chance of drawing a decent crowd. He knew, too, that such an extra race could be the difference in making money this year or not.

Jodell Lee had known Nathan Summers for better than thirty years. And he remembered the night when the track owner had suddenly decided on the spur of the moment that fifteenth place paid twenty dollars in prize money after all, simply because he knew a particular young driver who had finished fifteenth needed the cash to buy gas to get back home. Or the time they had shown up hungry and Nathan had fed them all free out of the concession stand. "Appearance food," he had called it, making it up on the spot.

That's one of the reasons that Jodell had not hesitated when the call came. A quick detour and some autograph time would hardly be too much of an imposition to help repay such a debt.

He owed it to his fans, too. He suspected they might not be thrusting programs at him to sign too much longer either. Many of the kids lining up in front of him weren't even born the last time he won a race. His friend, Richard Petty, had taught him the value of signing autographs long ago. Many a race, he and Richard would still be sitting on the back of a hauler when most of the other teams had begun pulling out, still jawing with the fans and signing.

"I seen you and old Bill Elliott get together that time at Charlotte."

"I was there the night you and Waltrip had that race to the finish at Nashville. I was pulling for you, but I guess it wasn't enough."

"I was watching you on TV when you hit that wall at Daytona. My, that was a hard lick!"

Every one of them seemed to have a particular Jodell Lee memory. He acknowledged them all, though most of it was a blur to him now. It went on for over two hours; ultimately, it was the thunder of the mini-stock engines cranking up that caused the line to thin, the crowd finally finding their seats for the beginning of the racing for that evening. With a quick glance at the weather, Jodell tried to rush the last few fans through so he could get back to the plane and head once again for home.

One of the track workers ushered Jodell up to the

promoters' box where Nathan Summers stood, happily surveying the big crowd in the stands, the bountiful harvest of racecars down on the track, and the thunderstorm that had so far cooperated by holding back. Jodell shook his hand and examined the catered spread that covered a big table by the side.

"You may as well have a sandwich, Jodell," he offered. "Momma ain't gonna have supper waitin' this late nohow."

If Hollywood had been casting a racetrack owner and promoter, they would have made sure the actor looked exactly like Nate Summers. He was short, dumpy, smoked a cheap cigar, and wore out-of-style polyester slacks, a short-sleeved white dress shirt, a wide tie that ended six inches above his belt buckle, and a fedora with a small green feather stuck in the band.

"You don't have any turnip greens and cornbread, do you?" Lee asked with a grin, already wondering how he could gracefully make an exit and be on his way.

"Naw, but I got some ham and cheese and stuff. Besides, you may want to stay and watch some of these boys run. We got some good cars and drivers for being so far out in the sticks and it being the middle of the week and all."

Jodell was bone-tired and ready to spend a night in his own bed for a change. But just then, a pack of cars pulled out onto the track with a roar, and the crowd stood to show their appreciation of the racing that was about to begin.

Jodell couldn't help it. He pulled a soda from a bucket of ice and stepped to the front of the box to watch the start of the first heat race.

The exhaust smell that rose on the moist wind to the booth was as intoxicating as any liquor. The old driver was quickly drunk with the aroma of it. He could imagine the tickling vibration of the gearshift as he cupped it in his hand, the way the gas pedal throbbed beneath his foot, the hot breeze that spilled through the window with its load of vapors, dust, and tire grit.

And as the green flag fell, it all came rushing back in full force. How stimulating it was to feel the power in the motor when he stomped it and made a beeline for the corner. How the vigor of it shoved him hard back into the seat until he could barely reach the wheel and he had to pull himself forward to grab for the next gear so he could pick off the old boy who lollygagged along in front of him. And how his heart raced as he guided the car to the front, for the lead.

Always straining for the front, for the lead.

As the mini-stock cars circled the track to start the second heat race he finally turned from the spectacle of it all and walked to the buffet. He filled a plate, and then as he ate he chatted with others in the box who were also enjoying the night at the track. Jodell knew that this was racing at its basic level: where those with a dream of moving up to the highest level of the sport honed their skills and waited impatiently for their big break; where those who had long since abandoned that dream still lived out their primal desire to run and to win, never mind the venue. But whether driving careers started or ended here, it was at tracks just like this one all over the country where the purest racing still took place, just as it had when Jodell Lee had been running for gas and parts money and a small, pewter trophy.

He missed it sometimes. It had been his roots, his

apprenticeship. But time and too many encounters with track walls had taken their toll. Still, deep down in his belly, the competitive fires burned as hotly as ever. Even as he munched his sandwich and watched the mini-stocks roar out of the corner to take the checkered flag for the end of the first heat race, he could feel the hairs on his arms stand up, his heart beat a bit faster.

For Jodell Lee, winning had always been everything. Second place was the same as dead last. As those wins became harder and harder to come by, he had finally been forced to admit that it took more than desire to get it done. The edge was gone and it was time to move on, to stop denying another young gun his own shot at the big time. Standing here, though, watching those little cars dart and dive for the lead, the old desire came bubbling back to the surface just as it always did. Just as it always would until he had run his last lap in life.

"Bet I can read your mind," Nathan Summers said as he walked up and put an arm around Jodell's shoulder. "Say the word and I bet one of them would give up his seat and let you drive."

The promoter's cigar made Jodell's eyes water.

"Shoot, Nate, these boys could drive circles around me these days."

"Hell if that's so! I still say you was the best driver I ever seen. And I don't just say it when you're standing here neither."

Down on the track, the crowd was cheering as the first of the three late-model heat races was about to start. The clouds still spat sparks out beyond the third turn and despite the show, Jodell was wondering how he could graciously break away and get started for home.

"Nathan, as always I have enjoyed your hospitality, but it's been a long week already. I think it's time for me to head on to the house."

"Jodell, you don't know how much your visits help," Nathan said sincerely, swinging his arm over the crowded grandstand. "I don't know any way I could ever repay you for all the help you've given me over the last couple of years."

"Now, Nathan, it's like I tell you every time. You paid me up front a long, long time ago."

"Jodell, that was so long ago that I can't even remember what it was."

"It was June of 1961 and that money let us get back home and fix the car to make the next three races. And we were in the top five in all three of 'em."

Down below, the late-models had lined up at the start/finish line, getting set for a heat race. Jodell bent slightly at the waist and leaned to catch the smell of the gas fumes again, to feel the rumble of their powerful motors against his chest when they cranked up. The bigger cars had clearly recaptured the old driver's attention. He had forgotten the sandwich now and was intently watching the drivers climb in and buckle up.

"Okay, Jodell, I sure ain't gonna try to talk you out of coming over to see us anytime you want to. But long as you're here, do me one more favor. I want you to watch these two drivers gettin' ready to run this heat. Both these guys are hot and I think they could have a shot at moving up to Grand National. Just look them over real quick in the heat race and then I'll have somebody run you back out to the airport."

Jodell had that look in his eye, that set to his jaw. A sudden streak of lightning unzipped the sky over the far side of the track but he hardly seemed to notice. The rolling thunder blended perfectly with the roar of the engines as they came to life.

"Okay. Fair enough."

"Good," Summers said with a grin.

With the competitive situation on the Grand National and Cup circuits these days, car owners were always on the lookout for fresh young driving talent. Jodell was no exception. While he was satisfied with the current driver in his car, an owner never knew when he might need a replacement, or when he might be pressured into fielding a second team.

"Which ones?" he asked, as he studied the nine cars that had lined up for the heat.

"That orange number 27. That's Slick Wilson. He won more than half the races I had last year and he's won a bunch this year already. That black 18 in the row behind him is the other guy, Stewart Asbee. He won four races last year and has split up the wins with Slick about equal this year."

"Slick, huh? Now that *is* a racer's name," Jodell said. Nathan Summers couldn't tell by the tone of his voice if he was serious or not.

Jodell carefully studied the two drivers Nathan had pointed out. Each had perfectly polished racecars, the lettering and numbering professionally done, with each toting rows of sponsor decals down their sides and on their gleaming hoods and rear decks. No doubt about it. They had money behind their efforts. He promised himself he would keep an open mind but it certainly appeared that their success could easily be the result of better equipment, not necessarily the talent of their drivers. He would find out once they got to racing.

Then, at the last instant, a group of kids pushed up

the battered red Pontiac with the number seven painted on its sides. A kid with a mop of blond hair wearing a dirty old driving suit ran alongside the car, pushing and steering, while the other boys helped shove it from behind into the last position on the track.

The old driver grinned. That sight looked eerily familiar to him. Except for the blond hair, that could easily have been him down there in the oil- and grease-stained driver's suit, scrambling to get in and strapped down for the start. And the other guys could have been his cousin Joe Banker, his friend Bubba Baxter, and the rest of their ragtag crew from a good forty years before. And the Pontiac could have been their own old Ford, not necessarily the prettiest car to take the flag, but often the fastest.

What would she have tonight? How about the others? Could sheer want and intuition take the win if the car wasn't right? Or would somebody else's silly mistake cost them a payday when they needed it so badly? So very badly?

"Jodell? Did you hear what I was telling you about those boys?"

"Sorry, Nate. I was looking at those kids with that red Pontiac. Who is he?"

"Aw, Jodell. Darn it, I can't even remember his name. Real nice kid, though. They showed up about a month ago with that old clunker of a car. They do okay for a little while but the car usually blows up on 'em before they can finish. If hard work paid anything, they would win every time. Somebody said they were from somewhere up close to the Tennessee line. You got to hand it to them for still trying."

Jodell had borrowed a pair of binoculars from someone and was studying the Pontiac's crew. Something familiar about them fascinated him.

"They do look like a hard-working bunch. Can't any of them be older than eighteen or nineteen," Jodell observed.

While they talked, the string of cars rolled off the line and began to circle the three-eighths-mile track behind the convertible pace car. The two hotshot drivers Nathan had pointed out kept gunning their cars' engines, swaying from side to side as if they really needed to warm their tires for a quick heat race. One of them suddenly zoomed up and threatened to pass the pace car, then the other guy darted up and gave the first one a hard butt in the rear end.

Was it really eagerness to get started or simple stupidity? Jodell held judgement until he could see them run. With the dollars behind them, they certainly didn't seem to have any worries about tearing up the equipment.

The green flag fell, and with a roar the cars dashed to the line as the crowd rose and cheered them past. The 27, Wilson, and the 18 of Asbee quickly jumped out in front of the others by a dozen car lengths. Jodell watched them for a moment before the red 7 caught his eye. On the very first lap, the kid piloting the car passed three other racers, putting himself in seventh place. The next time by, he executed a perfect pass to the inside going down into turn one and picked himself off another spot.

The two at the front were showboating, pushing and rubbing all over each other in their fight for the lead. They were so intent on smashing into each other that the driver of the 18 car, running second, missed several obvious opportunities to pass and take the lead. Jodell could only stand there and shake his head. These guys weren't especially good drivers at all, at least not from what he had seen so far. They were simply a couple of hotheads, more interested in running over the competition than in actually out-driving anybody for a win.

The kid in the Pontiac was a different story. Even on the tight three-eighths-mile track, he seemed to be concentrating on the car directly in front of him, and he was obviously picking his spots to make his moves. He would run hard up onto the back end of a car, then fade high or dive down low, forcing the driver to run a shade deeper into the turn than he wanted to. That would cause the car in front of him to kick up just enough for the kid to squeeze by cleanly on either side.

By the time the checkered flag fell after ten laps, the kid was parked right up on the back bumpers of the 18 and the 27, solidly in third place. He had come from last in the field to claim a nice starting spot in the feature. And the old driver, Jodell Lee, was duly impressed.

"What you think?" Nathan asked proudly.

"Nathan, that was some pretty good racing. The kid in the 7 car worked the field over beautifully."

"The 7? What about the other two?"

"Oh, those guys? Well, they run hard enough for sure. I'm just not sure they run smart." He checked the lingering clouds, glanced at his watch, and winked at Summers. "I tell you what. Let me call the wife, and I think I'll hang around and watch your guys in the feature. How about that?"

"Sure thing. That was just a heat race. You'll see how good them boys are then."

Jodell found a quiet corner and placed a quick call

on his cell phone. Catherine was still awake, waiting to hear from him. He knew better than to lie to her. She guessed from the excitement in his voice anyway that he had decided to watch the race at the track where he had only intended to sign some autographs and be on his way.

"Let me guess. You're going to stay for the feature."

Even through the slight hiss of the phone line, he could tell there was more amusement than anger in her voice.

"Yeah, there's a kid out here that I want to see some more of."

"Let me guess again. He drives like a young Jodell Bob Lee."

"I don't know that anybody will ever be that good, Cath. . . ."

She laughed then at the sincere tone in his words. She still had the most beautiful laugh he had ever heard.

As he folded up the phone, he almost motioned for Nate to send over the driver to take him on to the airport after all. He missed her terribly. He wanted to be with her. But then he heard the engines starting up again and there was the old feeling in his gut. He stepped back to the window and watched the cars pull away.

As they circled for the last time before the green flag waved, the public address announcer told the crowd that Jodell was staying around to watch the feature. Jodell acknowledged their ovation with a wave out the open window.

As he watched the cars get ready for the start, he glanced at his watch, then at the black clouds that still piled up toward the west, strobing lightning. He hoped that the stay would be worth it. Was what he had seen in the heat race for real or had he simply witnessed a lucky piece of driving? He had to find out. And the only way to do that was to sit patiently and watch.

Twenty-six cars had made the field. Two or three more had not been able to get repaired in time after wrecks in their heats. The kid in the red number 7 Pontiac was lined up in the seventh position as a result of his finish in the heat race, and that was directly behind the two guys Nate had pointed out. The officials elected not to invert the field. That meant that the starting order was based on the finishes from the heats.

Jodell studied the starting field carefully, sizing up the competition. He knew the two hotshots from the first race would likely beat and bang their way to the front, and he fully expected they would wreck several other cars in the process. The winner of the third heat looked as if he might be tough to beat as well.

The green flag flew over the field, sending the horde of cars off into the first turn with a deafening roar. From the start, there was the inevitable small-track give and take going on throughout the field as everyone jockeyed for position going through turns one and two. The leader, Slick Wilson in the 27 car, had clearly jumped the start and now pointed the rest of the field down the backstretch. The 18 had already pushed his way into third by rudely drop-kicking the car in front of him out of the way.

That old boy likely needs a bodyguard after a race, Jodell thought. *Wonder if he drives a bulldozer when he's not racing?*

But as he picked up the kid in the number 7, he was pleased to see that he was sitting there, waiting patiently in line, trying to stay out of trouble. Jodell smiled. There would be plenty of time in the fifty-lap feature to make a move. He seemed to be savvy enough to know that it was best to wait for the field to settle down for a lap or two, to let them get the bumping and paint-swapping out of their systems, and then he could start making his way up to the front. There was no need to be the cause of a wreck while trying to win the race on the first couple of laps.

Before the race was ten laps old, the 18 of Asbee was sitting in second place trying to run down the leader, who had pulled out to a four–car-length lead. The kid in the 7 had gotten around a couple of cars by then and now sat in fifth place. The field was finally starting to string out all the way around the track and that gave room for some serious racing. Jodell felt his own pulse quicken.

The start and the finish were usually exciting, but this was where the race got interesting!

The leaders were beginning to catch up to the back of the field, to those cars who had been lucky to even make the feature. As he blundered past one of the slower cars, the 27 punched the poor racer hard in the rear, spinning him out and bringing out the yellow caution flag. Jodell shook his head. There had been no cause for such a move. The guy could have skirted the slower car and put him down without resorting to a bump that could get anyone behind tangled up. And that could ruin the night for some folks who might not be as able to afford such bad luck as Wilson was.

Just then, though, Jodell caught his breath as the kid in the 7 barely slipped by the whirling car, making a nifty adjustment as he darted to the inside. He steered his Pontiac to a spot just below where he seemed to know the other car would be by the time he got there. The driver that was directly behind the

7 wasn't so lucky. He tagged the spinning car hard in the side and the crowd stood and groaned in unison at the viciousness of the impact.

The caution allowed the kid to pull up on the rear bumper of the fourth-place car as the track crew came out to drag the wrecked hulks off the course and shovel compound onto the spilled oil and gas. Jodell imagined he could see the grin on the kid's face. And when he picked up the binoculars, it was confirmed. Inside the car, the boy was smiling broadly, pounding the dashboard with his fist, and clearly having the time of his life.

He was a driver. The car seemed to be set up well. If she held together, it could get interesting out there before this race was over!

The caution allowed all the cars to catch up in a tight bunch, with the half-dozen or so slower lapped cars lined up on the inside of those that were still on the lead lap. Over the next twenty laps, those slower cars would keep getting snarled up with the ones that were leading.

Jodell stood up straight, stretching his tired back as he watched the cars flash past the start/finish line to take the green flag once again. The 27 jumped the re-start once again and took a three-car lead going into the first turn. None of the officials seemed to notice and the crowd cheered lustily as one of their local favorites had the lead, no matter how he had done it. The next four cars were lined up in single file as they tried to clear the lapped cars that chugged along on the inside.

Diving down into the third turn, the Chevrolet that was running in front of the red Pontiac tried to drive a little deeper into the corner, angling to get a run on the third place driver. The car obviously didn't maintain traction as it hit the turn and it slid upward on the track, barely missing the back bumper of the car in front of it. Jodell held his breath, then watched approvingly as the kid in the Pontiac anticipated the move and pounced.

Had the young driver been watching the Chevy already? Did he know from having followed it around the track that it would tend to lose its grip in a move like that? Was the kid that sharp or was it simply a lucky guess?

The 7 ran the same steady lap he had been running all along and pushed the nose of his car into the spot just as the Chevy pushed up and out of his way. It appeared as if the Chevy's driver was kindly moving over and letting him past, but Jodell knew better. The Pontiac muscled on past the Chevy through the center of the turn and easily claimed the spot.

Jodell watched the move carefully, amazed that such a young kid could show so much patience. Most drivers, including some in Grand National and Winston Cup, could benefit from such composure. The more he watched the kid drive, the more impressed he was. He grabbed a stopwatch from the desk in front of him, lined up the Pontiac with the flagpole, and clicked the start button. If what he suspected was true, the times for each lap would be remarkably consistent.

The next lap past, the kid pulled his Pontiac right up on the back of the Ford that was riding in third place. Coming off the fourth turn, the blond youngster pulled to the inside and outraced the Ford down the stretch and into turn one. The Ford's driver would have none of it, though. He tried to ease down the track and cut him off, bluffing that he would rather slam into him than give up the position. But the kid held his line like a pro and slid on by to take over the spot. Now all that stood between him and the lead were the two nuts in the 27 and the 18.

"Say, Nathan. Can't somebody find out that kid's name?" Jodell asked. The lap count showed there were ten more circuits to go. The watch confirmed that he was driving an amazingly consistent race.

"Hey, Steve!" Nathan yelled to someone else in the box. "What's that kid in the 7 car's name?"

"Let's see." The man shuffled some papers. "Wilder. Rob Wilder."

"That's it, Jodell. Rob Wilder. I don't know why you're so worried about him, though. He won't get past them other two boys if we run 'til Monday."

Jodell merely smiled.

"We'll see."

Asbee in the 18 was glued to the rear bumper of the 27, giving him a hard bump in the rear as they entered each corner. Neither driver seemed to be concerned about the car that had claimed third place behind them. They were more interested in their own private battle for the first spot. The kid appeared to have sensed it and took his time, looking high and then low, testing the line he would eventually need to follow to get by.

Jodell watched him laying back, testing different routes around the track each time through.

Is he doing what I think he's doing? he asked himself. *Is he looking for the best line?*

With six laps to go, the 18 ran hard into the back of the 27 once more as they drove off into turn one. The fans seemed to be enjoying the tussle between these two familiar drivers. It was one that was probably repeated often at this track, as either one or the other would eventually claim the race. With the bump, the driver of the 27 was forced to ease off on the gas to keep his car beneath him and under control. The kid seemed to intuitively see the opportunity as it presented itself. He took the outside line through turns one and two. That allowed him to pull even with the 18 as he ran in second place. But the other driver was more preoccupied with shoving the 27 out of his way. However, since he was holding the preferred line coming off the corner, the line he had already scouted out, the kid was able to nose ahead of him. Slick Wilson in the 27 pushed out to the wall as he recovered from Asbee's shove, but he kept the lead. It was clear, too, that the 18 was a good racecar and would not give up so easily.

The kid stood his ground when the 18 tried to bump him out of the way as they went into turn three. Wilson tucked his car down low, blocking Asbee and the inside. Wilder held his line in the 7 car, though, running deeply into the turn. Then the kid got a fender on the outside of Wilson, the leader. Wilson was so worried about Asbee in the 18 behind him that he never noticed the kid coming up on his outside. And he certainly wasn't expecting anyone there. The inside was the quickest way around this track, wasn't it?

The swirling mass of fans in the stands had changed their allegiance in a flash. They were on their feet, cheering on the kid in the old red Pontiac. For once, the two bullies who had been dominating the track for so long were in an actual race for the win. Wilder was somehow able to pull even with Wilson's number 27 on the outside as they crossed the start/finish line and they raced off side by side into the first turn. The track announcer was virtually screaming into the microphone, describing the struggle to those who could see it perfectly well for themselves.

Jodell stood there, smiling broadly. The Wilder kid was outfoxing the two hotshots as surely as some cagey veteran might. It was doubtful that his equipment was anywhere near what the other two drivers were chauffeuring. He was doing it with ability, intuition, and smarts, and nothing more.

The two cars, the 27 and the 7, rubbed fenders going down into turn one, kicking up puffs of smoke from where the tires rubbed against sheet metal. Then, as they exited the turn, the 27 tried to run the kid up and into the outside wall. Wilder held his line, even as the two cars slammed together hard. The 18 was still back there, too, and he bumped the 27 in the back end, getting him even more loose. That caused the 27 and the 7 to slam together again, even harder this time, as Wilson tried to gather the car back up and keep it from careening away.

Wilder sawed back and forth at the wheel, trying to hold his own car straight and keep it off the wall. He drove a little deeper into the corner than Wilson and pulled ahead by half a car length in the center of the turn. Wilson, though, was desperately trying to hang on as Asbee's 18 popped him again in the rear bumper. The kid used their dirty driving to his advantage as he pulled ahead finally for the lead.

But it was only by half a car length as they crossed the stripe with three laps to go. Except for a few lapped cars, the track ahead of the kid was clear. He would have to push his concentration level even higher now, show some wisdom, let his own instincts take over, and quell the urge to do something foolish.

Jodell Lee could clearly imagine what the youngster was feeling, as surely as if he was wired in; as if he had crawled into the kid's skin and taken hold of the wheel himself.

Don't push her too hard. How does the handling feel?

Lord, don't let the motor give out now!

What was that noise?

Think. Shove aside the tingling thrill that only comes to the one who is leading. Time for that in a minute.

Is that tire going down on the right front?

Concentrate now. Do what you know you have to do. What your gut tells you to do.

Do I want this win bad enough to step out and claim it now? Yes!

Think, dadgummit! And be smooth. Drive smooth!

It's our race now to win or lose.

And we are going to win it.

As if he could read Jodell's mind, the kid maintained the same smooth, steady rhythm he had run throughout the race. How rare to see someone so young and so obviously hungry for a win showing the patience to do the very thing he had to do to get the victory.

This kid Rob Wilder was a natural!

The side-by-side battle finally fell by the wayside and the kid pulled away to lead all by himself as he followed the line around the track that he knew was best for his car. The people in the grandstands were still out of their seats, urging the red Pontiac on en masse. They seemed to sense that they had seen something new and exciting this stormy night, some kind of special driver, not another fender cruncher with more bluster than racing ability.

In the box on the top of the grandstand, Jodell Lee could only smile and shake his head as he watched the 7 car take the white flag. One lap to go. Had he actually seen what he thought he had, or was even that last move merely a lucky pass for the lead? Was he so desperate to find new driving talent that he was seeing more than was there?

But then he watched Wilson drive up on the kid's rear and give him one last hard bump to try and break him loose. It was a hard enough jolt to shake most drivers, to cause them to over-correct or tap the brake to keep control. But Wilder held on as if it was nothing at all, kept his wits like a veteran, and drove on. He outran the 27 down the backstretch and then steered hard through three and four, never giving an inch to the trailing cars, using up the entire track to keep the other two from sneaking up beside him.

As he dashed under the wildly waving checkered flag the kid's left arm was already pumping outside the window. He had won! Jodell knew exactly how that felt. And he almost did a jig himself in his own elation at seeing such a race, such apparent talent.

Jodell grabbed Nathan's arm as soon as the checkered flag fell.

"Well, I'll be a monkey's uncle," Summers said with a grin.

"Come on, take me down to the infield. I want to meet this kid."

"Sure, Jodell," Nathan answered, a puzzled look on his face as they headed out the door before the boy had even finished his victory lap.

"Man, Nathan! That was something else. I can't believe you haven't noticed that kid before. He put your two hotshots to shame."

"Well, obviously he ain't run like that before. Like I say, he has usually blowed up. But I will say, that was as good a racing as we have had around here in a long, long time."

The celebration had already begun in the pits when Wilder pulled the car up to the start-finish line. A throng of well-wishers, most of them female and clearly glad to see a fresh new face in victory lane, immediately rushed him. As the excited youngster climbed from his car, the two young men who had helped prepare the car tackled him. The fans in the stands howled with delight at the scene, sharing in the unbridled joy the winners were showing.

With the help of several security guards, Jodell was able to navigate the grandstands and make it to the crossover gate. As a policeman unlocked it to let him through, the kid emerged from the pile like a halfback who had just made it over the goal line. He climbed up on the roof of the car, still pumping his arms in glorious triumph.

Jodell stood for a moment at the edge of the scene, remembering his own feelings when he had won his first race. It was a feeling the uninitiated would never be able to know. The marvelous satisfaction of knowing you had beaten both man and machine in a contest in which there could only be a single winner, only one who would finish first, while everyone else were doomed to be losers.

He remained outside the circle of celebrants, allowing the kid to savor the moment and all it entailed. Then, once it had settled down somewhat, Jodell made his way through the thinning crowd and held out his hand as he introduced himself.

"Hey, son. That was a fine piece of driving," Jodell said.

Wilder had a shocked look in his eyes. He tried to speak but nothing came out. He had heard that Jodell

Lee was at the track signing autographs but he had assumed that he would never have the chance to meet him, that he would have skedaddled much earlier to something far more important than this little old small-track race.

He finally seemed to find air enough to be able to speak.

"Thanks, Mr. Lee," he squeaked.

He was a handsome young man, maybe a little thin, and with a face that appeared to hardly need shaving, but his hand when Jodell shook it was rough and callused, likely from hard work, and his grip was strong and confident. And there was something else about the kid Jodell couldn't quite discern.

"I saw you make some moves out there that I haven't seen in a while . . . and especially from somebody as young as you are."

"Aw, Mr. Lee," Wilder said, modestly checking the toes of his tennis shoes. "Those weren't anything special. I just point the car and she seems to go to the right place."

"The name is Jodell, not Mr. Lee," he corrected.

"I'm Rob Wilder, sir." But now, he looked the old driver straight in the eye as he spoke. "I'm honored to meet you."

That was it. The eyes. They were clear, intense, and didn't back down when Jodell's own unwavering gaze met his.

"Well, Rob, it was a good race anyhow. How long you been driving?"

"A couple of years, I guess. Mainly just hobby cars though. This is our first year to try and run the late-models. We got a good deal on the car and the boys here work real hard on it. We're still learning. . . ."

"How'd you get the set up so right? I noticed . . ."

And then they were talking in a language known only to those who raced; about details only those who had sat behind the big engines and guided them into sharp turns could know. Even the first raindrops stirring little dust clouds around them didn't slow down their exchange, nor the flurry of activity as the other two young men politely asked them to move as they began pushing the Pontiac up onto the rusty trailer with the bald, patched tires; getting it ready to tow back to wherever they came from.

As they talked, the old driver couldn't shake an almost overwhelming feeling that seized him first in the gut and then spread quickly all over him.

The feeling that he was looking squarely into a mirror.

A mirror that had somehow given him a blond head of hair and had erased a good forty years from his face.

THE CALL

Jodell tried to concentrate on the blinking back-
lit instruments that swam in front of him in the
plane's cockpit, tried to force himself to listen
to the constant rattle of the voices in the headphones
that were clamped to his head. But he kept replaying
the night's events over and over in his mind. He was
even beginning to question his own judgement.

Was what he had seen at the little track as special
as he believed?Had the young driver really done the
things he thought he had seen him do?

As he dodged rain showers and lingering clouds,
Jodell finally decided to follow the one guiding prin-
ciple that had usually worked well for him. Whenever
he had had such a strong conviction about something
in the past, a feeling so powerful it would not be denied, then he had always done well to go with it.

"Trust your instincts and your eyes, old man," he
told his reflection in the plane's windshield. A distant

flash of lightning in a towering thundercloud seemed to confirm the pronouncement.

Still, he chewed it over until he had vectored the plane into the small Tri-Cities Airport, steered it to the hangar, and walked to his car in the parking lot. He tossed his bags into the trunk of the Lincoln and pointed it toward home in Chandler Cove, twenty more miles down the way. But before the beacon at the airport had even disappeared from his rearview mirror, he had pulled his telephone from his pocket and dialed a familiar number. It didn't even occur to him how late it must be until he heard the throbbing ring on the other end of the line stop and a thick, sleepy voice answer.

" 'Lo?" and the short word blossomed into a full-blown yawn.

"I've found him." Jodell said quietly into the mouthpiece.

"Found who? Who is this?" The voice was still blurred by sleepiness but was beginning to gain an edge. "Better yet, who did you really intend to wake up in the middle of the night?"

"I found you a driver, Billy. Instead of gettin' your beauty sleep, you need to go out and take the padlock off that shop of yours and get to work. This kid deserves a special car."

"What? Jodell Lee? Is that you?"

"This is your lucky day, Billy," Jodell whispered, trying to contain his own excitement. "I found that driver you've been looking for. I saw him win a race tonight."

Slowly Billy Winton was coming awake as he realized what Jodell was saying. And the fact that his old friend was apparently so excited carried considerable weight.

Winton had once been a top mechanic on Jodell Lee's racing team. He had joined up with them almost by accident. Another member of the crew had picked him up one rainy night while he was hitchhiking across the country. He was fresh back from his last tour in Vietnam and had no particular place to go so he had hung and around for a few days, helping. The few days turned into weeks; then he ultimately stuck around for nearly twenty years, indefinitely postponing his cross-country hike and wrenching for the Lee race team through the seventies and eighties. He only retired from the team after Jodell hung up his helmet.

Winton had always had a flair for more than the mechanical side of the sport, though. He was a natural for the business end of what had become a very big business indeed. He seemed to have as much aptitude for handling money and playing the sponsors as he did for tuning engines.

And he had an innate knack for working the subtler psychological angles, too. More than once, his cool-headed approach had held the team together when it had threatened to fracture and shatter. Through the years, he had talked Jodell and other drivers and crew down out of their trees, and often became father confessor to strung-out drivers and others who were at the end of their ropes.

It had actually been his business sense that had gotten him out of racing for a while. He had seen the coming of the desktop computer in the early eighties and had put some timely money into the right stocks. He decided he was financially secure and that the weekly grind of the Cup circuit had finally worn him down as much as he could tolerate, and so had simply walked away from the sport at the end of the season. Of course, that decision came the same week in which

Jodell Lee had decided to give up driving. He always denied there had been a connection. Then, later, he turned down Jodell's offer to help him field a team with a car he wanted to run.

"I'm gonna see if I can go without grease under my fingernails for a while," he had maintained.

Billy Winton's retirement didn't last much longer than Jodell's did. He spent most of the next year resting, playing at investing his money, taking care of the farm he'd bought just over the mountain from Jodell's in Chandler Cove, Tennessee. Before long, though, the shop in the barn out back held a racecar and he had to build a shed for his tractor when he brought in the second car. Even as he firmly maintained that he was only playing at racing, Billy tinkered with the cars far more than he worked at the cattle business or his investment portfolio. Soon, he was running Busch Grand National races every now and then, using some of the marginal Cup drivers or wild-eyed up-and-comers to man the cars for him.

Slowly but inevitably, he'd built up the operation over the years to the point where he now had a full-fledged race shop out back of his farmhouse, with four cars inside prepped and ready to go. He had access to a good crew on race days and had just enough sponsorships lined up and available to play at competing until he decided to take the big plunge into deeper, colder water.

The only thing missing was the right driver.

There were plenty of journeymen who would have gladly climbed into any car prepared by Billy Winton. He heard from them almost every day. But if he was going to seriously mount an effort, he knew he needed a special driver. He had the résumé he was looking for pictured in his head: someone relatively young and

malleable but still mature enough to protect an investment that could run into the millions. Someone
with a good head inside his driver's helmet, and with
natural instincts and abilities, of course. Someone
knowledgeable enough that he could tell the crew if
there was a pound or two too much air pressure in
the right front tire simply from how the car felt to
him. And if he was willing and able to grab a wrench
and help out in a tight spot that was fine, too. But
there would have to be something else, something not
quite tangible. This special driver would have to have
a fire burning in his belly, a desire to win that was
almost as strong inside him as was the will to live.

Yes, the driver would have to crave winning in an
almost unnatural way if he wanted to steer a racecar
for Billy Winton.

So far, he had come up dry. There were those who
were hungry enough, but they lacked the raw talent.
Others knew how to win but weren't willing to make
the ultimate sacrifices in time, work, travel and single-
mindedness. And there were plenty of average drivers
out there.

Billy Winton was committed but things were on
indefinite hold. As badly as he wanted to get serious,
he had stubbornly decided to wait until he found his
kind of driver before he ratcheted things up. Lately,
he had been wondering if he ever would.

Now, Jodell Lee's words had Billy suddenly wide
awake and sitting up on the side of the bed, ready to
hear more. He idly ran his fingers through his thinning red hair as he listened to the excited voice on
the telephone.

"Billy, I think I found you a driver tonight. Young
kid, eighteen, maybe nineteen tops. Watching him
drive was scary. Just plain frightening, like seeing a

ghost. He looked so much like me at that age, Bill, or like one of the others we used to drive against that have gone on. I saw the kid do things with the racecar tonight that I don't think he even understands."

"Okay, so he can drive. But can he win? Does he want to win as bad as Jodell Lee did?" Billy asked. He suspected what the answer was going to be.

"Let me put it this way. Our old friend, Nathan Summers, wanted me to watch a couple of his hot-shots run tonight. This kid came from dead last to third in a ten-car heat race. And he did it with a piece of junk car and some of the prettiest driving I've seen in a while. Then, he beats the two hotshots who have won everything at the track over the last year or so. And he does it by passing them cleanly . . . on the outside."

The line was quiet for a moment. Jodell could hear static over the road noise inside the car.

"You say the outside line?"

"Yeah, the outside line on a third-of-a-mile track. I tell you I haven't seen anything like it since Joe Weatherley or Tiny Lund or some of them boys. I told you it was scary."

The two of them were still talking when Jodell pulled into the driveway that led up to his house, next to the house where he had been born and raised by his grandparents. He smiled when he glanced next door and saw that the lights were still burning brightly at his own race shop. The boys were getting the car ready to pull out in the morning and head for the Pocono track in Pennsylvania. He told Billy goodnight and, tired as he was, started toward the shop to speak to the crew and check on things before he called it a night. He felt rejuvenated somehow, as if the night at the small track and seeing the kid put on a show had given him a boost.

But as he walked across the yard, he glanced back toward the west, back in the direction from which he just flown in. And there was sheet lightning everywhere, still illuminating the distant night sky like some kind of joyous, celebratory fireworks display.

J odell Lee's coffee had long since grown cold in the cup. Billy Winton had not touched the doughnut on his plate. Jodell had just recapped once more what he had seen at the track the night before, and the kid's exploits had grown even more spectacular with twelve hours' worth of aging.

"Jodell, I do believe you have seen the reincarnation of Fireball Roberts himself," Billy finally teased.

Jodell paused then, smiled, sat back, and finally took a sip of the tepid brew before he spoke again. He reveled in the excitement in his old friend's eyes. Getting back into racing, deciding to get serious again, had clearly agreed with the man. There was a look on his face Jodell had not seen in a while.

"Tell you what. I'll fly down from Pocono Saturday and pick you up and we'll go see him run. I kinda want to confirm I wasn't dreaming myself."

"Naw, you got a race to run Sunday. I appreciate

it, but you need to be thinking about your car and crew, not finding me a driver. Besides, if you say he's good enough to take a look at, that's good enough for me."

There was a firmness in the set of his jaw that Jodell found very familiar. The man had lost none of his fire. Billy had maintained his fighting weight by jogging the length of the perimeter fence on his farm daily; and, even though it had thinned considerably on top of his head, there was no gray at all in his long red hair or in his close-clipped Van Dyke beard. Doing exactly what he had wanted to do over the years had obviously kept him young. Getting back into serious racing would likely make him younger still.

"He is."

"Then all it'll cost me is some travel and track time, at the least, and a busted race car at most. You met him. You wanna introduce us?"

Jodell nodded and pulled a slip of paper from his shirt pocket. Billy handed him the telephone and dialed the number.

"Brandon Cabinet Works. Hello?"

The kid was a cabinetmaker. That had seemed to indicate that he had a good work ethic, that he would be likely to pay proper attention to detail.

"Rob Wilder, please."

"Who's calling?"

"This is Jodell Bob Lee."

There was a moment's pause on the other end of the line, then a snort.

"Yessir, and this is old Santa Claus on this end." The guy laughed heartily. "Robbie with all his talk about meetin' the real Jodell Lee last night and now he's got you callin' up playin' like you're him. Is this

you, Roy? 'Least Robbie could have got somebody
that sounds a little bit like Jodell Lee!"

Jodell smiled and winked at Billy. Such a reaction
was common. Many people on the telephone told him
he wasn't who he claimed to be. He would often give
up arguing and agree it was all a hoax just so he could
go ahead and talk to whomever it was he had called
in the first place.

"Okay. You're right. I'm not him. Could I speak
with Rob, please?"

He could hear the man laughing as he walked away
from the telephone. There were also the buzzing of
power tools and hammering noises in the background.

"Hey, Robbie! You got a call. Some feller says he's
Jodell Bob Lee."

"Hello."

The kid's voice was hesitant, clearly wondering who
was playing what kind of trick on him.

"Hey, son. Jodell Lee here. I see the boys at the
shop are giving you a hard time this morning."

He could almost read the boy's mind across three
hundred miles of telephone wire: *That sure sounds like
Mr. Lee. Maybe it is. But why . . . ?*

"Yes, sir. They take special pride in giving me a
rough time."

"Well, I got somebody here I want you to talk with.
His name is Billy Winton. He's a friend of mine going
back a long way. He has a little proposal he'd like to
lay out for you."

Jodell passed the phone over to Billy and they chatted for a while. It was hard to tell how it was going.
Winton led the conversation and did more listening
than talking. When Billy finally set the phone back in
its cradle, he looked over at Jodell and smiled.

The old driver liked the sparks he saw in his friend's eyes.

Sawdust settled like thick smoke as the men all flicked off the switches on their machines and waited for the kid to come back from the office. Word had spread about the telephone call. When Rob stepped back into the shop, they all erupted into a crescendo of whoops and hollering, slapping their knees and pointing at him.

"First, he claims Jodell Lee came by and talked racin' with him all night!" one man giggled.

"Then, he puts old Roy Poole up to callin' and actin' like Jodell wants to talk some more," yelped the man who had answered the phone in the first place.

Trying his best to ignore them, Rob simply grinned and floated on back to his workbench, his face flushed and hot. But it was not from embarrassment. It was from sheer exhilaration. He had just had the most exciting five-minute conversation of his young life.

In a week, he would finally have the chance to show somebody who mattered what he could do behind the wheel of a car. He had no idea what the test drive might consist of, but he was already deciding who he would tell and how. His buddies who made up his crew most races would be happy for him, but they would have to wonder if this was the end of their short racing careers. None of them had any desire to drive the old red Pontiac if Rob went up. But how would he break the news to his boss here at the shop? He would have to get off work for a couple of days, and they were so far behind and so short-handed already.

But a couple of things he was certain about. He would duly impress Mr. Billy Winton. And he wouldn't be able to sleep a wink between now and the most important few laps he had ever driven.

THE TEST

A big jet roared overhead, temporarily blotting out conversation as it made its final approach to the airport across town. Below, wisely seeking the shade of a huge eighteen-wheel transporter in the heat of the day, a small group of men waited in the infield of the Nashville Motor Speedway for the plane to get on past so they could hear each other again. One of them, a blond-haired young man, shifted from one foot to the other, not nervously, but clearly in anticipation. He seemed ready to go, to get on with what it was that had brought him here on this clear, white-hot day. Meanwhile, with the noise gone, the others resumed their plans for how they wanted to set up the racecar that waited inside the hauler, for what they hoped to do during their allotted time out there on the track's surface.

Billy Winton had contributed little to the discussion so far. He simply stood by, watching how the kid pre-

sented himself, what he said when he did speak, and
how he said it. From what he had seen up to this
point, he had to agree with his friend, Jodell Lee.

At first observation, the kid seemed to be pure
sponsor bait. Though he was a bit thin, with a little
work on his hairstyle he would be drop-dead handsome and downright photogenic. The women would
love him. So would the people who produced television commercials. He spoke well, too, using good En-
glish and without an objectionable amount of drawl.
Southern fans would accept him as one of their own
but folks from other parts of the country could understand him when he talked, too. The questions he
had asked and the comments he had made thus far
had been knowledgeable without being pushy or
cocky, and he seemed to know his way around a car
and a racetrack. Or he was darn good at bluffing.

Now, was he too good to be true? And, most importantly, could he drive a racecar? It was time to
find out.

Will Hughes, Billy's crew chief, had his head stuck
in the driver's-side window while Rob leaned in the
other. Hughes maintained an expressionless face as he
patiently pointed out what everything in the car did,
went over the safety equipment, and made sure Rob
understood how the belts hooked up. And, maybe
even more importantly, how they unhooked in case
he had to get untangled in a hurry. He also showed
him the levers for the fire extinguisher, where all the
switches were and what each one did.

"We don't leave anything to chance," Hughes said
in his low, monotonous voice. "We haven't killed a
driver yet and we don't aim to start with you."

Billy had already warned Rob about Will.

"He's direct to a fault. Don't read him the wrong

way. He's just all business when he's at the track. He comes off mean and gruff sometimes but he's just into his job. You get him away from the track and he's as nice as can be. And there's a bunch of Cup teams that would steal him away from me in a second if they thought they could."

Hughes had come to Billy's team by way of the Jodell Lee Racing team. He'd shown up five years before, directly from a college engineering program, and had parked himself at the front door of the Lee Racing shop until someone invited him to come on in and get to work. He had offered to sweep the floors, clean the restrooms, do whatever grunt work needed doing, just to break into the sport and put what he had learned in school to work. That had been another one of the times when Jodell Lee had had one of his strong feelings and had issued the invitation, just as he had with Billy Winton almost thirty years before. He did not actually have an opening at the time, but he showed Will where the tools were and explained what he wanted done and that was that.

Jodell had been correct in his assessment then, too. Will's work ethic was as good as Jodell had anticipated, his perception uncanny. And then, when Billy Winton needed a crew chief for his fledgling team, Jodell made sure Will Hughes was the first and only candidate for the job, even though it took a valuable man off his own car. Unselfishly helping young wrenches get a start had always been a hallmark of Lee Racing.

Will, with his degree in mechanical engineering, brought a fresh perspective to the job of crew chief. With the older, tried and true techniques he had learned at Lee Racing and the more technical knowledge from his engineering background, he was able to bring a totally different approach to his work on Billy's Grand National cars. That fresh angle had already shown up on the track, where Billy had gained a reputation for bringing top-notch equipment every time he pulled a car to a race—equipment that, so far, had been far better than its series of mediocre operators.

Having seen all he could without actually strapping on the racecar, Rob Wilder climbed up into the hauler to change into his driving suit. Meanwhile, Will and the two other crewmembers made some minor adjustments on the car, setting it up for the peculiarities of the Nashville track. The bright midmorning sunshine and quickly rising temperatures meant they needed to tighten up the setup of the car. The hot track surface would make the car loose, its rear end more prone to slip and slide in the corners, and that might be too much of a challenge for the skills of a young driver his first time in the car.

Billy watched as the other two boys worked on changing the rear springs while Will installed a different shock absorber at the right front. The men worked quickly despite the heat, swapping out the pieces, happily bantering with each other as they did, seemingly oblivious to the boiling temperature, stifling humidity, and knuckle-busting work. As he observed, Billy couldn't help reflecting back on the days when he had been their age, living the gypsy life that the Grand National racing circuit had been back then. Even now, in 1999, there were still no set hours or time clocks to punch, no overtime pay or holidays off, little time to spend at home, lots of hotel rooms and roadside restaurants and all-night work sessions in the garages and shops from Chandler Cove to the West Coast. Sometimes he wondered if he was totally insane, getting back into the game when he could very easily sit in the swing on his front porch, checking his stocks and counting his dividends, and going to an occasional race as a guest in the pits. That should be enough of a gasoline-vapor fix for any rational man. But he knew there was no way he could stay away from racing. All he had to do was feel the way his pulse pounded every single time the car was cranked, just as it had the very first time someone had fired up Jodell Lee's racing Ford in the barn out behind his grandmother's house. He had been hooked immediately and had not thrown the lure since.

Rob stepped out of the changing room in the lounge at the front of the hauler. He caught a glimpse of himself in a mirror and thought he actually looked like a racecar driver, even if his old suit was stained and tattered. As he walked past on his way out of the trailer, he marveled at the banks of equipment, the racks of parts, the storage cabinets, and all the work surfaces that had been built into the hauler. Everything was neatly stacked or strategically placed to be readily available, in its place, should it be needed. The work counters were so clean and antiseptic that they looked more suited for a restaurant than a mobile automotive garage. He shook his head and smiled as he thought of his own pickup truck, parked on the other side of the hauler. That's where they typically piled all the tools and equipment they could scrape up and then hauled them to a Saturday night race.

He strode out the back of the trailer and into the blinding sunlight. Billy waited beneath the shade of the deck that lowered the racecar down from its traveling spot in the top of the hauler. As the kid approached, Billy looked over the dirty, worn driving suit Rob wore and made a note that the first order of business, should they strike a deal, was going to be to get him a new track wardrobe. Fans and sponsors expected a driver to look like a star, not like some scruffy grease monkey who had just crawled from beneath a car.

And shoes, too, he thought as he checked out his feet. The boy wore tennis shoes with knotted strings and rips and tears down their sides. Winton suddenly realized that Rob had apparently just asked him something he had not heard.

"Mr. Winton?"

"Oh, sorry," Billy said, looking the boy in the face now. "I didn't catch what you said."

"I was just wondering if you wanted me to pitch in and help them with the changes on the car."

"No. No, no. Thanks for volunteering, but you just stand there and think about the track and how you'll drive it. They'll be done in a minute."

"Okay. I just feel funny standing around when there's work to be done on the racecar."

Was the kid putting on a show for him? He certainly had a sincere enough look on his face.

"Maybe you'll get a chance to help out some other time. Today, you are here just to drive. I want all your focus on the track and showing us how you might get around this place," Billy answered as the two crewmembers slid from underneath the rear end, their changes completed.

"I guess standing around makes me a little nervous, that's all. It just . . ." Rob said, turning his head away from Billy to watch Will Hughes roll from beneath the right front wheel well.

Billy looked at him quizzically, his hand cupped behind his ear.

"Sorry, I didn't catch that, son. What were you saying?"

It was only then that Rob realized that Billy Wilder was practically deaf. Years and years of listening to unmufflered racing engines had apparently robbed him of a great deal of his hearing.

"I just said that I'm a little nervous if I'm not helping out. Working on the car always helps to relax me, keeps me from being distracted."

Billy simply nodded and smiled. The kid sure knew all the right things to say. Each thing seemed to make him like him more. He was young and green, for sure, but that also meant he was hungry and willing to learn the right way to do things. He didn't appear to have an ounce of prima donna in him. Many a racing career had been snagged on ego. Billy Winton had culled a few potential drivers for that grievous sin already.

Now if Rob Wilder could just drive a racecar as skillfully as Jodell Lee had reported, then they could get down to trying to plan their next step. And there was only one way to see if that was the case or not.

"You've never driven on this track, have you?"

Rob shook his head.

"No, sir. I've watched a lot of races here and dreamed about driving it, but I've never had the chance. I have watched how they drive it, though. Many a lap, in fact. Sometimes I feel like I've driven it myself." He looked around the empty grandstands. "Feels kinda weird for there not to be anybody here but us, though."

With everything redone and tightened back up, Will placed the jack while the other men removed the jack stands and the car was lowered down onto its tires. Will let down the hood and one of the others fastened the hood pins. The racecar was ready for the kid to go out and show what he could do.

Rob Wilder took a short stroll around the Ford. To the casual observer, she might have been considered downright ugly as she sat there in the hot sun. She still wore only her dull gray coat of primer, not the usual bright-red color scheme she would eventually carry on race day. There was no number painted on her yet, either. She was still anonymous. That would come later, too, just before they left the shop for her first real contest.

But to Rob, she was about the most beautiful sight he had ever seen. The car even smelled new, and to him, she appeared to be a caged panther, ready to sprint and pounce as soon as she was given her freedom out there on the circling track.

"She's all ready to go," Will said thumping the car's roof with the heel of his hand. "Reckon you can bring her back in one piece?"

Rob ignored the question, as well as the sideways looks from him and his two wary crewmen. They had been around a while, too, and had seen hotshots come and go. Youth and good looks and a bushel of "yessirs" didn't mean anything to them at all. The kid still had to drive the car to impress them.

"Well, son," Billy said from behind his sunglasses, "let's see what she'll do."

"I'm ready, Mr. Winton."

"For the last time it's 'Billy,' son."

"Okay, then it's 'Rob,' Billy."

He said it with a sincere enough smile and Billy quickly returned it.

"Alright. Glad we got that straight. Now go out there and run a couple of laps to get comfortable, then bring her back in and we'll decide what we want to do."

"Okay . . . Billy."

It still didn't feel natural to call someone who was his elder by his first name. But Billy was the boss.

Wilder walked over and swung his legs in through the open driver's side window of the racecar as if he had been doing it all his life. He settled down into the seat and stretched his legs out to see how he fit. It seemed perfect! The seat was set at almost the exact angle and distance from the steering wheel necessary for his legs to be comfortable. He shuffled around in the seat and it seemed to have been contoured to fit him, and it felt more like the upholstery in a luxury car. There was padding everywhere, unlike the seat in the car he was used to driving. They had used duct tape to add some extra foam for padding in the old Pontiac, but the springs still poked through in places if they stayed in the race long enough. Sometimes after their better showings, when the car would last more than half the race, he couldn't comfortably sit down again for several days.

Will reached in to help him with the safety belts. It took Rob a moment to figure out how they buckled up. Will patiently assisted him as he checked them for snugness and made sure the snap was fastened and securely locked.

Then he went over the gauges and explained where the arrows were supposed to line up: straight up for everything but the tachometer.

"You sure you're all set?" Will asked.

"I believe I am," Rob said. He actually spoke the words with more confidence than he felt. Butterflies were having a wild party somewhere inside his gut just below his breastbone.

"Comfortable?"

"Yeah, the seat is set just right and this thing fits like a glove."

Will smiled. Jodell Lee had estimated the kid's height for them. Using that, they'd been able to place the seat to where they figured it would be close to a fit. The kid would likely be nervous, have far more things to worry about than how the seat and wheel were adjusted. Yet, once he was out there, such details could be a factor in how well he could drive.

Rob put the earplugs for the radio in his ears as Will had instructed and placed a small piece of tape over each one. He pulled the helmet on and began to fasten the chinstrap. Then, he was struck by a wave of calm that suddenly rolled throughout his body. He had been nervous as a cat ever since he had climbed out of bed early that morning, so nervous he had not even been able to eat the sausage and biscuits he had bought from a fast food place along the way. He hardly slept the night before, spending most of the night shifting and steering in his half-awake dream world. Then, all the way up to Nashville, he had played his tapes extra loud, trying to drown out the voice in his head that kept telling him how important these few laps would be to his career as a racecar driver.

Since arriving at the track, he tried to concentrate on listening to what Billy, Will, and the rest of the crew were telling him so he wouldn't go out and do anything stupid. Even then, the jitters had stayed with him, suppressed, denied, but there nonetheless. He only hoped they couldn't see it, that they only saw the confidence he tried so hard to show.

But now, when he felt the snap close on the helmet, he suddenly realized that he was in the one place where he always felt most comfortable: behind the wheel of a racecar. And he grinned broadly when he realized it didn't matter if that car was entered in a Wednesday night heat race at a tiny track somewhere or if it was in the first row leading the rest of them out of the turn to take the green flag at Daytona. He was born to race. And in the next few minutes, he would show these men that irrefutable truth once and for all.

"You got a copy on me?"

The loud voice crackling over the radio startled him. He jumped in the seat. It was so clear that for an instant, he thought it was actually inside his head. He stretched his thumb to hit the switch on the steering wheel that keyed the microphone for his own transmitter.

"I read you clear as a bell."

"What about you, Billy? You got a clear signal?"

Billy had already climbed up to the viewing platform on top of the hauler while Will had gone over the final check with Rob. From there he would easily be able to see the car all the way around the speedway.

"I got both of you five-by-five, but this is your show. I'm just gonna sit up here and work on my tan and be quiet."

That was Billy Winton's way. He had a young crew chief that he trusted. And he wanted to make certain the rest of the crew knew it. He let Hughes and the driver make the decisions. He supplied them with whatever equipment they needed to get the job done. He carefully avoided being a meddlesome owner, constantly interrupting, always trying to tell everyone how to set up and drive the racecar. He was there as a sounding board if they needed him, as a senior advisor, but other than that, they were on their own. And if he had a different opinion on something, there was a time and a way to let it be known without second-guessing his crew chief and driver in front of everybody. Most likely it had been his military training that had shaped Billy's management style. He knew for certain that the quickest way to undermine a leader was to have him questioned by a commanding officer in front of his troops.

"Okay, kid," Will Hughes said into his ear. "Just go out there and take it easy for the first few. Let's see how the car is set up and then we'll take a look at what you can do."

Rob reached over and touched the starter switch, took a deep breath, then flipped it. The motor instantly roared to life with a rumble that felt as powerful as any earthquake. The vibration of the big engine shook the entire car as it sat there, innocently idling, waiting for instructions on how to behave. Rob patted the gas pedal a couple of times, revving the engine, feeling through his foot and calf and leg the promise of raw power that waited for his command. He had never even been close to a racecar with a motor as strong as this one, and now, in a minute, it would be his to do with what he could.

Even atop the hauler, Billy Winton felt the power of the motor, too. He knew it was a good car, state-of-the-art, the best machine he had been around in a while. And there were three more back in the shop equally as good. He said a little prayer that this Rob Wilder would be what he had been searching for—and that he would have the judgement to know for certain if he was or not.

Downstairs, Will Hughes got the familiar rush he always did when a racecar's engine fired. He, too, knew it was a fine car, and that they had the equipment to compete with the other Grand National teams. It was the culmination of a dream he had had since before he left high school for college. He had been around racing all his life. His dad had been a dirt track demon, winning championships all over the eastern part of the Carolinas before cancer ended it all when he was an otherwise healthy fifty-five. Will decided to pursue an engineering degree as the best way to get to where he wanted to be: the crew chief of a winning team on the premier Cup circuit. Catching on with Jodell and his team, then coming over to chief for Billy Winton had put him exactly on the path he knew he had to follow. Now, so much depended on this tall, slim, blond-headed kid, and Will couldn't help worrying about it.

He was a little apprehensive about putting a driver this young and inexperienced in his fine new car, but that had not been his call. He trusted Jodell Lee's recommendation, though. And Billy Winton's. But now, as the kid eased off on the clutch and pulled slowly down the pit road in his pride and joy, lugging just a bit as he figured out the gearing, he couldn't help but worry. He, too, sent up a little prayer: "Please, Lord, let this kid be a driver."

Rob eased in the clutch and shifted into second gear, giving her enough gas to keep her from bucking any worse than she had already. He hoped they had not noticed his bumpy start. But any jitters had faded completely away by now as he reveled in the power that he had at his beck and call. When he goosed the throttle as the car exited the pit road onto the track, he was yanked hard back into the seat. He couldn't help it. He let out a whoop as he stayed hard on the gas as the car rolled through the middle of turn one.

"Take a couple of easy laps and get all the temperatures up before you crank her up a notch," came the calm voice of Will over the radio.

Rob had to fumble with the steering wheel to try to locate the switch for his mike. He finally managed to key it and reply.

"Ten-four!"

Will stood there in silence then, watching with the other two crewmen. He didn't want to talk too much on the radio to the youngster. He didn't know how well Wilder might be able to concentrate and that would only distract him, taking his mind off learning the car and the five-eighths-mile track.

Out there in the car, Rob Wilder was concentrating just fine. In fact, he felt as alert and alive as he ever had before, despite the lack of sleep and food. He glanced down at the gauges as he came around past the pits at the end of his second lap, still going only about three-quarters what he figured maximum speed would be. The needles were all standing straight up, except the tach, and it seemed to flutter impatiently, wanting to soar. Suddenly, he took a deep gulp of the blistering air in the cockpit and rammed his foot down hard to the floorboard. The tach needle danced and the car leapt forward as if a rocket beneath her hood had just been tapped.

Now quickly gaining speed, he dived low going down into turn one, exactly the way he had seen other drivers do it all those times when he had been a paying customer up there in the stands. He yanked the wheel to the left as he negotiated the turn, leaving the car hugging the white line that ran around the inside of the track where the banking met the apron. The heavy car stuck there as if it was no problem at all for her to totally ignore centrifugal force and go anywhere as fast as she and her driver wished. The Ford held the bottom line and sailed through the corner.

Shooting down the backstretch next, Rob concentrated hard as he set the car's line for the upcoming corner, guiding her once more right down to the bottom, the left front tire next to the white line. The car thundered through the corner, the sound of the powerful engine echoing off the empty grandstands and the metal roof that covered them.

Oh, Lord, he felt at home! As much at home as he had in the old red Pontiac, racing along while his buddies were down there in the pits cheering him on. He tried to keep his mind on what he was doing but he couldn't help it. He grinned broadly and gave the steering wheel a joyous slap.

Billy Winton watched those first couple of slow-speed laps with an experienced eye. He held the stopwatch tightly, ready to clock the first hot lap when it came. Then he heard the throttle pitch change as the car exited turn four after the second time through. As the car crossed in front of his position, he clicked the watch, beginning to time the lap. The kid charged off into the first turn as if he had driven this old track all his life. Billy smiled as he watched him run, then realized that he had been holding his breath for the last lap and a half.

Rob set the car right on the white line, intentionally taking the fast way around the bottom of the track. The gruff rumble of the motor changed slightly as he got out of the throttle to exit the corner. Over the bump where the tunnel had been cut beneath the track, heading for the backstretch, he was back into the gas and the car eased up the track and to within a few feet of the outside wall. Through turns three and four and past the position on the pit road where Will and the crew watched, Rob shoved the car hard.

Billy clicked the watch again as the roaring Ford zipped past.

He glanced down at the time and his eyes widened. Then, in his headset, he heard Will call his name on the radio. When he looked down, his crew chief was at the foot of the ladder, motioning him to take off the headset.

"Billy, did you time that?" he shouted up to him. "He was within two tenths of the speed that won the pole here back in March."

"That's what I got. He's sure smooth in the corners."

Billy looked out at the track again as Wilder guided the car around again to finish another lap. Down below, Will clicked his watch again and studied it. He had an uncharacteristic grin on his face when he looked up once more at Billy.

"That last lap was just a whisker off the pole speed. This kid can drive!" Will yelled. Billy had never seen the man so animated. It took something unusual to break his normally dour demeanor.

And Billy loved the enthusiasm for a number of reasons. He desperately needed a driver who could build some excitement and chemistry with his young crew chief and the rest of the team. Everything else was in place. Now, as he watched young Wilder work his car through its paces, he suspected that he had finally found the catalyst he had been seeking.

After twenty laps, Will radioed Rob to bring the car in. Reluctantly, he obeyed the command, slowed the car down on the back straightaway, and dropped it down to the apron to hit the entrance to the pit lane in the center of turns three and four. He shut the engine and coasted down pit road to a stop.

It was eerily quiet now with the car's engine silent. Rob tried to read Will's face but it was once again indecipherable. Billy Winton was climbing down the ladder, his back to them, so it was hard to tell what he might be thinking. And the two crewmen had dived under the car immediately to take a look at the tires and check for fluid leaks.

Had he done what they expected? Was the car so good that they had anticipated even more than he had shown? Had the laps that had seemed so wonderfully fast to him actually been disappointingly slow to these men?

"How did she feel?" Will asked as he kneeled next to the driver's side of the car.

"Well, she was a little bit tight in the center of the corners and then she was just a tad loose coming off the turns. Otherwise, she was like a pod racer out there."

"Like a what?" Will asked with a blank expression.

"Sorry. *Star Wars*. She felt good except for the corners." Rob blushed.

"You would never know she was anything less than perfect by the times you were running."

"What do you mean?" Rob asked.

"You were a tenth of a second under the time that won the pole here last March, and the track is a whole lot hotter today than it was then."

"Really? I was trying to take it easy. I didn't want to put your brand-new car into the fence on the first run."

"Appreciate that," Will said, and stood, still hiding his excitement well.

Rob reached up and grabbed the edge of the roof of the car and pulled himself up and out of the window of the racecar. Billy Winton was standing there waiting for him with the same question as Will Hughes. Rob gave the same answer. And Billy reported the fast laps, too, also with a non-committal expression on his face.

Meanwhile, one of the other crewmen went around the car checking tire temperatures. He measured the heat on each tire on the outside edge, in the center, and at the inside edge, then he carefully wrote each reading down on a tire sheet clamped to a clipboard. When he had finished the task, he handed the information over to Will who then studied the numbers as if he was working out some complicated calculus problem. Then he joined Rob and Billy in the shade of the hauler.

"Tire temps are fine all the way 'round except for the right front," he reported.

Billy stayed quiet, not offering a suggestion unless asked for one.

"What does that mean?" Rob finally asked.

"That we probably need to go back to our original shock setup."

"It's not something I did, is it?"

"Not at all. But if we run too long with that shock under there, we'll likely blister a tire and you'll find yourself being introduced to the wall, I expect."

"If it's all the same to y'all, I'd rather not do that," Rob said with a deadly serious face.

The other two men laughed out loud then and slapped Rob on the back, showing their emotions to him for the first time that day. They had realized how uptight they, too, had been, hoping that the car was ready and that the kid was the real deal.

Then they stood there out of the sun for a while, discussing some other slight changes they wanted to try for the next run while the other two men went to work on the shock absorber at the right front tire. Will was duly impressed at some of the things the kid said; he showed a much better understanding of a racecar than Will could ever have hoped for. He was also surprised at Rob's willingness to try changes. He only had one question about each one: "Do you think it'll make the car go faster?" If the answer was yes, then he was enthusiastically for it.

With the changes made, and with Rob full of sports drink from a big cooler in the hauler, they sent him back out in the car to run off another set of laps. After ten circuits, they could see that some of the changes they had made had done more harm than good. Will radioed for Rob to come on back to the pits.

They spent most of the rest of the day that way. Billy primarily sat under an umbrella on top of the hauler, keeping out of the way but maintaining an eagle-like vigilance on all that was going on as he timed the laps. He made a few notes and compared them to a baseline they had established from the first run, but mostly watched the changes and guessed where Will was going with each one. He also watched with considerable interest how Will, Rob, and the two crewmen meshed, how they seemed to be working together. After the first hour or so of tension, there was considerable change. The four of them were working together well, typified by the joking and banter that went on during their quick break for sandwiches at a midafternoon lunch.

As they experimented, they were able to find ticks of speed here and there, and maintain it in the longer runs they began to make. By late in the afternoon, Will proclaimed that they were ready to do a simulated hundred-lap run. That was about all they would be able to do on one set of tires, but it would serve their purpose perfectly.

Now Rob found himself severely tested. The short twenty-, thirty-, and forty-lap runs had given ample opportunity to set a rhythm, but they had also given him time to catch his breath and get some fluids between workouts. This longer run, set late in the heat of the afternoon, would be different. He didn't mention it to anyone, but he had never run as many laps in his life as he'd already run today. The hundred laps still to go would be twice as long as any race he'd ever driven.

Will Hughes suspected as much. He figured the long stretch would tell as much about the young driver as it did their racecar. Could he be as consistent over such a long run as he had been in the sprints? How would he react when the tires got slick and refused to hold traction? Would he get tired and make a mistake or give up and start slacking off, playing it safe? Or would he be just as fast and fired up at the end of the run as he was at the start?

Rob climbed back into the car one more time and proceeded to buckle up. He didn't hesitate, and once he had pulled out onto the speedway he quickly began to reel off one hot lap after another. Will gave him the times periodically on the radio and counted off the total he had completed in five-lap increments. Trip after trip the kid ran remarkably consistent laps, varying by only a tenth or so each time. The times slowed a bit as the tires wore down, but the fall-off was consistent with what they expected as a result of the loss of rubber.

Inside the car it was insufferably hot, and that made it difficult for the young driver to concentrate. It took everything he could muster to keep his mind's eye focused on the track, on hitting his braking and acceleration marks, on studying the gauges and the feel of the car. The last twenty or so laps went by in a blur as he began to wear out as surely as the tires beneath him. He knew he was driving as much by instinct as awareness. His arms and legs felt like lead weights and it seemed to take all the strength he could muster to continue wrestling with the steering wheel. Still they ached and cramped and twitched spasmodically, and he desperately needed to go to the bathroom. He was drenched in sweat, his eyes stinging from the salty perspiration that had trickled down beneath his goggles.

But then, somehow, he seemed to get his second wind. He imagined he was leading a pack through the last few laps, ready to take the checkered flag and claim his first Busch Grand National race. Quickly, all the pain and discomfort faded away.

He was driving. Driving for the win!

When the call for lap one hundred came, Rob was psyched, and he was almost disappointed to end the practice, even though the car had begun to slip and slide all over the track on the worn tires during the last couple of circuits. He had known from the first hundred feet on the track that he was in his element. Just him, the racecar, and the track. And if Billy Winton and Will Hughes ultimately decided he was not to be their driver, then that would be fine. Somebody else would eventually find him. Rob Wilder knew now, more assuredly than ever, that he was born to do what he had done today. All he needed was for somebody to give him a chance.

The grin on Billy's face had grown wider and wider the deeper they got into the long practice run. Jodell Lee had been right once again. Unless he had them sorely fooled, the kid was a natural. He was one of those drivers who didn't seem to be doing anything spectacular at all, but who was always up near the front ready to take the victory. Their style is not to bang and shove but to drive smoothly, find the proper groove to run for whatever point it is in the contest, pursue it when it inevitably changes, then win the danged race. He had seen other young guns do it already, naturals like Jeff Gordon; Dale Earnhardt, Jr.; Tony Stewart; even Casey Atwood, who was barely old enough to have a license but was winning Grand National races. Now he appeared to have found his own young gun, and Billy couldn't wait to see him in a shootout with those guys in the middle of Main Street at high noon!

Rob pulled the car behind the wall, rolling to a stop next to the truck. As Will pulled down the window net, Rob threw his gloves up on the dash and wrestled with the strap on the helmet. He finally got it unfastened and tossed it nonchalantly up on the shifter like a veteran. Will passed him a cold towel to wipe his face.

"How you holding up there, cowboy?"

"I'm hot and so thirsty I'm spittin' dust," he reported, then took a big swig of ice water. "But I'd love to bolt on another set of tires and run a hundred more. That was great!"

"My kind of driver," Will said and slapped the kid on his wet shoulder. The words didn't sound false or patronizing at all, coming from Rob. Hughes didn't doubt for a minute that the boy would truly love to go right back out there and run 'til the sun went down. "If we had another set I might just take you up on it. But look, we've accomplished everything we came over here to do today. Everything."

He gave Rob a big wink.

"You have one fine racecar here, Will. You know I'd be honored to drive it for you."

"You just get out of there so we can get her back on the truck. That is, unless you want to ride in there all the way back to east Tennessee."

"Don't tempt me," Rob said with a grin as he undid the last of the belts and reluctantly climbed out of the Ford for the last time that day.

He had to stand there for a moment, leaning against the car, getting his balance. It felt as if he was still hurtling around the track at speed, darting and dancing for the right angles to get around the course at the best possible clip.

And at that moment, Rob Wilder wasn't at all sure that he ever wanted that feeling to end.

The old pickup continually jumped out of gear all the way back to northern Alabama, and that kept interrupting Rob's constant replay of the day's events. He kept dwelling on the times where he missed a mark or shaved off too much speed taking a corner, all spots where he could have gotten even better times out of the wonderful racecar that Billy Winton and Will Hughes had allowed him to chauffeur around for the better part of a day. Still, he felt it had gone well for the most part.

Several times he glanced over to the old, tattered scrapbook that rested in the passenger seat next to him, but it simply lay there, not offering any advice or confirmation at all.

"We need to get you on a track with some other folks in a real race before we get too far down the road, son," Billy had told him, and promised to call

him in a day or so to let him know when his first
opportunity would be to do that.

But the closer he got to home, the more he fretted
that it was the old, "Don't call us, we'll call you."
What if they simply needed somebody to test their car
for a day and he was actually way down on their list
of desired drivers? Why, of all the people they could
likely get to run their car, would they want a total
unknown, a snot-nosed novice like Robbie Wilder? A
raw kid who had won a grand total of one race in his
whole life? Somebody with his background and up-
bringing, for Pete's sake?

By the time the lights of his apartment building
were in sight through the dusky mist, he was dead
certain he would never hear from Billy Winton again.

Billy and Will rode back to Chandler Cove in Billy's
Lincoln, the others following along behind in the
eighteen-wheeler with the hauler in tow. The two men
stayed mostly silent as they pulled out of the speedway, down the short run to the freeway entrance, then
on east toward the airport and out of town. As Billy
negotiated traffic, Will studied the notes he had taken
on the day's activities.

"So, what did you think?" Billy asked pointedly as
they finally took the ramp onto I-40 toward the east.

"It's not what I think, boss. What did you think?
You own this team."

Billy cranked the air conditioner up one more
notch before he answered.

"With just a touch of experience, I think we may
have found us a driver we can take and go out and
win ourselves a championship."

Will sat back and watched the airport exit whiz
past. That was high praise indeed for a kid neither

one of them had ever seen before that very morning.

"We still don't know how he does in traffic."

"Besides what Jodell says he saw."

Will nodded. That did carry considerable weight.

"And I was wondering where we're going to find a major sponsor so we can go and hire us enough people to move things up to the next level."

"I have a few ideas in that area, Will. You leave that up to me. You just start figuring on where we need to run this kid first so we can get him some seasoning." He took a swig from a can of soda he had resting between his legs. "I've got to get the sponsorship thing done pretty quick, though. I can't afford to run all this out of my pocket if we try to run a full schedule. It's not like the old days when we lived off what we won."

They rode in silence for a while longer with only the radio playing quietly in the background.

"You know who Wilder reminds me of?" Billy finally said. Will knew, but he let Billy tell him anyway. "Jodell Bob Lee. Same fluid style, same consistency, same confidence without being cocky so it doesn't rub anybody the wrong way."

"I just hope we can get as many wins out of him."

Billy Winton grinned and his eyes danced when he turned to look at Will.

"I fully intend to, Mr. Hughes. I fully intend to."

THE QUALIFYING

Early August thunderclouds piled up in the west like snowballs stored for an impending fight. But there was certainly no snow and so far the clouds had not diminished the warming Midwestern sun one bit as it bore down relentlessly on the frenzied activity below.

The Winton Racing crew was too busy unloading their own hauler to take note of all the other racecars that swarmed around them. The makeshift garage area at the half-mile speedway just outside of Indianapolis filled with crewmen working on the vehicles that had come there to race. The trucks had run the night before; the Grand National cars were on tap for tonight. And all that racing was merely a prelude to the Cup contest that would be run on Saturday across town at the famed Indianapolis Motor Speedway.

For Billy and his team, this trip capped off a frantic couple of weeks. They had not previously planned on coming here to race at all. But then, once the team had taken a hard look at Rob Wilder in Nashville weeks before, they decided they needed to try to make the next available short track event wherever it might be. The schedule pointed them straight to central Indiana. This would be a good opportunity to fine-tune the setup on the car, true, but Wilder was the primary reason they had decided to run a race as quickly as they thought they could get a car ready. They wanted to get the youngster some experience on the shorter tracks before they turned him loose on one of the big, fast, and dangerous superspeedways. And they wanted to find out as quickly as they could if Rob was their man or not.

Will and the other boys at the shop had rushed to get the car ready. After the way the car had run on the track at Nashville, Will had been totally in favor of making the trip here to see what they could do under race conditions, so he and the rest of them had pitched in for some long nights. Now they felt they had a car that could certainly challenge.

Rob took the rest of the vacation time he had built up at the cabinet shop and drove over to spend three days before the race at Billy's shop, then rode to Indy with the rest of them. He helped out where he could, but mainly, at Billy's insistence, stayed out of the way. His assignment was to learn all he could about the cars, how they set them up, what kind of tweaking was possible during practice, before qualifying, and during the race itself. And he was to build lines of communication between himself and Will, who would be running any race from the pits.

Rob also spent a lot of time with Billy and the others, trying to pick their brains for anything he could get. He decided early on that it was impossible to know too much. A driver could never tell what tidbit of information or knowledge could serve him in good stead in a crisis during a race. So he asked questions over breakfast in Billy's kitchen or sat with him on the wraparound porch of his sprawling one-story log farmhouse until late into the night, listening to him tell stories until the others finally walked up from the shop for a cold drink and reminded them how late it was getting.

And in his spare time he rested under the big shade tree next to Billy's racing shop, thumbing through racing magazines or the old scrapbook he took with him everywhere he went. Sometimes Will would call him into the shop, showing him something on the car, describing what effect it would have on how she performed, how it would feel or sound or smell if it went haywire. Or they would fire up the engine, make a bad adjustment, and demonstrate to Rob what the subtle difference in sound it caused or the influence it would have on the gauges on the racecar's dash.

The more time Billy spent with the kid the better he felt about his decision to give him a chance in the 6 car. The kid was a sponge, soaking up anything and everything concerning the cars, the tracks, or the other drivers. The only thing holding him back was his lack of experience racing at this level. But they were going to do everything they could to accelerate his move up the racing curve now that they were going to an actual race.

Inevitably, members of the other teams came up to Will and his crew as they worked to get the car out of the truck. The question was always the same: who was going to drive the car this week? They all knew that with the importance of the race across town none of the usual Cup drivers would be stepping down to drive in this one. And Billy had about used up the marginal drivers who were always looking for any chance to run for a payday.

When they asked the question, Will would simply smirk and say, "We got us a new guy. You'll meet him soon enough."

Rumors were spreading all over the garage already. Hardly a Cup driver without a ride didn't get tied to the 6 car. Several names of drivers who had long since been put out to pasture emerged as favorites. There was actually a good reason for Will and his men to be so evasive: they wanted to try and keep as much pressure as possible off Rob. They suspected they were going to struggle just to make the race with a brand-new driver, but they didn't want the kid thinking that way. Better he should go out there confidently, assured in his own mind that he could qualify in the top twenty his first time out, even as long as the odds of that actually happening might be. They would need every edge they could get if they were going to have any chance to make the race on Friday night.

"Easy now, boys. Bring her down slow," Will called as he directed Donnie Kline to continue lowering the car on its lift on the back of the hauler. Kline was a relatively new addition to the crew, a big man with a shaved head who looked perfectly capable of lifting a car all by himself, never mind the jack. He and Rob had hit it off immediately, though their continual banter didn't sound exactly friendly all the time.

Rob stood with his hands in his pockets, watching them as they eased the lift to the ground. He already thought of the Ford as "his" car and he wanted to make sure she got gentle treatment.

"Donnie, be careful. I'd like to still have those fenders and a bumper on her when we qualify, if we could."

"Hear that, Will?" Kline growled. "The rookie knows what fenders and a bumper are. He ain't nearly as dumb as you and Billy was tellin' me he was."

Rob still didn't like to stand around and do nothing but now that they were at the track, the others would have none of his help. He was to only think about driving this weekend and nothing else, and he'd be in real trouble if anybody caught him with a wrench or a screwdriver. Billy had told him to relax and get used to all the hoopla and confusion that went with being in the infield of a track bigger than what he was accustomed to.

But all this standing around and watching was making him nervous. He needed to get his hands dirty working on the innards of the car. That would keep his mind clear. When it came time to drive, he would be much more ready if he had done his share in preparing the car.

"What's wrong, cowboy?" Will asked as they finally rolled the car off the ramp. Rob was pacing back and forth like an expectant father.

"I can't stand all this waiting around, doing nothing. You got something I can do to help? Anything."

"Once we get to practicing you won't have time to be bored. This first practice is going to be crucial with only one round of qualifying."

"I hope you're right. I'm used to driving up to the race and pushing the car out on the line and climbing in and running. No waiting required."

"Trust me, you play at this game long enough and you'll be begging for times when there's nothing to do. Tell you what. You dying for something to do, go in the trailer and help Rick unload some of the gear."

Rob brightened.

"Thanks, Will."

But as the kid started up the trailer ramp, Will yelled, "But hey! Don't drop anything heavy on your accelerator foot."

Wilder grinned and waved him off.

Will figured the kid was telling the truth when he pled nervousness. Giving him something simple to do might help. It would be tough enough making the transition from bumping and banging on a local track to big-time racing without having to cope with a case of the nerves.

He hoped, too, that the kid would remain free of any cockiness, even once they had actually begun to win races. This youngster was as unassuming as anyone he had ever seen, and his demeanor seemed absolutely genuine. If he could maintain his humility when he started winning races, it would make their effort that much stronger, their team more tight-knit. Will Hughes hated bigheaded, self-important racecar drivers who thought they were more important than any other cog in a well-oiled set of gears. Such ego could ruin a team's effort as fast as fouled plugs or a full-speed crash.

Finally, it was time for the cars to take to the track for practice. Rob stood there in his new driving suit, still shifting impatiently from one foot to the other, while Will went over some last-minute instructions for what they wanted to accomplish in these first sets of runs. There would not be much time to get comfortable in the car, so everything they did had to focus on getting the car ready to qualify for the race. If they didn't at least qualify, the whole trip had been a waste and their plans for testing car and driver would have to be postponed for awhile.

Rob couldn't help noticing the sideways looks he was getting from the other teams, trying to figure out who he was, where he came from. A couple of them even stopped by long enough to come right out and ask.

"Will, who is this guy you got here?"

It was Elton Sawyer, one of the regulars in Grand National who also had run some on the Cup circuit. He was looking Rob up and down as if he was inspecting an alien from outer space.

"Oh, hey, Elton. This is Rob Wilder. He's a new driver we're taking a look at."

"Well, hey there, buddy," Elton said, extending his hand in Rob's direction in a friendly enough gesture. Rob had not known what kind of reception to expect from the men he would be driving against. "It's nice to meet you. You couldn't be driving for a better bunch of guys."

"Well, thanks," Rob said, hoping his hand didn't tremble when he took Sawyer's. It was difficult, too, meeting and associating with drivers he had watched for years on television or heard racing on the radio.

"First race?" Elton asked. He surely could tell the answer to his question from the paleness of the kid's face.

"Well, yeah. In Grand National, anyway."

"Good luck, Rob. If you need anything, let me know," Sawyer said, and then turned and marched off toward his own car. He suddenly stopped and turned to say something over his shoulder. "Watch those corners. They're a lot flatter than they look. You break it loose in one of them and you'll be hard into the fence. I just don't want you taking me with you if you do."

Rob nodded thanks and filed that tidbit away

alongside all the other tips he had been getting. He stood and watched then as Will and the others finished getting the car ready for their first trip out onto the track. There were only a few minutes before the practice session was going to start and the garage area was now frantic with activity.

What in the world could they all be doing now? Rob wondered. With the Pontiac, once they had checked the water and oil and the air in the tires, they were ready to set sail.

"Okay, cowboy, you about ready to go for a little ride on this bronco?" Will asked. He figured it was high time he got Rob in the car. That, no doubt, would help calm his nerves more than anything else.

"Ready to go!" the kid called and his voice squeaked as he literally leapt into the car. Will shook his head. The kid looked and sounded more like an eager teenager than ever.

All around them, engines began to fire and cars started pulling slowly out onto the speedway. Will was still doing some last minute checks on the car while, now buckled inside the car, Rob tested his restraining belts for the third time. He realized how familiar it all was to him now, the belts, the cockpit, and the hood of the car out there in front of him. He looked around to see if there might be anything he had overlooked.

"Come on, come on," he whispered, hoping Will and the crew would hurry up so he could get the car out onto the track with the others and not waste a precious second of practice time.

He was still looking around the cockpit, tapping impatiently on the wheel with his fingertips, when the earphones in his helmet crackled.

"Fire her up. Let's see if she'll even crank."

"Roger," Rob radioed back, then quickly reached over and hit the starter switch.

The engine immediately awoke. Will stepped to the window and checked the protective netting one last time. Donnie rolled the jack away from the side of the car. Rick Clevenger, the other crewman, gave the hood pins one more check and slapped the sheet metal to show everything was battened down. Rob gave them a little wave and pushed the shifter up into reverse and backed out of the spot.

He rolled the car down the pit road, onto the apron, and finally pointed her out onto the surprisingly wide and flat track. Although it looked totally different from this angle, Rob recognized at once that this place was much like many of the tracks he was used to racing on back home. Immediately comfortable, he pushed the bright red Ford up to speed and began to reel off laps.

Billy preferred having his cars painted fire-engine red if the sponsors would approve. It was a good contrast to the dark blue cars his friend Jodell Lee always raced, but, from a practical standpoint, it was simply easier to follow the car on the track.

The first few laps he ran on the track felt good to Rob. The wide, flat surface didn't give him any trouble at all. Neither did the other cars. Everyone seemed to be working to stay out of each other's way until they could figure out their cars' setup and the track itself.

Billy watched the practice run from atop the grandstand, anxiously clicking his stopwatch, timing the car on every lap. Rob was running relatively fast but the car seemed to be pushing up a bit off the exits from the corners, the nose of the car not wanting to turn into the curve. That was no big deal. They could fix that most likely with a slight wedge adjustment.

"How's she feeling, cowboy?" Will asked on the two-way.

"Pretty decent. Only thing is she's wanting to push just a little in the corners."

"I was afraid of that. We'll loosen her up a bit when you bring her in."

The response from the driver was exactly what Will had hoped to hear. They had actually laid in a little trial for Rob, setting the car up tight at the start on purpose to see what his response would be. Besides, they didn't want it too loose at the start of the practice either. For all they knew, the kid would get excited and try to knock down the fence with the rear end of their beautiful new racecar.

Young Rob Wilder had just passed his first test.

Rob stayed on the track awhile and followed Dale Earnhardt, Jr., Matt Kenseth, and some of the other more experienced Grand National drivers around, taking mental notes the whole time. He mirrored the lines they took, the spots on the track where they would come out of the gas, where they were back into their throttles as they exited the corners. As Billy and Will had suggested he do, Rob was doing his best impression of a sponge, unashamedly soaking up everything he could learn from the others that might eventually help him to get around the track just a little bit faster.

They finally brought the car in and began to adjust, to make the first changes. Will would make a suggestion and they would give it a try. Then Rob would go back out and report quickly on how it had worked. That was a refreshing change for Will. The other drivers they had used before had usually been impatient, only interested in driving the car in the race once everything had been set up perfectly for them. The hit-and-miss of practice was not very glamorous and was sometimes downright tedious. But it was totally necessary. Will was glad to see their driver had both the patience and the aptitude for it.

From Rob's point of view, many of the changes they were making didn't seem to make much sense at the time. But he didn't say anything. He figured these guys were the experts and he still had plenty to learn. And he also knew he was in the best position to report back on the results, so he kept an open mind about every little tweak and correction. He had decided early on that the racecar and the team worked much better together when he kept quiet. He needed to listen and learn, not talk.

Sure enough, some of the adjustments they tried worked and others didn't. Each time, Will would tell Rob what to look for, what to expect from the change, then the kid would take the car back out and run a few laps. All the while, Will coached him on the radio. Billy stood by, watching, occasionally adding an idea or two, but mostly observing the mutual respect that was building among his crewmembers and driver.

And even as he was trying the changes, Rob was learning more and more about the car and gaining even more confidence in his ability to steer it around the track. His speeds were already within the range they thought would be good enough to make the race. Finally, practice ended and the qualifying run was imminent.

Will and the crew were busy making their last minute preparations while Rob sat on the back stoop of the hauler watching them. They clearly knew exactly what they were doing and Rob figured the best thing he could do was stay out of their way. He would have plenty to do shortly.

Billy appeared then, emerging from the front lounge in the trailer. He had been on the telephone for most of the past hour, talking with potential sponsors. He eased down next to Rob and watched his crew swarm all over his racecar.

"How'd that first practice feel, Robbie?"

"I'll admit I was a little nervous at first, but once I got a feel for the track and the car, it was fine."

"It just takes time and patience. Sometimes drivers try to force things. So do crew chiefs. And owners, too, for that matter. Patience is a virtue."

"Yeah, I'm learning that. There was a time or two when I tried to push it and run down into the corner real hard and she almost got away from me. I had to say 'whoa' and put a governor on myself. I can see how those little lapses in concentration could get a driver in trouble."

"That's what's important here. With the level of the competition you'll see, you make even the smallest of mental mistakes and these guys will drive right on past you and not look back."

"I found that out. A couple of times I made just the slightest bobble out there and the next thing I'd know, three or four cars would get by me."

"You make a mistake, get over it quick. You have to stay focused. Everybody out there makes a mistake occasionally. That's how you learn. But get wrapped up in a mistake for too long or try to make it up too fast and you may blow the whole race."

Rob had been concentrating so hard on what Billy was saying that he hardly noticed that someone had walked up beside them and was eavesdropping on their conversation.

"So, Billy Winton, I assume that this must be that new driver I've been hearing about, the one that you've been hiding from us."

It was a female voice. Rob turned to see a very attractive young blonde-haired woman standing there, smiling, a notepad and tape recorder in her hand.

"And one more thing. Rule number one, Rob," Billy said with a wink toward the kid. "Avoid the press at all costs, even if they are as good looking as Miss Susan Maguire here."

"I'm glad to see you're still as politically incorrect as always, Billy," she said with a smile, but she still wrinkled her brow a bit as if she wasn't totally kidding.

"One of the privileges of getting old. Susan, this is Rob Wilder. We're taking a look at him for a few races. So far, so good. Rob, meet Susan Maguire. She writes for one of the weekly racing papers."

"Pleased to meet you, ma'am," Rob said and extended a greasy hand. He suddenly realized how dirty it was and quickly pulled it back, jerked a rag out of his pocket, and tried to wipe it clean. "Sorry," he apologized, blushing.

"That's okay. Happens a lot. I don't mind a little grease. It goes with the beat, after all."

Billy couldn't help but notice the way she was surveying his driver as she shook his hand, taking in his lean tallness, his long hair, his youthful face. And he was certain he could read her mind.

"Don't worry. He's old enough to have a driver's license," he said in anticipation of her next question.

"You sure?"

"And he seems to be a pretty fair racer," Billy added.

"Or else I wouldn't expect Billy Winton to put him in the cockpit of one of his cars. Mind if we chat a minute before you have to qualify, Rob?"

He looked first at Billy, saw only a blank look on his face, then realized he was on his own.

"Sure. What can I tell you?"

"Well, let's start with the basics. Where you from?"

"I'm from Hazel Green, Alabama," Rob responded.

"So where is that close to? I'm from Charlotte and if they don't have a Cup or a Grand National track there, I'm afraid I don't know where it is."

"Oh, it's kind of north of Huntsville, the Rocket City. I usually just tell people I'm from Huntsville, though. Most people have heard of that."

"You drive like I saw you doing in that first practice, putting up those kinds of times, and I think a lot more people will know where Hazel Green, Alabama is. And who Rob Wilder is, too."

Maguire's comment brought a small smile to Billy's face. So, others in the garage had been watching, timing his driver. Reporters already sniffing around after only the first practice? That was a good sign. Now, if they could only get the car qualified and in the field. That would really get their attention!

And the attention of other folks, too. Folks with checkbooks.

Susan finished up her short interview with Rob in only a few minutes but promised to come back later for more. Maybe enough for a full story in next week's edition. Billy knew that depended on how he did in qualifying and the race but he could see the lights go on in Rob's eyes. He gave his driver a tap on the shoulder.

"Why don't you go on in and get yourself a cold drink and rest for a little bit. Qualifying starts right here shortly."

"Okay. You want me to bring y'all something?"

"No, thanks," Billy said, winking again at Susan. A good driver and polite to boot. "Just go rest up and be ready to put that car on the pole."

Rob told Susan goodbye, shook her hand once more, and told her again how happy he was to have met her.

"So where on Earth did you find him?" Susan asked as soon as Rob had disappeared into the back of the hauler. "He's so young, but he comes across as genuine. The fans and the sponsors are going to love him . . . if he can drive."

"Ain't that always the case? To tell you the truth, I didn't find him. Jodell Lee did. The kid was driving at a race where Joe Dee was doing an appearance, racing in some old beat-up car, but he managed to whip a couple of the local hotshots and do it in a way that impressed Jodell more than somewhat."

"You don't say? But aren't you taking a big chance with him? It's a long way from some little bitty old local track to here. You think he has what it takes?"

"I don't know, Susan. You tell me after you see him run." They'd known each other long enough that she was familiar with his struggles with some of the journeymen Cup drivers he had been forced to hire. And she knew, too, that if Billy Winton and Jodell Lee were both willing to take a chance on such an unproven quantity, they had to have seen something special. Winton looked her in the eye. "What are they saying about the kid that made you look us up and ask all those questions after only one practice? I figured you'd be out tracking down Earnhardt, Jr. or that Atwood young'un. Seems like that's where the stories are that your readers would want to see. Not over here with the unknowns and the has-beens."

"Well, Billy, your guy could be right up there with those guys. They're saying he looks like he cut fifth-period study hall to come up here and race and yet he's putting up times out there and handling the car like he's been doing this for years. You know how hungry the fans and sponsors are for a young gun they can get behind. And every man-jack out there in those pits wants to say they spotted him first."

"Off the record, okay? Jodell says the kid is the most natural driver he's seen since Little Joe Weatherley. And, thank God, he doesn't have all of Little Joe's peculiarities. That's high praise indeed."

Joe Weatherley had been one of the earliest superstars of stock car racing. He had died in a tragic crash at the Riverside track in California at the height of his career. Twenty-four of his twenty-five wins in the old Grand National series came in the five years before he was killed. Billy had never gotten the chance to see him drive but he had heard plenty about him from Jodell Lee and his crew. And about his legendary parties and practical jokes, too.

"Yeah, that sort of puts the onus on the kid, doesn't it?" Susan said, shaking her head. "It's kinda like Buddy Baker saying on television that Casey Atwood drives as well as Fireball Roberts did. Gives these young guys a lot to live up to."

"Well, if they have the touch and the heart and the competitive spirit, they'll do it. And if they don't, they don't belong out there on that track in the first place."

Just then, the call came on the public address for the cars to line up for qualifying. Billy told Susan goodbye and stood, ready to get going. Will stepped over, nodded politely in Susan Maguire's direction as she headed away for the press box, and spoke to Billy.

"High number."

"Shoot!"

They would have to attempt to qualify late in the session. They had hoped to draw an early number in the lineup. That would have put Rob out before he had time to get nervous or see some especially good times posted ahead of him already. And that might have kept him from pushing too hard once he was on the track.

But so far, the kid seemed cool as could be. Billy tried to keep him distracted as the first of the cars rolled off for their qualifying run. He recounted the interview and told him how proud he was of how he had handled himself. He also gave him a few tips on things he should try to do or say when talking with reporters: what to reveal and what not to, the differences between those on deadline for daily papers, radio, and television and those who would have several days to file their stories, and how he should give them different information. And, primarily, how important it was to mention the sponsor for the radio and TV guys and to speak in short thoughts to everyone so he could be easily quoted or more likely to make the eleven o'clock sports report.

But, primarily, the reason for the tutorial was to keep Wilder's attention off the others who were already qualifying. The hope was that he could simply go out and make a good, clean lap as if he was simply practicing at whatever small track he most often ran. Billy and Will were convinced that if he did relax and simply do what he seemed to know how to do, if he was smooth and hit his marks correctly, then the car's speed would be there and they would at least have a shot at making the field.

But if he tensed up and drove the car too hard, they would most likely be loading her up in the back of the hauler and heading for home in a few minutes. Or loading up what was left of her if he found the wall in his desperation to show well.

Finally, it was time. The crew pushed the car slowly out to the line. Rob jumped up to help. He'd never driven a single race before without having to help push his car out to line it up. Billy just smiled and allowed him to shove along with the rest of the crew. He saw no need to tell him that at this level, the driver wasn't necessarily expected to push the car around.

Qualifying times were fast from the very first competitor to roar away. Will looked at Billy when the first time was posted. They read each other's minds. Most of the drivers had somehow picked up more speed since practice. Will checked the times for the second and third qualifiers and fretted. They were going to have to have a near-perfect lap to guarantee them a spot in the field. It was now clear that the times they had been running before that had seemed adequate would be marginal now, based on how fast these guys were qualifying.

One by one, the cars were waved out to run their hot lap. Green, Sawyer, Parsons, Atwood, Earnhardt, Kenseth, and the others roared away and, to a man, posted impressive times. As the results were announced, Will and Billy continued to exchange glances over the top of the car. The odds were getting stacked higher and higher against them as each car shot beneath the checkered flag. They were careful to not allow their young driver to see the looks on their faces, though.

Then, when there were only three more cars sitting in front of them, Will motioned for Rob to climb into the racecar. He wanted the kid in place early to allow him time to get acclimated, to allay any jitters he might be feeling from attempting to qualify a car at this level. And they had been observant enough to notice that a deep, confident calm seemed to envelop Wilder anytime he sat in the cockpit of the racer.

Will leaned through the window to help him buckle up. Rob was already pulling on his helmet, totally unaware of the concerns the other two men had about his mental state, the success of all the others' laps, and their own concerns about making the race. He had put his nerves behind him now that the time had finally come to actually do something rather than sit on his hands and wait. He was ready to go, ready to take this powerful racecar out there on the track and show them what he could do with her.

"You about set, cowboy?"

"I've been ready, Will. You know what? There's too much standing around up here!" he answered and flashed Will a big grin, showing his perfect white teeth as if he was posing for a picture. Ironically, Billy was snapping his photo at that very moment, chronicling what could possibly be a memorable moment: their first successful qualification run together. After the flash, Rob pointed toward the track with a gloved hand. "Let's get this thing qualified so we can start gettin' her ready for the race tonight."

Will looked at him sideways. For the first time, he realized that the kid might be understandably nervous about being here, but he was also supremely confident that he would drive this car right into the race. He was already thinking about later this evening.

"Just go out yonder and get me a good smooth lap like we've been running in practice and then we can go about getting the race setup under her."

"I'll get you that lap, Will. No problem there."

The set of the kid's jaw confirmed that he was certain of his promise.

"You're the next car out. Just run like we been running, okay?"

"Got it!"

Will slapped Rob on the shoulder and backed his head out of the car, then pulled up the window net and clipped it into place. There were only a few cars left behind them to qualify. The car directly ahead of them roared off then, leaving Rob looking out the windshield at nothing but the open lane that led out onto the track.

And out onto the rest of his racing career.

He sucked in a deep breath and let it out slowly. It was now the time to show them all what he had, that he was, indeed, ready for this level of competition. Sure, he could go out and try to push the car beyond its capability and try to claim the pole itself. Most rookie drivers would do just that. But he knew he had to finish the lap to have any hope of qualifying. Put her into the wall and they'd have nothing but a bushel of body damage to show for their trip to Indianapolis. And he would be nothing more than another charging, reckless young racecar driver with more foot than head.

No, he was a racer. And there was a big difference.

Rob smiled. He knew what he could do. And now he had a good feel for what the car was capable of. Will and Billy were most likely biting their nails right about now, but Rob Wilder was confident. He couldn't wait for the official to wave him out. He was still driving a mental lap when the call finally came. He revved the engine up a couple of times, then eased off on the clutch and rolled the car out onto the speedway just as the other car qualifying ahead of him flashed by.

Behind him, as soon as the car had rolled away and he was certain he was no longer in Rob's rearview mirror, Will Hughes looked over to Billy Winton and showed him a pair of crossed fingers.

Rob rolled through the first turn, already pushing the car hard to get to speed and warm up the tires. He had to be at top speed when the car crossed the start/finish line to take the green flag that would signal the start of his qualifying lap. Everything felt good beneath him as he circled, then he focused his attention on the first turn, a straightaway ahead, as he came roaring out of turn four to take the flag.

He stayed hard in the gas until he felt that the car was likely on the edge of losing its grip, skewing upward, as he turned the wheel into the first turn. Then he eased off a bit, touched the brakes, set the line, and sailed boldly through turn one and right on into two. He kept his driving as smooth as he could as he pushed through the turns, knowing a mistake here could cause him to lose traction and fractions of a second on the timing at best, or spin the car at worst. There would be no second chance to recover from such a mistake, no place on this track to make it up.

Then, he was through the first two turns and was back on the gas as the Ford hurtled out of the sharp curve of turn two and was pointed down the backstretch, already set up in the perfect position to resume acceleration. The run so far was so smooth, it seemed to him as if the car was driving herself, as if she was smart enough to know where on the track she would run the fastest, what the quickest possible speed she could manage would be. But Rob knew it was only because he had such a good feel for the car. He was still in control and he wasn't asking the car to do anything she wasn't capable of doing.

Now, with the next turn coming up quickly, he put the car right down on the white line on the inside of the track. She stuck as if she was actually supposed to run there. Then, exiting the fourth turn, he steered the car right out to the wall, only inches away from the barrier as he stomped the accelerator again and roared down the front stretch to take the checkered flag. He didn't let off until he was already at the entrance to the first turn again.

Back in the pits, Will and Billy each held stopwatches and clicked their buttons simultaneously. And they both avoided looking at the results for a moment after the run was done.

As the kid had driven the lap, they had watched him get a good run down into turn one and then saw him put the car right in the line they knew was the fastest through there. He seemed to have a good exit from the second turn, too, and then, when he put the car so low in the third and fourth turns, Will had pumped his fist and yelled.

"Attaboy! Attaboy! Come on, now. Finish strong!" Will hollered.

Billy's eyes left the track for an instant to check out his crew chief. It was not like Will Hughes to show any emotion at all. Now he was jumping and kicking and yelling like a cheerleader.

Then, after Rob took the Ford beneath the checkered flag, they both finally checked their stopwatches, but still refused to believe them until the official word came over the public address system. It seemed like it took an hour to make the announcement, and even then, they weren't sure they were hearing right through the grumbling of the engine of the next car pulling out to qualify.

But then the PA announcer added a bit more information and the two men happily high-fived, then hugged each other unashamedly.

". . . And currently with the fourteenth fastest time, rookie driver Rob Wilder."

The time flashed on the scoreboard and that confirmed it. With only a few more cars left to make a run, they knew they were solidly in the middle of the field for their first race as a team.

The small crowd in the grandstands applauded politely. They knew the effort necessary for a rookie to make the field here in his very first start. Over by the Billy Winton truck, the hoots and yelps could be heard throughout the garage. It might have been their first qualification ever, judging from all the excitement. But everyone in the crew knew what this meant. They had found themselves the final piece of the puzzle. They had themselves a team.

Will sprinted over to the car and bear-hugged Rob as he calmly climbed out of the Ford.

"Alright! Great job!" Will crowed as he picked his driver up off the ground and danced him around.

"Whoa! Wait a minute, chief," the startled kid laughed. "We haven't won anything yet. The race is tonight."

"We did win the first race. We made it into the field. You are going to race this evening!"

He let the kid go then and slapped him on the back. Rob was looking at him oddly. He had never seen Will Hughes so emotional. The man was normally a flatline on the emotion meter. And all this whooping and hollering for just making the race? Wasn't that what he was supposed to do?

"Well, of course I am. I thought that's why we

came up here in the first place. Did you actually think I wouldn't make the field?"

Everyone standing there erupted into laughter. Billy Winton joined in. The kid had never doubted that he would make the race. Billy shook his head as he stepped over to congratulate Rob. If only he had had the same confidence, the last day or so would have been far less stressful.

He was finally ready to admit that maybe—just maybe—the kid was a real find, a natural.

Across town, inside the Indianapolis Motor Speedway, a cell phone beeped shrilly from where it lay on top of a toolbox. An obviously harried Jodell Lee almost ignored the blamed thing. His car had been struggling in practice and everyone on the team, himself included, were neck-deep in a frantic search for speed. The car was a couple of tenths of a second off the pace and nothing they tried had seemed to pick it up.

Then he thought it might be Catherine. Maybe an emergency back home. He fished the thing out of his pants pocket and answered it with an irritated growl.

"What?"

"Well, a hardy hello to you, too," Billy said. "What you got stuck in your craw, old man?"

"Aw, Billy, we're struggling for speed and I'm fixin' to pull this thing back on the hauler and go home with it and save the gas and tires. So to what do I owe the honor of this call?"

"It's that kid you hooked me up with."

There was a short take on the other end of the line.

"So, he didn't make the race for you and now you're calling me up to give me a hard time about it, huh? Well, I got to tell you, I've got enough of my own blamed problems right now to take any of the credit for yours," Jodell snapped.

"Didn't make the race? Is that why you thought I was calling? Hah! I was calling you up to thank you, Jodell. That kid just went out there and qualified us in the top fifteen."

"What? You pulling my leg?"

"I'm telling you, Jodell. This kid is the real deal. He drives like a ten- or fifteen-year veteran."

"Well, I'll be," Jodell said into the cell phone. "Maybe you'll learn not to doubt ol' Jodell Bob Lee when it comes to sizing up racecar drivers."

"Never, my friend. Reckon you'll have time to come over and watch him later on tonight?"

"I sure will. If they don't arrest me for impersonating a race team owner between now and then, that is."

They talked a few more minutes before they hung up. Then Billy Winton sat there in the hauler lounge, nursing a soda, trying to think who all else he wanted to call to tell about this kid he had behind the steering wheel of his racecar.

THE RACE

Rob Wilder didn't think the lull between the end of practice and the start of the race festivities would ever end.

Billy Winton and Will Hughes thought time was passing like a runaway truck on a downward slope. There was more they wanted to do to the car but the race was imminent now and there was always the risk of messing up something and not having time to fix it. Rob still couldn't understand why the car was never finished.

"When do y'all finally quit working on the car?" he asked Donnie Kline late that afternoon.

"When she'll go a thousand miles an hour and still stay all hugged up to the track. That's when." The big man winked and went back to his ratcheting.

The last practice was done and Will led the crew on his detailed pre-race check of the car while Rob looked on. The racecar itself rested on jack stands directly behind the team hauler. There were checklists taped everywhere on the car, under the hood, in the wheel wells, in the trunk, and in the cockpit, all flapping in the breeze like captured birds.

Now, while the crew did their job, Rob did his, sitting in a director's chair, getting himself interviewed by the racing beat reporter for the *Charlotte Observer*. Word had gotten around about the good qualifying run, that Billy Winton had found himself a driver. Now, the requests for interviews had jumped from nothing to plenty. He had spoken with three newspaper guys, a crew from ESPN, a television reporter from Indianapolis, and someone who ran an Internet racing site. By now, he was running on automatic pilot but it still felt good, actually having someone interested in what he had to say. He tried to keep in mind what Billy had been telling him, but the reporters mostly asked the same questions over and over so he just kept repeating the same answers.

Billy stood in the back of the truck watching the crew and Rob work. He was proud of the kid. He seemed to be taking all the new attention in stride, keeping his poise and polish and giving the reporters exactly what they wanted. Despite his rural background, he showed no signs of the media jitters that plagued so many young drivers, and some old ones, as well. He kept his answers brief and to the point, spoke his opinions without being cocky, appeared humble and cooperative, and politely thanked each reporter when the interview was completed. One of the newspaper guys even asked for his autograph and for him to write the date next to it.

"I don't usually do this," he groused, "but someday, you may actually make it in this sport and I'd like to say I interviewed you 'when.' "

Billy couldn't believe his ears. That particular writer was one of the toughest in the business. His boy had apparently won over one of the old dogs. He smiled. If they ultimately decided to take the program up to the next level, the kid seemed ready to take on these kinds of demands.

Early in the evening, the drivers' meeting just completed and the final checks made on the racecar, Jodell Lee came sauntering up. He brought along with him several members of his over-the-wall pit crew to help Will with his pit stops. It was clear that on a tight course such as this one, quick stops would be critical. Otherwise, a car could lose laps in a hurry during tire changes.

Jodell put his arm around Rob's shoulders.

"Feel like takin' a walk, kid?" he asked.

"Sure."

He led Rob around the track, showing him a few things he might not have noticed and giving him a few tips the other drivers would have paid good money to hear. All along the way, he preached the gospel of patience.

"I know how bad you want to win the whole thing," he said. "But for a first run against competition like these old boys, just finishing is a victory for you. Show 'em you can drive and it'll help you more than you can imagine from now on. You get their respect, they'll move over for you when you got the faster car and they'll think twice about trying to pull any junk on you. They think you're not up to it, they'll punt you right off the track if you get in their way."

Rob listened carefully to everything Jodell told him. The old driver was right about one thing. Rob certainly did have the burning desire to go out there and win this first start. He knew his own limitations, but he was confident he had a chance, and especially in the car Will had built.

But he was also smart enough to know he had plenty to lose, too, by going out and showing what many people expected, that he was only another raw rookie, a danger to himself and everybody else on the track. Despite all the backslapping Billy and the rest of them had done, he knew he was still under a microscope, still very much on trial.

"I appreciate it, Mr. Lee. I just want to show Billy and them that I can do this. You, too, for all the faith you've put in me. I do appreciate that. And I got to tell you, if I can win this race, I intend to do that very thing. But I also know I can't mess up. I know I need to finish. Then I'll have plenty of chances to show the rest of them I've got what it takes to finish first."

Jodell stopped for a moment and looked the kid in the eye.

"Son, sometimes I wonder if you're shooting us all a line of bull manure. You sure say all the right things. But the proof is right out yonder." He pointed toward the asphalt track that encircled them. "Either you can or you can't. You either want it as bad as you want to breathe or you don't. We may not know tonight. Lots of things can happen out there. But Billy and Will are smart enough to know. You just go out there and relax and have a good time. You got it, they'll see it. You don't, they'll see that, too, and you don't need to be out there anyway or you'll get your young butt killed."

Rob tried to hold the old driver's gaze.

"Mr. Lee, I've never wanted anything so bad in my

life. I intend to make you all proud. And some other folks, too."

"Good. And call me 'Jodell,' not 'Mr. Lee.' "

"Yessir."

The kid looked away then, just as a couple of fans recognized Jodell and stopped for an autograph.

"You better get this kid's, too," Jodell told them, pointing a thumb in Rob's direction.

"You a driver?"

Jodell didn't give Rob a chance to answer.

"You're dad-blame right he's a driver!"

Everyone was rattling off so many last-minute instructions that Rob completely missed Miss Indiana singing the National Anthem. It was almost a relief to finally be in the seat, strapped in, with no one else jabbering except for Will on the radio. And even he had cut down to just the basics on pit stop strategy.

Rob wiped his forehead one more time with a rag before he dropped the visor. There had been a time when all he had had to do was show up at a track, roll the car off the trailer, and drive a race. Not here! It had never occurred to him what all was involved in getting the car ready, getting the driver's head in the race, plotting strategy, lecturing and practicing the crew, and all the other things that cluttered up a simple evening's drive. No, it had been much simpler, just showing up, driving fast for awhile, and leading the field on the last lap.

Oh, but forget going back. He was where he wanted to be. Man, was he where he wanted to be!

"Gentlemen, start your engines!"

"They're playing your song. Fire her up, cowboy."

"Roger," Rob answered. He reached over, hit the starter switch, and felt the car vibrate as the big engine coughed and started. He could not actually hear it over the accumulated thunder of all the other cars, but he saw the needles dancing on the dash and felt the reassuring shivering of the Ford's frame.

There was also radio chatter in his ears once more as Will and the rest of the crew checked out the communication circuit. Finally, there was the spotter, one of Jodell's men, who was standing on a rooftop overlooking the track.

"Rob? This is Clarence. You and me are going to be best buddies before this night's over," the voice said.

"Hi, Clarence. Good to have you along for the ride."

Then the official who was standing between the two rows of rumbling racecars was motioning with both hands for them to roll out and hit the track, to take their pace laps and get ready to race. Rob sat in the front third of the field on the inside row and his windshield was full of the rear ends of swerving, swaggering cars. Rob sawed away on his own steering wheel, cleaning his tires, trying to get them warm for the start.

"How are all the temperatures looking?" Will asked.

"Coming up fine."

"Good. I know I've said it before, but be careful on the start and remember that you can't pass to the inside until you cross the line."

"Got it."

"Now watch your pit speeds if you have to come in. Do them just like we practiced."

Everyone knew that would be the trickiest part. Pitting the car had not been something Rob had done much of in his previous experience. And that could be tricky for even the more experienced drivers.

"Ten-four."

The cars slowly tailed the pace car as they all paraded down in front of the grandstands. Out his side window, Rob could see a large crowd, standing, waving, popping hundreds of flashbulbs. There had been times that he had scanned the crowd at races, looking for particular, familiar faces. But tonight, there would be no one there specifically watching him. A couple of his buddies had talked about coming up but had not made it. Those were all strangers up there. Maybe, before the night was over, some of them would know his name, would pick him out in future parade laps and pull for him to do well. Not tonight, though. All his fans at this racetrack were down there to his left, in the Billy Winton slot in the pits, crowded around their toolboxes and stacks of tires and standing on the pit wall nervously waiting for him to go.

The frenzy that had been building for hours was finally set to begin. The flagman held up one finger as they rolled beneath him, meaning one lap to go. The lights on the back of the pace car were extinguished, telling the drivers that the next lap they would be racing.

Rob took a deep breath, thankful all the preparations for his coming-out were finally over. Now it was all up to him. He wiggled in the seat a bit, getting as comfortable as he could, making sure the belts were good and tight. He steeled himself for the hellacious land rush that was about to break out in front of and behind him. This was it, the culmination of all the hard work and hours of small-track racing he had done so far.

For a moment, he allowed himself to flash back to a time when he was only twelve years old. He had somehow found the nerve to crawl behind the wheel of a hobby car, lying about his age, telling the owner he was fifteen and a half. After a couple of races with Rob in the car, the owner quit asking to see a birth certificate.

And there had been familiar faces there, then. At least, in the beginning. Someone to rush across the track when it was all over, grab him, give him the kind of hug and handshake that only a mother and father could.

Now, the powerful cars slowly rolled through turns three and four, like horses straining at their bridles. The pace car suddenly took a hard left turn and dived down to the inside of the track out of their way. The field bunched up tightly, bumpers touching bumpers, as the drivers strained to see the green flag unfurled from the hand of the starter, standing high up in the flagstand up ahead at the start/finish line. They were too far away to see the look on the starter's face, but they knew he was watching them intently, making certain someone didn't jump the start, didn't do anything to gain unfair advantage over the others.

Rob pulled up as tightly as he could manage on the back bumper of the Chevrolet that was rolling along in front of him. He felt a slight tap in the rear from the car behind him as that driver tried to stay on his bumper, too. The dry heat that rose off the header pipes beneath his feet was already toasting the floorboard and quickly warmed up the inside of the car. He could smell it, feel it, and he imagined this must be how a sauna would feel if he had ever been inside one.

He was sweating already, and felt sticky inside his fireproof driving suit. He put the discomfort out of his mind, though, and gripped the wheel tightly as he looked ahead, searching for the green flag amid the swirl of color in the stands behind the flagman. He knew he needed to get the start of this race right or he was liable to find himself drop-kicked from behind by the cars that ran so tight on his rear end that he seemed to be towing them along. But before he could do too much searching, he spotted a green blur and heard Clarence's voice, shrieking in his earpiece.

"Green, green, green, green!"

Rob had already stomped down hard on the accelerator before the first "Green!" had been finished. He set his sights on the far turn, and watched the cars in front of him skew and plunge forward, and from the corner of his eye, saw the other cars that darted and danced wildly all around him. His immediate concern, though, was the car that ran directly on the outside of him. The driver steered sharply downward onto him as they raced off toward the first turn. The other driver actually brushed against him, leaving a puff of smoke in their wake and a black tire doughnut on the side of the 6 car.

Rob twisted the wheel instinctively, fighting to hold his spot in line, and the two cars roared off through the corner in perfect tandem, neither giving an inch. Except for the two lead cars that had already broken away from the pack, the rest of the field ran two by two through the corner, exactly as they had roared beneath the flagstand at the start.

Rob smiled inside his helmet. It was nothing new to him. Grand National division on a track before thousands in Indy or a quarter-mile oval in Podunk before a couple of hundred, the start was exactly what he was used to. The cars on the outside did all they could to push their way down into the inside line, the faster route around the track by far. And the drivers on the inside did all they could, short of launching hand grenades at their competitors, to hold onto what they had.

Ten laps into the two hundred that would make up this race, Rob Wilder realized how much fun he was having. True, he could not remember ever working so hard or having to maintain so much concentration on so many different things at one time. But he was living the stuff of his dreams, a fantasy he had harbored since that first day in the cramped little seat of the hobby car when he had felt that intoxicating rush of adrenaline as he passed an opponent for the first time and left him behind in his dust and exhaust smoke. And driving against these guys, young guns rapidly rising up through big-time stock car racing's second tier, still left him a bit breathless.

Oh, he didn't doubt for a second that he belonged here. It was simply the magnitude of it all that gave him pause.

And he had quickly realized that it was much more difficult than a Saturday night feature on the tracks back home, and it looked *much* easier on television. These guys were good! They seemed ready to pounce on even the slightest mistake.

Rob drove down into turn one too hard once, the car pushing up ever so slightly on him when he did. In an instant, the car trailing him had its nose beneath him and had pulled right on past. And even before the spotter was able to yell to him on the radio that there was a narrow slot there if he wanted to pull back down in line, six cars had sailed right on by him while he spat out tire grit and pounded the wheel in frustration.

But he remembered what Jodell Lee had told him

and quickly got back in line and did all he could to keep pace.

His first trip onto the pit road, even under the caution flag, was an adventure, too. They had practiced the maneuver as much as they could without all the other cars around them, but now, in the madness of the fruit-basket–turnover that a pit stop resembled, it was a totally different thing. As he pulled off the track and onto the pit road, all he could see was pandemonium everywhere. Looking down the length of the pit road with all the cars swerving into their stalls, others up on jacks getting serviced, and still more screeching away to get back in line on the track, he couldn't even see where he was supposed to stop. Clarence had to guide him in like an air traffic controller landing a plane in a storm.

The over-the-wall gang quickly went to work, jumping across even before he had completely stopped in the stall. The tire changers from Jodell's team were amazingly quick about their job. Rob only had time to stop the car, shift it up into first, and grab the offered water bottle that came in to him through the gap between the window and the upright door bar. He was still fumbling with the tube on the bottle when he felt the car drop off the jack and Will's voice screaming over the radio.

"Go, go, go, go, go!"

Rob was too careful about avoiding stalling the car when he popped the clutch, almost getting himself run over by another car charging past him down the tight pit lane. But he caught sight of the car in his mirror and yanked the wheel, then stood on the gas and peeled away, running side by side with the other driver down the short run back to the track.

"Good job, cowboy, good job." Will sounded sincere, even though Rob felt at the moment that he had made a mess of his first pit visit. "You got fresh tires and a belly full of gasoline. We took a pound of air pressure out on the right side and did a quarter turn on the wedge adjustment."

That meant they had changed the air pressure in the car's right-side tires and added a little more tension to the springs on that side. The car had been handling relatively well, and Rob had reported that to the crew, but Will felt they needed to make the minor adjustments as the track conditions changed.

"Ten-four," was Rob's only answer. He was concentrating now on merging back into traffic without getting himself run over or bulldozing into some other slower cars that were just now coming out of the pits ahead of him.

Only then did he notice that his right foot felt as if it was resting in the hot coals of a fireplace. The heat was still radiating up through the floorboard from the headers and it was impossible for him to keep his foot on the throttle pedal without having it contact the scorching metal. He could only try to block out the searing pain and focus on driving the car. He could put the thing in a bucket of ice water once he had won this race.

The cars continued to circle while they cleaned up the debris from the crash that had brought out the caution flag and led to the first round of pit stops. Rob was running in twentieth place. When Clarence informed him of that fact on the radio, he didn't know whether to be glad or upset. Upset because he had lost some spots since they had started the race. Glad because if felt at times as if the entire field had passed him already. At any rate, he was a rookie, and he had managed to stay on the lead lap, ahead of people who had been doing this for a long time.

Still, it gnawed at him that he wasn't leading. That's what he desperately wanted to do.

Billy and Jodell stood watching him exit the pits and get back in line for the restart.

"Not bad, old partner," Jodell grinned.

"He's been a little impatient a time or two and it cost him," Billy said, "but with some polish and experience, he might be all right."

"Yep, I figured on an old tight track like this one and with the kind of drivers and cars they have in Grand National nowadays, he'd drift right on back to the rear and ride along learning. Instead, he's held his own pretty good. The kid's a driver, Bill. Notice how the car seems to drive itself, seems to know exactly where to go on the track without him even telling it to? That's how you tell. You ask a driver how he made this move or that and he'll just shrug his shoulders. He can't tell you. It's a gift. And I believe Mr. Rob Wilder has the gift."

Another fifty laps into the race, fatigue suddenly slapped Rob hard in the face. He had never run a race this long before. And he had certainly never driven this intensely before. The close-quarters racing never gave him an instant to relax, to think about anything other than getting around the car in front of him or holding off the driver that was coming up quickly from behind to try to get around him.

The constant bucking of the steering wheel had caused his arms to ache and spasm and it felt as if the seat belts were slicing into the skin of his shoulders. Even the seat that had been so comfortable at the start now seemed to be padded with rocks and bricks instead. And his right foot still felt as if it was being rotated slowly on a spit over a charcoal fire.

Will could tell that Rob was wearing down. He began to talk to him more on the radio, giving him lap times, counting down how many were left, and mixing in some words of encouragement. Eventually, he had dropped several laps behind the leaders, the four or five cars who had been setting a furious pace since the get-go. He was struggling simply to hold on, doing all he could to keep the car in the top twenty. But Will was convinced now that the kid was doing his best driving in the last laps. Tired, hot, and likely very frustrated, he was still making moves, holding off challengers, racing.

It was little consolation that the heat and humidity were taking a toll on even the most experienced drivers. Crashes and mechanical failures were ending the night for some of the teams as well. So far, Rob had steered clear of the wrecks, once or twice with truly breathtaking skill, most of the time by sheer luck. Running where he was, in a pack of drivers trying to stay in the bigger money and points, all running about the same speed, it was almost inevitable that he would get caught up in some kind of smash-up. But so far he had steered around all the carnage.

Will knew, too, that with only thirty or so laps to go and the last pit stops already done, there would be plenty of hard fender banging from now until the end. He radioed Rob to be sure to give the leaders plenty of room to race against each other. He certainly didn't want the rookie, *his* rookie, to get in their way as they dueled for the lead.

The checkered flag finally fell. Will and Billy held their breath, waiting for the final standings to be posted. Then, with the results in, they smiled at each other one more time. Their kid had held on for a top-twenty finish in his very first Grand National race!

Jodell slapped Billy on the shoulder then shook his hand. Billy was beaming. Qualifying was a victory. Finishing ahead of more than a dozen far more experienced teams and bringing the car home in one piece throughout a brutal race, was more than they could have ever hoped for.

Even Will Hughes allowed himself a bit of a smile when Jodell hopped off the wall and hugged him.

"Work with the kid, Will. He'll take you a long, long way."

"Joe Dee, you might just be right," Will said with a wink, and then he smiled again.

Twice in two minutes. That was an astonishing display of spontaneous emotion for Will Hughes!

Rob steered the car slowly around the track for its cool down lap. Inside, the driver knew nothing of all the celebration in his pit. He was disappointed that the checkered flag had fallen before he had had an opportunity to improve his position. He'd been back in the middle of the bunch since he had made the careless move early in the race. Nobody but the leaders had really gotten by him, but neither had he been able to get back the positions that he had lost. And even though he was as tired and sore as he had ever been in his young life, he was still having a blast driving the car, right up until they made him quit by ending the race.

He pulled the car in to the garage and up to the back of the truck, shut off the engine, and slumped down into the seat. He wasn't sure he had the strength to lift the steering wheel off the column or unsnap the belts and yank off his helmet. But suddenly, someone jerked the window net down and a pair of strong arms reached into the car to help him get disentangled and to climb out. Donnie Kline pulled him out and set him down against the side of the car while someone else produced a towel soaked in ice water and a cold drink.

"Not bad for a rookie," Donnie said, and tapped him on the shoulder. Rob knew the big crewman well enough to know that was practically gushing praise, coming from him.

Will leaned down, looked into his driver's tired eyes, unzipped the front of his driving suit, and draped another towel around his neck.

"How you holding up?"

Rob managed a weak grin.

"Reckon they'd let us run a hundred more?"

"I don't know if you or the car would break first."

Rob tried to shift his legs and grunted.

"I think I may have burned my foot a little."

"Here, let's get this shoe off. Donnie, get us a bucket of water."

Will knelt down and began to untie the driving shoe. The shoes themselves were plenty thick and de-signed to be fireproof, but they weren't really intended to protect the foot from all the heat radiating up through the floorboard.

Rob grunted involuntarily when Will slipped the shoe off over his heel.

"We'll have to put some padding down or do some-thing for next time to keep it from getting so hot on you." Once the sock was off, he could see that the heel was blistered and red. "It's not burned too bad. Might interfere with your dancing for a day or so. Soak it here a minute and we'll put some ointment on it. You'll be ready to go next weekend."

Rob was still sitting there, swigging sodas, wiping the sweat out of his eyes, soaking his burned foot, when Billy and Jodell returned from congratulating the winning team. Jodell knew from experience how the kid must have been feeling. Hurt, hot, sore, exhausted, and no trophy to show for it. A nice check, maybe. Certainly more money than he ever got for a top-twenty finish at those backwater tracks.

But no victory. And that was why people like Jodell Lee and Rob Wilder drove racecars. Not to finish somewhere in the middle.

"Good run, kid." Billy said to his exhausted driver. "You showed us a few things out there tonight."

"Thanks, Billy. If I haven't said so already, I appreciate more than you'll ever know you giving me the chance to drive that car. It was a lot harder than I expected, but it sure was fun. I just wish I could've gotten you a win."

"You'll get us some, I reckon."

Rob looked up at him.

"You know I wanted to run some more tonight."

"From the looks of you, they probably dropped that checkered just in the nick of time," Jodell Lee offered.

"You may be right. Only thing is, I run to win, sir. I had a good time tonight but I also got my butt kicked. I'll be ready next time," Rob said, his jaw set and his eyes squinted. "And more ready the time after that. I'm gonna get you a win, Billy. Stick with me and I'll get you a win sooner than later."

The kid's voice quavered on the last few words. Billy and Jodell both reached, grabbed an arm each, and helped the kid to his feet. Then, without a word, they each got one of his arms around their shoulders and helped the youngster hobble into the trailer to see about his foot.

Will surveyed his own injured racecar. The dough

nut on the right side, a few dings and a crumpled left fender were the only noticeable wounds.

It looked as if both horse and jockey would live to race again.

Someone else noticed the job Rob had done at Indianapolis.

Billy Winton was seated at his desk early Monday morning, sipping from his big coffee mug as he waded through a stack of bills. When the phone on his desk pealed, he almost let it ring itself out. There was no one in particular he wanted to talk with. Will and the rest of the crew were in the shop where they belonged. He had already talked with Jodell Lee that morning, letting him talk some more about his own car's disappointing showing in the big race at Indy on Saturday.

But then, he picked up the thing and tried to manage a civil "Hello." Maybe it was a potential sponsor who wanted to throw millions of dollars at him.

"You have any idea how many times our car got on television the other night?"

It was Jim Locklear, the president of ArchTech

Products. He made electronic parts for the automobile after-market as well as wired up circuit boards for the military and computer companies. And he was the primary sponsor of Billy Winton's racing team.

"I'm afraid I didn't get to watch too much television that night, Jim."

"They must have mentioned the kid a dozen times, had a slo-mo of him getting past one of the wrecks, and even followed him all the way through one of your pit stops. It was just about the *Rob Wilder Show* right there on national TV."

Locklear was clearly pleased with the unusual exposure his logo on the hood of the car had received. Several of his key customers had commented on it to him already and a couple of his marketing people had noted an upsurge in orders, and it was still early on a Monday morning. And then, Locklear shifted gears, wanting to know what Billy's plans were for the new, young driver and for the rest of the Grand National season.

"Well, Jim, I'm glad you asked. We'd like to take the kid to the rest of the races this year so we could get a running go for next season," Billy reported. "If we could get some more sponsorship to supplement our twelve-race deal with you, of course. We've got the equipment to do it now, I reckon. We just need to bring on a couple more full-time people and be able to do the travel without it breaking us. And have something to fall back on if we get some cars torn up, as we almost certainly will."

"I wish I could budget more," Locklear said, "but I'm doing all I can right now. This thing is going great for ArchTech but we're not that big, you know. You get the figures. With the plant we're building in Texas and the new motherboard assembly facility in Utah, we just don't have the liquidity right now. We're not a public company like some of them. We can't just go print up some more stock and sell it and raise a bunch of cash."

That's one of the things Billy appreciated about Jim Locklear. He didn't beat around the bush and he was honest to a fault. That's one reason Billy had become an early investor in his startup company, a gamble that had paid off handsomely. But he knew without a doubt that Jim was a sponsor of his car because it was good business, not to return any favors. And he knew Locklear was shooting straight when he admitted that he couldn't help much more than he was already. The relationship had worked fine for both of them when they were only running the occasional race, helping Billy get his competitive fix. But a full-time commitment would get expensive in a flash.

And without either one of them having to say so, they both knew that the promise shown by Rob Wilder had now forced the issue.

"You know I want to give you first shot at it, Jim. I'd love to see you step up with us."

"Billy, to be honest with you, I don't see any way we could take on the whole thing. I know I can add in a few more races by redoing some of our advertising and vendor dollars. We had some money earmarked for a promotion that I'm not all that wild about anyway and I guess the boss can still pull rank on something like that around here. After that, I can't guarantee anything."

"I appreciate your honesty as always. See what you can do and maybe I can scratch around and dig up enough so we can at least do what we want to do for the rest of this season. Maybe we'll find us a sugar daddy in time to gear up for next year."

"There's one other thing I can do, Billy. Let me do some asking around. Maybe I can come up with something you'd be interested in."

"I'd be much obliged."

"And you keep that kid safe. He's going to be a star."

He smiled when he hung up the phone and took a big swig of the lukewarm coffee. He deliberately shoved the bills aside for the time being. It was time to go to work.

Billy had already mentally committed the next couple of days to a renewed sponsor search. While stock car racing was flush with money, it was still getting harder and harder to find fresh new sponsors willing to put up the money to do things right. Most wanted to dive in, get all the pop they could for the least amount of money, then dash to the next hot team as soon as they figured out who it was. And that was doubly true for Grand National. If the potential sponsor had the kind of dollars that it took to back a good effort there, they most likely preferred finding a ride in the Cup with its greater television audience and potential for exposure. At this level, most teams traded sponsors around like baseball cards. But that was not what Billy was looking for.

He knew how hard a sponsorship was to come by and he wasn't about to go out and steal someone else's. And like a cheating spouse, if the subsidizer could be so easily stolen away from another team, he knew somebody else could come right back and return the favor.

Billy wanted somebody new, someone with deep enough pockets and sufficient patience so they wouldn't be afraid of long-term investing, wouldn't flinch and start looking elsewhere even if the stake didn't pay off on the very first lap of the very first race. That was the only way to win consistently given the competitiveness in the sport. Anything and everything was long-term. It was tempting to take the first stack of offered money and worry later about actually keeping the donor, especially when he was so anxious to get going in a big way.

But Billy Winton refused to approach racing that way. Even though it cost him sponsorship money, he always shot straight with the companies and brokers who brought him the offers.

"I need X dollars for X years, folks. If you don't want to commit to that, I can't commit to handing you a winner."

And he grew accustomed to the dismissing click on the other end of the telephone line.

THE PHONE CALL

Things didn't improve much in the sponsor
search over the next three weeks. They were
approaching the stretch run of the season and
Billy had nothing, not even a nibble.

There was good news on the track, though. They
had run two more races and Rob had done well
enough in each contest to more than keep his name
on everyone's lips. How well the kid was doing remained one of the chief topics throughout the garage
each week.

The trip to Michigan had been especially eye-
opening.

It was the first time Rob had driven on a track
longer than the standard one-half to five-eighths of a
mile of most of the smaller venues. The long straightaways and the wide, gently banked turns gave the
youngster the opportunity to run at speeds he had
only dreamed about before. Billy decided to run the

race at Michigan for that very reason, because he knew it would be a relatively easy transition for his rookie from the short tracks to the bigger speedways.

On the other hand, the sweeping turns lacked the high banking of Daytona or Talladega. That made the track seem deceptively easy to negotiate and sometimes drivers would push and push until they had achieved speeds that were unsafe. Several bad accidents in the past ten years had shown tragically how deadly the track could be, even for the more experienced. Ernie Ervan had almost been killed there; then, five years to the day later, he had crashed again during practice and was hurt too badly to drive on Sunday.

Jodell had made sure his young discovery understood. He detailed each individual accident for Rob, described exactly what the driver had done or what had happened to get him in trouble.

"These are the trickiest turns you'll find," he preached. "You'll drive into one of them at full speed and think you're okay. Next thing, you're skatin' for the rail and hanging on for dear life. You get out of the groove and lose your grip, brace yourself for a mouthful of wall. And as fast you'll be goin', it's gonna be a lick you'll still be feelin' next week. If you're still feelin' anything next week."

Billy walked up about then.

"You trying to scare the bejesus out of my driver?"

"I certainly hope so!"

Rob listened, nodded a lot, took it all to heart, then went out and drove the track as if he had been doing it all his life. He whooped out loud when he took the first turn at speed and felt the Ford take hold and sail right on through. For a moment, it felt exactly like the times he had run wide open on some of the rel-

atively flat country roads back home in Alabama, but
here, he was traveling at almost twice the best speed
he could muster back there.

Then, just to prove that he knew how to handle
the track, he reeled off another good qualifying run.
He couldn't have picked a better time or place. This
race was to be another companion event to the Cup
event and the track was crawling with reporters and
television crews looking for something to write about
until the big boys raced. Rob didn't disappoint in the
event either, finishing again in the top twenty for the
second time in as many races and, to his great joy, on
the lead lap.

Will pulled him aside and apologized after the television cameras and print guys had gone on in search
of more interviews.

"This one's on me, cowboy. I let us get a mis-
matched set of tires on the car and we were running
eighth about then."

"Hey, I got wide over yonder a couple of times and
it cost me two or three spots both times."

"You drove one heck of a race, son. We get it all
together, you're gonna be dangerous," Will said, and
used up one of his rare smiles.

Bristol was a totally different kind of challenge. The
short track was nestled between the remains of two
mountains and both Billy and Will expected Rob to
struggle on the high banks. Those slopes made Bristol
lightning-quick for such a short circuit. Some of the
drivers had described racing there like piloting a jet
airplane around the inside of a gymnasium.

Rob, on the other hand, found that it felt very similar to the track at Nashville. It was a bit quicker,
though, and left a driver with no time to react if there
was sudden trouble. It would be what Jodell liked to

call "an instinct track." A driver was often best served by slipping his brain into neutral and relying on his innate impulses, if he happened to be blessed with any. Otherwise, he tended to drive tight, always ready for something to happen in front of him, and that was no way to win at Bristol.

The team had some trouble getting the right setup under the car and Rob could only qualify toward the back of the field. But then they found that they had stumbled onto the perfect setup for racing, and Rob quickly worked his way up to the top ten by the time they hit the hundred-lap mark.

Billy and Jodell stood atop the Lee Racing truck watching in awe as the kid made move after move. They looked at each other without speaking. They didn't have to. They knew they were watching a true driving talent out there.

Then, just when he was about to pass his way into the top five, a couple of slower cars in front of Rob crunched together and went spinning all over the track. He tagged one of them hard enough to shove a fender back against a tire and it took them awhile in the pits to get it hammered back out of the way. The repairs cost them several laps.

A third good finish brought the reporters around again, as soon as they had interviewed the winner. More fans sought out Rob, too, and he was busy for a good hour after the race signing everything they thrust at him. Billy listened proudly as his driver carefully mentioned ArchTech and the other minor sponsors they had picked up, then he thanked his crew, most of them by name, and gave Billy and Jodell Lee full credit for all the advice they had given him before he ever took on this track.

The only time the kid got rattled was when one

reporter asked if he had a wife or girlfriend who came to watch him run. He stammered and stuttered before he finally realized that all he had to do was say, "No." But he blushed brilliantly crimson for the camera.

Billy hoped to capitalize on the double benefits of good runs in key races and on the accompanying coverage they were getting. It could only help his sponsor search, he figured, but so far he was still coming up dry. Thankfully, Jim Locklear had managed to round up enough extra money for them to be able to run most of the remaining races. Practically all of it had come from vendors he dealt with and what extra advertising money he could scrape together. These deals came to fruition the week before the Bristol race, just in the nick of time. It gave Billy some breathing room and let them concentrate on getting ready for the races. But everyone knew they needed to do something quick and more long-term if they were going to run the full schedule next year.

Billy and Will knew they should be ordering more cars now and firming up the extra crewmembers they would need. They already had their eyes on the men they wanted to hire, but they needed something solid, a multi-year sponsorship deal, before they would even consider asking those men to leave the positions they were in already.

It was still early morning, the Wednesday after Bristol, and the first hint of autumn had begun tempering Indian summer ever so slightly. Billy was up early, bringing a sweet roll and his big mug of coffee out to the small log cabin he used for an office. He'd built the cabin himself, raising it up out behind the house, with the intention of making it his investment office. It held an antique desk, a new computer, shelves filled with books, a wall full of pictures, and a television set that was always on with the sound turned down, always tuned to one of the financial news cable channels. Of course, he had built the cabin well before he'd added the big new race shop next to the barn, but he had kept his office there even now, away from the noise of the shop.

He almost felt lonely this morning, even with the sounds of all the activity down at the shop. For some reason he was in an odd, melancholy mood. The boys had left early the afternoon before to help Rob move some of his things. He was staying in a room at Will's for the time being, until he could find himself a place of his own. It had been Will's wife's idea to empty out the spare bedroom and let him stay there. It certainly suited Billy. It would either help cement the relationship between his driver and crew chief or make them so sick of each other they'd quit speaking. And if that was going to be the case, better to find out now before he got some big sponsor on the hook.

Rob usually showed up early every day at the shop, eager to help the other four regular crew members with whatever they had to do that day, and he would inevitably be one of the last to leave. After the race at Bristol, he'd told Will in no uncertain terms that if he tore the car up racing it then he was darn sure going to help them fix it.

Will didn't argue with the idea of Rob helping out either. He figured it would help his young driver in the long run if he understood how the cars were built and how they set them up. Will suspected that, at this stage, Rob needed to be absorbing any and everything related to racing. Besides, the truth was that they also needed the extra help in the shop. Setting up and preparing cars for this many races and test sessions had just about worn out the small crew.

And though it was unspoken, they all knew that when they landed a sponsorship, Rob Wilder's time would suddenly be in much more demand for chores totally unrelated to the underside of a racecar.

As he sipped the strong coffee and enjoyed the quiet morning, Billy reflected back on the last seven or eight weeks and pondered his options for the next year. Instead of running one race, as they had originally planned, they had actually run three. And they had also tested the car once, down in Nashville, when they had given Rob Wilder a look-see.

Billy Winton knew he was at a crossroads. He'd now been officially retired from the sport for better than seven years. The six or eight races he'd run in each of the last two years had allowed him to dabble, to keep a hand in the sport without having to seriously commit to it. Between his own money and what Jim Locklear could come up with, he could keep playing at the game halfway, get enough of a whiff of gas fumes and hot metal to keep him satisfied if he really wanted to. But it was like a casual girlfriend who was now suddenly demanding marriage.

Sometimes he thought he was an idiot for not wanting to stay in the game on a much smaller scale, for even considering giving up his pleasant retirement. He truly enjoyed raising his few head of cattle, puttering around in his vegetable garden, playing at his investing, much as he would a low-stakes poker game. But now, in his mid-fifties, he realized that maybe he had not gotten rid of the stock car racing bug after all. He still loved the feel of watching a car that he had helped put out there as she circled the track and picked off the other competitors on the way to the front. It was something so strong in his gut he doubted he could purge it any other way than by diving into the whole business in a big way again.

He couldn't explain it. He just knew the visceral thrill of it all was still there, strong as ever.

All the recent frantic activity in the shop and at the tracks had immediately brought back to him the reasons he had stuck with racing in the first place, back when he had been drafted by Jodell Lee, Jodell's cousin Joe Banker, and their friend Bubba Baxter. It had grabbed hold of him then and it clearly was not yet ready to let him go.

Lately, since Jodell had pointed them toward Rob, he found himself waltzing into the shop and actually grabbing some tools and helping the boys with the cars. He had already admitted to himself that the few years of retirement had bored the dickens out of him. He relished the fast pace of the racing business and nothing pleased him more than being back in the thick of it once again.

And besides, it gave him a perfectly good reason to be up early, enjoying the cool hint of fall on this beautiful Indian summer morning in the foothills of the Smokies.

He leaned back in the office chair, propped his feet up on the desk, rested his mug on his chest, and scanned the far wall of the cabin. Pictures and racing memorabilia covered the entire surface. Most of the framed photos were from his days as part of the Jodell Lee team and had been taken throughout the seventies and mid-eighties. There was the picture of him at the White House with Jimmy Carter. With President Reagan in Daytona. Victory Lane at Darlington, Talladega, and Charlotte. Clowning around with Petty, Earnhardt, Baker, and Allison. A sad photo of him fishing with Neil Bonnet only a month before he was killed. A far happier picture of him talking with a young Jeff Gordon somewhere he couldn't quite remember now, but during the youngster's breakout season.

There was another pair of photos, hung close together down low on the wall, each with a young redheaded GI in its center. In one, he stood with a group of buddies, all in fatigues and lined up beneath a palm tree. The other showed the same baby-faced soldier in a similar pose, but this time there were different friends in the photo and they all wore cutoffs and swim trunks and stood in a line on a ratty beach somewhere. Sometime along the way, he had placed small black dots on the chests of the half dozen men in the pictures who he knew had not made it back home. A couple more he wasn't certain about. He had given them the benefit of the doubt and left them dotless.

As he surveyed these familiar photos, Billy felt a renewed rush of determination bubbling inside him, the desire to build some new memories to add to those represented on the cabin wall. He suspected that he might be regaining his own youth from all the new blood that was reinvigorating the sport these days. And especially from the new enthusiasm that had clearly infected his team lately.

The ringing phone interrupted his thoughts.

"Hello?" he answered curtly, fumbling for the phone as he swung his long legs down off the desk.

"Billy! Jim Locklear here. Hope I'm not calling too early for you. You got a second?"

"Oh sure. I was just . . . looking over some things."

"Good. Then do you think you and your new driver can meet me in San Jose on the Tuesday after Labor Day?"

"What? What are you talking about, Jim?"

"I asked if you and the kid can meet me in San Jose, California?"

"What for?"

"Well, one of those guys that partnered up with us on the car at Bristol was tickled with all the TV coverage Rob got for him. The CEO saw his company's name on the side of that Ford when it was racing side by side with the others, and boy was he hooked! The guy is ready to start a Rob Wilder Fan Club right this minute."

"You don't say."

"I faxed him a bunch of those marketing demographics and lifestyle statistics you gave me and some of the pictures of the kid. Now he suddenly wants to take a closer look."

"So, what are we talking here? Adding a couple of races or what?"

"I am talking the whole shootin' match, man. This is big! Do you think you can get me a proposal up here in the next couple of days that I can forward on to him?"

"Well, I reckon I can. Where and when you want to meet again?" Billy sat up straight and scribbled the details furiously on the note pad in front of him. "You'll have the proposal Friday morning."

"I'll look for it. Talk to you soon."

Billy tried to temper his excitement with a dose of logic. It was only a lead and he had seen plenty of those before that had never panned out. And he thought he knew of every potential serious sponsor out there, Grand National and Cup, too, and the well had pretty much run dry.

But this felt different. It came from Jim Locklear

for one thing. And Locklear never promised more than he could deliver.

Which one of the partners could it be? Did they really understand what kind of dollar commitment it would take to be the primary sponsor of the 6? Or would it be yet another wild goose chase?

Quickly, he quit his idle speculation, booted up the computer, and went to work putting together the various spreadsheets and documentation he had worked up already for others who had pretended to be interested in backing his team. It was well past noon when he finally came up for air, snapped the materials into a binder, then an envelope, called the parcel service for the pickup, then stood, stretched, and headed out onto the small porch that ran along the front of the cabin.

On the way, though, he stopped for a moment and wiped a speck of dust from one of the photos on the wall before he finally stepped outside. It was a glorious day, the sun already starting its descent on the other side of midday. He crossed the porch and headed for the shop. Several cars, including Will's big Buick and Rob's old pickup, were parked in the shade of the building.

It was cool inside the shop, the air conditioning cranked up. Will was standing at a table, measuring some parts with a micrometer.

"Where's Rob?" Billy asked him.

"Over yonder," he replied, nodding to where a pair of sneakered feet stuck out from underneath one of the cars.

"Rob, you under there?"

"Yes sir," he answered eagerly as he rolled out on the dolly from beneath the racecar. "You need me for something, Billy?"

The kid's blond hair was dusted with grit and grime. He had a big smear of grease across his right cheek and Billy noticed for the first time the freckles across the bridge of his nose. At that moment and from that angle, Rob Wilder looked about fourteen years old.

"Yeah, I have a chore I want you to do for me every day for the next week or so."

"Sure. Anything you say, Billy. You need me to make a parts run to town or something?"

"No, nothing like that."

Will had wandered closer, pretending to be checking under the open hood of the car that Rob had been working on.

"So name it. You know I've been wanting to finally do something to earn my keep around here."

It was true that he was paying no rent for staying with Will. His wife, Clara, had insisted he eat every meal with the family, had thrown his dirty clothes in with all the rest of theirs, then ironed the ones that needed it, and had even sewed some missing buttons on a couple of shirts for him. He had had little place to spend his driver's share money so far.

"I want you to spend a couple of hours every day out back of the house on the patio, working on your tan."

Rob looked at him blankly.

"You want me to do *what?*" he finally asked, his voice breaking into a squeak on the last word.

"I got a lead on a sponsor out in California and you and I are going to have to fly out there after Darlington. I want you to look like you belong out there."

"I don't look like a Californian," Rob protested.

"Farthest west I've ever been is a race one time in Memphis."

"You may or you may not. But let's see if we can give them that impression anyhow," Billy said.

He had overheard the comments, especially from the ladies, about how someone with his blond good looks had to have come from California. He had also seen some of the rumors in the papers about how Rob Wilder had apparently begun his racing career in Southern California, up near Sacramento, out there in the desert near San Bernardino, down close to the Mexican border. Several of them had even claimed to have firsthand knowledge of the kid's West Coast roots.

He had not bothered to correct anybody so far. Let them add to the mystique if they wanted to.

But just then, a disturbing thought seemed to occur to the kid.

"How are we going to get there?"

"We'll fly out of Bristol I suppose."

And Billy noticed the sudden look of stark terror pass over the kid's face. He had never before seen anything even approaching fear in the boy's eyes. Now, it looked as if he had spied a ghost floating somewhere over Billy's head.

"I've never flown in an airplane before, Billy. I don't know if I can get on one of those things or not."

His voice actually trembled. Billy choked back a laugh and he could hear Will making a clucking sound from beneath the car's hood. The kid had done close to two hundred miles per hour lap after lap at Michigan, surrounded closely by a mad herd of stomping, snorting machines doing the very same thing, and he had not even flinched. Billy had watched him bravely steer through corners, dodge violent collisions, and dive into tiny openings that looked half as wide as the car he was piloting, all with no trepidation whatsoever. Now, the prospects of sitting in first class on a 767 had the boy spooked but good. He actually looked as if he might burst into tears.

"You better get used to it, son," Billy advised. "I expect you'll someday spend as much time in an airplane as you do in the racecar."

The kid swallowed hard.

"Okay. Whatever you say, Billy. If I gotta, I gotta," Rob said, but his eyes were still wide as he dug in his heels and began rolling back under the car to return to work. Or to hide.

"Hey, where you going, hotshot? The sun's out. I'd say now is a good time to get started on that Golden State suntan."

"I was just going to . . . aw, never mind."

He climbed to his feet and began unbuttoning his shirt as he quickly headed outside. Billy and Will tried their best to hold their laughter until he was well out of earshot.

Somebody's left the oven door open."

That was Donnie Kline's assessment of the heat that slapped them in the face when they opened the truck doors in Darlington, South Carolina. It was sweltering.

Rob had ridden down in the team hauler, sandwiched between Donnie and Will Hughes, and the two men had held school the entire way. They wanted to drill Rob on the intricacies and nuances of one of the trickiest tracks on the circuit, one that had gotten the best of even the most talented and experienced drivers. Rob took it all in, filed it away, and asked even more questions. But he was still somewhat in awe that he, a lowly cabinet maker only a few months before, was about to slide out of the hauler and step foot on what was, to many stock car fans, sacred ground.

The track had suddenly appeared to them as they

approached, shimmering in the distance like a sudden mirage, rising up from nothing among what used to be pine flats and fields. The new towering grandstands of the front stretch gleamed in the early morning sun.

Will and Donnie were finally silent as they steered the hauler through the tunnel and into the infield. All three had the same unspoken thought. They could almost feel the presence of the ghosts of Fireball Roberts, Curtis Turner, Little Joe Weatherley, Davey Allison, Alan Kulwicki, and Neil Bonnet beckoning them in, welcoming them. Will broke the spell and spoke first.

"Well, Robbie, this is the place. Petty, Pearson, Yarborough, Waltrip . . . they all made names for themselves here. And there's plenty more you never heard of who decided that if they had to run twice a year at this bad boy, they'd just not bother."

"Look at how narrow those corners are!"

Rob had just spied the legendary first and second turns.

"I think it was Waltrip that said he'd been on wider jogging paths. See how they narrow up right there in the center of the corner? That's what we've been telling you about for the last four hours. You get in there too hard and you'll earn yourself a Darlington stripe. If you're lucky, that is. Or you'll bring the car back to us in a bucket if you're not."

The retaining wall looked innocuous enough. It seemed unmarked from where they stood but that was only because it was wearing a fresh coat of white paint. That hid the evidence of all the racecars that had foundered there like wrecked ships on a shoal. But it was also the spot where, in the old days, if you hit it just right, a slight bump or tap with the right rear fender, a savvy driver could use the impact to help propel the car through the corner without losing as much speed. That treacherous maneuver was how the famous "Darlington Stripe" first got its name. It was impossible to win there if you didn't know how to take advantage of the wall.

Excited as he was to take to the course, the next two days were a struggle for the kid. The track was slick and the racecar perilously loose from the first lap. It was certainly nothing like the sweeping turns at Michigan or the high banks of Bristol. This was far trickier, the best line through the corners seemingly changing from one lap to the next as if in defiance of anyone cocky enough to think he could tame the place after only a few trips around.

Rob talked with Dale Earnhardt, Jr. in the garage for a while and he mentioned some of the things he had learned from his dad. A couple of the other drivers were a part of the same conversation and they passed along some things they thought might work. Rob immediately tried some of the tips out on the next practice run and he picked up a few tenths of a second. Still, they were several tenths off the speeds being posted by many of the faster cars. And that was enough to potentially keep them out of the race altogether.

Will and Billy watched the run from the top of the truck parked in the infield. Will would normally be with the crew on the pit lane or in the garage during the practice sessions, but with their driver's inexperience on display out there on this tricky track, he wanted to better observe what both car and driver were doing.

"The kid's struggling," Billy said, stating the obvious.

"Yeah, he's all over the track. We keep tightening

the car and he keeps complaining it's too loose."

"That's just inexperience. I remember watching Jodell struggle here, even when he was winning at other places. Most of the time, though, we'd make one little bitsy change and *voilà*, the car would suddenly be perfect. Sometimes I think we might have just hit on the right setup, sometimes I just think Jodell found the right line and the car had been fine all along."

"Well if we don't find that little bit of magic in a hurry, we're gonna be watching the race on television back home."

"He'll find the groove. He just needs some more laps. And so do you, Will."

It amazed Will how calm Billy was, and especially when they were clearly struggling to make the race. With a high-profile sponsor meeting set for the very next Tuesday, Will was well aware of the pressure the team was under to make the race this weekend and then to go on and have a good run.

"Well, what if we don't?"

Will was so driven to perfection, it was his nature to fret every detail. Billy put his hand on his crew chief's shoulder.

"I look at everything as a battle plan. Line up everything you know. Decide what you want to try and in what priority order. Do it. Somewhere along the way, if you follow everything logically and in the right order, you'll win the battle. And if you win enough battles, you'll eventually win the war."

"Whatever you say." Though his boss was usually correct, it sometimes seemed far too simplistic for Will. He had already tried all he knew to do and still couldn't figure out why the car was still so loose. Just then, Rob was on the radio again.

"This thing is so loose I feel like the back end is

gonna come around on me on the straightaways!" the kid complained.

Will curtly ordered him to come on in. The crew went to work, making another round of changes to the car. They adjusted the sway bar, changed out the shocks once again, and put a different spring in the right front. Meanwhile, Billy motioned for Rob to climb out of the car and get a cold shot of water. As the kid drank, Billy coached some more.

"Maybe you ought to try to let the car have its head a little bit. Let the car go where it feels like it needs to go. Maybe you want to let the car find its own line instead of fighting to rein her in and keep her down on the white line in the turns. Trust your instincts."

Robbie swallowed a swig of the icy water and looked up at Billy.

"That's what has me bumfuzzled. I drive off into the turn and the car seems to want to go all over the track."

"That's exactly what I mean. Go low as you get into the corner and then let it drift up in the center. Don't try to fight it. Concentrate on staying smooth and getting a good run coming off the turn."

"I'll try, but it won't be easy. I guess I'm used to trying to peg it down to the white line. That's usually the fastest way around."

"Most places that's the plan. But here, it's a little trickier than that. Go out there and run some laps behind Dale Jr. and watch how he attacks the corners. He seems to have this place pretty well figured out."

"I will if I can keep him in sight. He's flying."

"A little more experience here and so will you. Even some of the veterans can feel as lost as you are here. Eventually they figure it out. Just takes time. It's laps and experience and a willingness to learn, that's all."

Rob looked down at the toes of his driver's shoes for a moment, then turned his head sideways and looked up at Billy Winton.

"Billy, you ever think what a big chance you're taking with somebody like me that you didn't even know?"

"I've already tried all the drivers I know. Can't a one of them drive like you can."

"Naw, I don't mean just driving. You don't know what kind of person I am. What kind of stock I come from. What my family's like. I could be a drug addict or a drunk or a bum. You don't know."

Billy eased down into the director's chair next to him. He couldn't imagine what had brought this on.

"Yessir, you certainly could. But I learned something when I was in Vietnam, Rob. You learn to be a damn good judge of character when you walk a night patrol near the DMZ with a bunch of grunts who are as scared as you are. You trust the wrong person, you end up dead. You think I would have ever put you out there on that track with my car if I didn't trust you?"

The kid took another long swallow of water. For the first time since Billy had known him, the boy avoided his gaze and studied the ground between his feet instead. He could hardly hear him when he spoke again.

"But you don't know where I come from, Billy."

"We did some checking. We may know more about you than you think we do. But you want to tell me some more?"

The crew was crawling from beneath the car and Will was standing there impatiently, waiting to help

Rob climb back in and see what they had accomplished. The kid looked up then and grinned crookedly.

"Maybe some other time. I got to go out there and pound this old momma into shape."

Rob quickly found Dale Jr. and pulled in behind him, following along for several laps. He did all he could to emulate the line the 3 car was taking and he was surprised to feel his own car seem to pick up, as if it was chasing happily after the other one.

Back in the pits, Will studied his stopwatch carefully and noted an additional tenth of a second. It was their fastest time of the day. Will accidentally smiled slightly as he watched the car head off into the first turn.

They continued picking up speed right up until time for the qualifying runs and he could hear the confidence grow in his driver's voice on the radio as they finally seemed to be on the right course. But then, time had run out. Will was concerned because even though they had been picking up speed, their last times were still not good enough to guarantee them a starting spot on the grid.

The qualifying session was long and intense, with some of the other teams holding their breaths, too. Rob drew a late number in the qualifying order yet again, and the day was turning into a real scorcher. That gave Will Hughes still another thing to worry about. The heat was making the slick, greasy track even more loose and precarious. Heat was a killer on speed. Handling would claim a better starting spot before raw power on this day.

Rob, though, was cool and calm and confident. He didn't seem concerned at all about making the field. He couldn't understand the worried expression on

Will's face. He was usually the one who had to convince everyone that the car was fine.

Will was still kneading his hands when Rob pulled away for his qualifying run. He watched as the kid did fine through the treacherous first and second corners, allowing himself to actually feel some confidence. But then, Rob apparently pushed the car a tiny bit too hard in the final turn. That caused him to have to crack the throttle ever so slightly to not risk losing the car. And that tiny bobble was enough to cost him a couple of tenths of a second. A couple of tenths they really couldn't spare.

The scoreboard showed the cold truth on such a hot afternoon. They were currently thirtieth fastest and there were still ten would-be qualifiers to go, some pretty good cars, and all of them with designs on driving them lower and lower and possibly out entirely. There was a good chance now that they would have to try and re-qualify the next day if they wanted to make the show. And that was far more pressure than they really wanted to put onto their young driver and the rest of the team.

Rob was not happy with either the run or himself and it showed on his face as he pulled himself out of the car. He knew the Ford was a tick-slow compared to many of the others. What the team had needed was for him to go out there and run as close to a perfect lap as he could, but instead, he had tried to do it all himself. He had overdriven the car and that had led to the slipup in the corner that had cost them several positions, and placing any kind of a starting spot in jeopardy.

Billy Winton walked over and got into step next to his driver as he headed for the hauler.

"You're gonna trip over that lower lip if you're not careful."

"Sorry, Billy. That one was on me. I just pushed the car too hard coming through the corner there and had to crack the throttle."

"Kid, remember one thing. I pay you to race hard. Smart, too, but we have got to run the car right up to the edge if we expect to win any races. We'll get them in the second round. Don't worry about it."

"I promise you I won't let you down, Billy. I do learn by my mistakes. You can bet I won't make that one again."

"Mistakes are not quite so bad as long as you learn something from them. We'll get 'em tomorrow. Don't worry."

For some reason, Billy felt supremely confident. He knew Will would spend all night figuring out what setup they would need. And he never doubted Rob's vow not to repeat his mistake of the afternoon. They were not beaten yet. Their margin for error was only just getting a little tighter.

Sure enough, the next morning Will had some new things he wanted to try. As soon as the crew members were able to enter the garage, they set to work in a flurry, changing things out.

Meanwhile, Billy took his driver to a leisurely breakfast, primarily to keep him from the pressure as the team worked on the car. Over platters of eggs, sausage, country ham, grits with gravy, and biscuits, Billy talked about everything but the upcoming attempt at a better qualifying time.

"So what did you end up doing last night?" Billy asked as he spread a big mound of jelly across a buttered biscuit.

"Some of the boys took me out to eat at a place

they know here. We ran into some folks from some of the other teams. What about you?"

"Me and Will sat up in my room 'til all hours looking over our old notes. We even had an old buddy of yours drop in. Jodell Lee stopped by and we picked his brain for a while."

"You mean y'all worked all night?"

"Well, I don't know that you'd call it working. We ended up telling more tall tales than anything else," Billy said. "But we had to figure out what you need so they could put it under the car this morning. And Will thinks he may have found the right combination."

"I hope so. But I feel bad that I was out having fun while y'all were back at the hotel working."

"Hey, you need to be out there meeting your public."

Rob grinned sheepishly.

"I kind of got some of that last night. I was having to sign autographs while I ate. But I don't mind, I don't guess. In fact, it was kind of neat. Some of the Cup drivers were in there and people started asking for their autographs and the next thing I knew they wanted mine. I can't believe people would want my name on a scrap of paper."

"I know it can be a hassle sometimes but you should always be gracious and give the fans time. How do you think Earnhardt and Petty sell all those hats and T-shirts? The folks will take care of you when you're a big star."

"I guess I'm just having a little trouble getting used to even having fans who know my name. We had a few, I guess, in Huntsville and Birmingham and Chattanooga and a few of the places where we used to run."

Billy noticed it sounded as if it had been years since the kid had raced those tracks, not a few weeks.

"Well, get used to it. With a little luck, next week we're going to turn you into a household name."

They finished up and hurried to pay the check. They didn't want to get caught in traffic on the way to the track. They needed every minute of practice they could get.

"I see the tanning is coming along nicely." Billy said paying the cashier.

"I guess so," Rob said, subconsciously checking the skin on his forearm. "Let me go on record as saying that I would a thousand times rather be in the shop working on the car than sittin' out there in the sun."

"Well, keep in mind that if things go well next week, your days of working in the shop are pretty well over. You won't have time to do much of anything else but jump when our new sponsor calls."

"Gosh, Billy, I don't necessarily want to be another Gordon, or Elliott, or Earnhardt. I want to race them, yes. Beat them, too. But mainly I just wanna race."

"And it takes a good sponsor to make it so you can afford to stay on the same track with those guys. If we're going to get serious about this thing, we have to have serious commitment from everybody, including the folks who write the checks."

"I know, Billy," Rob said with a smile. "All I wanna do is go out and win a bunch of races."

"And that you will, Mr. Wilder. That you will."

It turned out to be a tense second round of qualifying. Most of the cars stood on their times from the first day. However, the slower cars had no choice but to go out and re-qualify. Rob was among them. They had already determined that the car could run much faster with the changes they had made. All Rob had to do was go out and knock down a good lap and they would be much better off.

Of course, if something went wrong, the trip to Darlington would be over.

Finally, the Ford sat in the middle of the queue of cars, all lined up nervously to re-qualify. Many of the teams were struggling, still searching for a better combination, and their times showed it. Occasionally, though, one of them would roll out and run faster than the day before, moving themselves up in the starting grid and, at the same time, bumping one of the other cars that had stood on its original time.

The official waved Rob out and he rolled away, more than ready to take his lap. Billy and Will stood watching as the car accelerated around the track to take the green flag. The rest of the crew looked on anxiously, too, praying that they could get the lap they needed.

It was difficult to tell how well he was doing as Rob came around to take the checkered flag. What was the time? Would it be fast enough?

Billy nervously fiddled with his stopwatch as they waited for the official time to be posted. By his watch they were good enough, but his time didn't count.

When the time flashed up on the scoreboard, the team jumped in unison. They were in! They had improved on the day before and there were not enough cars left to run to push them out of the field.

Inside the car, Rob was yelling before he even dashed beneath the flagstand. He knew it had been a much better lap than before and that he had not made a single mistake. He made a mental guess of his time and Will confirmed that he was pretty close when he popped on the radio to give him the good news.

"Good job there, cowboy. You ran a thirty-seven.

That's several hundredths better than anything we've run yet."

"Alright!" Rob yelled back to him and to everybody eavesdropping on their scanners in the crowd. "I'd rather have the pole but I'll take it."

"Good job, kid," Billy said into his own microphone as Rob pulled the car to a stop in their stall.

There was plenty to do now. They would have little time to get the race setup under the car for the two hundred-mile contest. Billy talked quietly with his driver as they watched all the activity. The qualifying run had done wonders for Rob's confidence, then they picked up even more speed during the final practice session. They all knew they needed all the velocity they could find once the race started. The thirtieth-place starting position would be tough to overcome, but it could be done. They still had a shot at a good finish on Saturday.

They were back the next morning as soon as the garage opened, partly to get a running start on the things left to do to the car and partly to beat the crowds that would be showing up at the speedway early, so as not to miss a thing. There were plenty of stories of drivers or crew who got a late start and ended up missing the start of the race, stuck outside somewhere in the traffic.

Will was still apprehensive. Even if the car was much better, it would be difficult for a young driver like theirs to work his way up from the rear of the pack. Great instinctive driver or not, it would be hard to avoid the certain get-togethers that would take place out there in front of him. He had preached to Rob the gospel of patience over supper the night before and was still evangelizing as they drove back to the motel.

"Get aggressive early and you'll run up somebody's tailpipe. And whatever you do, watch out for the ones up ahead of you that haven't had the advantage of my wise counsel. You're just as out-of-the-race if you get caught up in somebody else's silly wreck. Patience!"

Billy was pleased with the progress Will and the crew had made from the previous afternoon. The car was at least competitive now. But he also knew that, with all the good cars there, they would need a perfect run and some lucky breaks to win the race. And Darlington was a treacherous old track that could turn brutally fickle even on drivers with far more experience than his.

They had the luxury of using the Lee Racing team's over-the-wall crew once more. That could only help.

The garage area teemed with activity. The Cup crews were occupied with their early practice while all the Grand National teams were busy preparing their machines for the start of their afternoon race. The grandstands were already brimming over with enthusiastic fans that had come, despite the pervasive heat and humidity, to watch a race. Any race. Cup, Grand National, or wheelbarrow, they didn't care so long as there was wheel-to-wheel competition.

Jodell Lee showed up and took Rob on another of his tours of the tracks he would be driving. As they sauntered back down through the garage on the way back to their stall, Rob thought to himself once more how wonderful it felt to glance from side to side and see the faces of men he had idolized since he was old enough to watch a televised race. One of them walked beside him, stride for stride, and must have noticed where he was looking. Or maybe he saw the look in the kid's eyes.

"You ain't star-struck are you?" Jodell asked with a grin.

"Naw. I'd just love the chance to drive against those guys."

"You prove yourself in Grand National and you'll get the shot."

"I don't know. Waltrip and Elliott and some of the others are hinting they might give it up before long."

"Who knows? You may be one of the very young bucks that helps them make up their minds."

Rob was still thinking about Jodell's words when he climbed in and strapped himself to the car. It would be something to be practicing this afternoon for the race the next day, to plan strategy against Gordon and Labonte and Jarrett and Burton and the rest of them. But he also knew he had his own race to run, and before he knew it, he was pulling away with the others, two by two, and heading off into turn one. The nerve-wracking hoopla, the endless driver introductions, all the pre-race festivities were finally all over.

Once again he realized how impossibly narrow the first turn was at this track. Even with only two abreast on the warm-up laps, it seemed barely wide enough for them to get through at the same time. How in the world could they race through there, side by side, at high speed? Practice was one thing. He was about to face the real thing. And he almost had to fight the instinct to simply close his eyes and hold on.

And then, before he could even catch a good breath, the green flag was waving, and, with a cloud of dust and a deafening reverberation, they were off.

Will stood on top of the team's tool cart watching nervously as the early laps played out. Rob was boxed in from the start and had to do all he could simply to hold on to his position. The cars in the middle of the pack were racing furiously for position even before they rolled beneath the flagstand, seemingly determined to wreck before the first round of pit stops.

Will shook his head. There would be plenty of time to race later on. Why didn't they settle down and put some track behind them?

Rob was doing his best to fight off frustration. He was simply trying to patiently pick up spots when the opportunities presented themselves. He knew better than to force something that might or might not be there. Back where he was, the cars were mostly still running side by side, exactly as they had started. He was pleased to see that the Ford was running beautifully. If he could only clear some of the slower cars in front of him, he was sure he could run with any of them out there. Anytime he felt the strong urge to bolt out of line and try to split a couple of cars that blocked his way, he heard Will's words from the night before.

"Patience!"

He mouthed the words as he tucked back in and took the safe way through turn one, yet again.

"Looking good, cowboy," Will's voice suddenly crackled in his ears on the radio. "The pack directly ahead of you is racing hard. Be smart. You're just running six seconds behind the leaders."

"Ten-four."

Rob did manage to pick up a couple of spots over the first ten laps or so and that brought him right up to a good view of a furious battle between a half-dozen cars directly ahead of him. Will watched his driver closely but kept a wary eye on the battle being waged in front of Rob. Those yahoos were driving on the ragged edge, clearly in danger of scattering themselves and everybody behind them all over South Carolina if one of them suddenly broke loose.

Rob manhandled the steering wheel as the car sailed through a corner. He already had picked up a couple of doughnuts, one on each side of the car, clear indicators of the tight racing he had been doing already. And now there was more of it ahead, standing between him and the front where he felt he rightfully belonged.

He tried to keep his concentration on the minefield he would have to navigate first before he could think about scaling the next hill. The machine-gun chatter from the spotter and the occasional terse comments from Will were all that he allowed to break through his fixation on the cars directly in front of him and the line he wanted to take into and out of each of the track's dangerous corners.

"Turn two! Turn two!" Clarence, the spotter, suddenly screamed over the radio.

Will spun instinctively to see the smoke that had instantly shrouded turn two. He listened to the radio and crossed his fingers as he lost sight of his car as it plunged into the throat of the turn.

"Come on, kid, come on," he half-prayed. "Find a way. Please find a way through."

"They're in the wall! Go low! Go low," the spotter cried, doing all he could to steer Rob away from where it looked like the spinning cars would be heading.

Rob had just been entering turn one when Clarence's warning had come. He never actually saw the accident itself, only the huge cloud of tire smoke and dust, and before he could even react, it had swallowed him up completely. He was driving as blind as if someone had turned out the sun, following the rear bumper of the car in front of him and heeding the spotter's warning to steer low.

Then, magically, the swirling smoke thinned just enough to give him a view of several of the whirling cars. Now that he had some idea of where they were, Rob relied on his own instinct to steer for an opening where some kind of ingrained logic told him the cars would not be by the time he got there. And he adjusted his pressure on the throttle to time his own arrival at the opening, too.

But there was one thing he could not know. There was at least one other reeling, out-of-control car not accounted for. And at the instant when Rob thought he had cleared the carnage, there was a flash of movement to his right, something hurtling down from the wall directly toward him. The hole Rob had been making for suddenly slammed shut and he, instead, drove hard into the side of the late arrival.

The cars smashed together brutally. Dazed by the impact, Rob still tried to steer the car and keep it straight ahead on the track, conscious all the time that other racers were bearing down on him from behind. But the Ford seemed to have a mind of its own and headed off toward the inside of the track. The hood had been shoved upward, obscuring his vision, and so did the immediate plume of steam. Then, with a sharp jolt, he felt another car pile into the back of him, shoving him even farther down and off the track and, ultimately, to a shuddering stop in the midst of more dust and smoke.

He felt dizzy, and a strange otherworldliness tried to claim his senses. And he kept telling himself to breathe, even though the air was dirty and tasted of tire rubber and burning oil. And he felt as if he was floating, treading hot water.

"He's in it," Clarence reported matter-of-factly to all listening in on the radio circuit. "Damn track closed right up on him. Not his fault."

Will didn't answer. Instead, he started barking orders to the other crewmembers that were sprinting toward the garage already to wait for what was left of the car to either come on around under its own power or to get towed in on the hook.

With the crew off to get ready for major surgery if the patient could be saved, Will finally keyed his mike and spoke.

"You okay, cowboy?"

There was nothing but silence on the circuit except for bit of robotic cross-talk from someone else talking on a frequency near their channel.

"Cowboy, can you hear me? Talk to me, buddy," he tried again. "Clarence, you got an eyeball on him yet? Is he moving?"

"Car don't look too healthy. Front nor back. I'm afraid she's finished. Can't see the driver for all the dust and smoke."

"Rob, you alright? Talk to me, cowboy."

Someone punched a microphone button on their channel but paused ten seconds before talking. It was Wilder.

"I'm okay." The kid sounded short of breath, deflated, dejected. "I sorta got the wind knocked out of me. The car's pitiful."

"We can fix the car."

"Not by the time the green flag comes back out. Sorry, Will, Billy."

"We're just glad you're okay. You feel like climbing out so they can get a hook on her?"

"I reckon."

He was still a little wobbly as he slid to the ground,

and felt even sicker when he circled what was left of the car and surveyed what torture she had taken. He tried to tell himself that they had three more just like it back in the shop in Chandler Cove; but somehow, he still felt it was his fault, that he was almost certainly in big trouble with the boss.

If he had only anticipated the other car. If he had only had the presence of mind to back off another few RPMs and let the thing slide by in front of him; or if he had stomped it and passed it by before it got into him. Never mind that he had had no idea it was up there getting ready to get in his way in the first place.

He would still be fussing at himself, silently and aloud, for the rest of the weekend. And nobody could convince him he had done all that was humanly possible.

It was his job not to crash. And he had not done his job.

THE MEETING

Rob was still muttering to himself as he and Billy made their way Monday afternoon to Tri-City Regional Airport north of Johnson City. He was so disappointed in the way the Darlington race came to such an abrupt end that he hadn't had a chance to be nervous about the airplane ride that awaited him. It all came flooding back, though, when they made the turn into long-term parking and he spied a plane sitting on the tarmac next to the terminal.

Billy was talking about the plans for the trip, rambling on, but all Rob could hear was a throbbing roar in his ears that he suddenly realized was his own pulse pounding in mortal fear.

". . . and Jim Locklear will meet us out there. He's already out there on business and wants to make the introductions," Billy was saying. He glanced over at Rob and was shocked at what he saw. "Son, you alright? You're white as Murphy's ghost. You're not carsick, are you?"

Then he realized how odd it would be for a racecar driver to be susceptible to carsickness. But something certainly seemed to have his driver spooked.

"Aw, I'm okay, Billy," Rob answered, but there was an unmistakable quaver in his voice.

Then Billy remembered Rob's admission that he had never flown before, that the only thing he was afraid of was climbing into an airplane and zooming off down a runway to be hurtled into the sky. He tapped the kid on the knee as he maneuvered the Town Car into a parking slot.

"Next thing you know, you'll be flying one of those things yourself, like Rusty Wallace and them. Just sit back and relax and imagine you're riding a bus."

"I'm not crazy about them either, Billy. I don't much like not being in control."

Billy laughed as he slid out of the car and stepped around to claim their overnight bags, his briefcase, and a cardboard box out of the trunk. Rob had had to borrow a bag from Clara Hughes. He had never needed one before. He had shown up in Chandler Cove with his clothes in a couple of grocery sacks in the back of his old pickup.

Their meeting was scheduled for ten the next morning in Los Altos, a small town between San Jose and San Francisco, and in the middle of Silicon Valley. Billy had managed to wheedle out of Jim several weeks before the name of the company they would be talking with, though Locklear had been reluctant to tell him.

"I don't want to jinx the deal," he had said. "Or give you a heart attack."

The potential sponsor turned out to be one of the

major software houses, a company that was currently soaring in the high-tech world. They had managed to create several applications that had caught on immediately with the advent of the Internet and now enjoyed a quickly growing share of the market among the more technical minded. But now they saw the need to keep pace with the casual Internet users, folks who used their computers more as appliances, and that was a potential customer base they didn't want to concede to cheaper or more visible competitors.

Jim Locklear had been telling their marketing folks that automobile racing would be a perfect way to do that. And they were interested enough to have set the meeting with Billy Winton and his young driver. Of course, Locklear had a vested interest in seeing such a deal consummated. He knew he could stay on as a secondary sponsor, but a big commitment from someone like these guys would assure a better, more successful team. And his logo would be right there, along for the ride.

Billy knew the company well already. He was actually a stockholder. Computers and related companies were hardly a mystery to him. As a natural-born tinkerer, he had helped computerize the Jodell Lee Racing operation when the first personal computers appeared in the early eighties. They had installed a computerized inventory system back when many teams were still simply keeping piles of parts in the corner so there would be no danger of running out. Billy actually helped program much of the computer code once he convinced Jodell how much money they were wasting. It wasn't long before other teams were doing the same thing.

That was one of the reasons Billy felt so comfortable marching in and selling the merits of his race team to these people. If the company's marketing department was as forward-thinking as their developers, then it should be no problem showing them the possibilities of signing on as the primary sponsor. But Billy knew nothing was for certain. More than once, he had seen sponsorships fall through at the last minute, when all that was needed was a string of ink on a dotted line. Or others disappointingly disappear into the ether when some accountant somewhere who didn't know a track from a yak nixed the deal, not understanding the value of hooking up with such a clearly "redneck" sport.

Thankfully, Rob settled down quickly once they were off the ground and was soon engrossed in a racing magazine Billy had brought along. Somewhere over Kansas, the kid fell asleep and then snored quietly most of the way to the coast. For most of the flight, Billy had his laptop computer unhinged on his tray table, surveying the prospectus of Ensoft.com and reading all the reports on the company that he had been able to download.

They touched down in San Jose shortly before dark, then Billy picked up the rental car and drove the two of them out to Los Gatos, a quaint town a few miles south of San Jose on the highway toward Monterey. The town was tucked right up against the range of mountains that hugged the coast. While Billy checked them into the hotel rooms Jim Locklear had reserved for them, Rob went exploring. His only impression of California had come from *Baywatch* or *Adam 12* reruns on television. He didn't really think busty blondes in bikinis walked the streets of California towns in droves, but he wouldn't have been surprised to see just that. It was interesting to note, though, that this particular part of California didn't look all that radically different from the scenery back home with its broad fields and distant mountains.

They met Jim Locklear for dinner, and between bites of fresh-caught sea bass from the Pacific and the artichoke salad from the nearby San Joaquin Valley he briefed them on what they would likely encounter the next day at Ensoft.com.

"Bill, I'm going to tell you again. These boys are a different breed," he said after a sip of wine. Rob was carefully eavesdropping, still disappointed that he couldn't get pre-sweetened iced tea to drink, and then, when the tea did come, it had been flavored with raspberry or something foreign that didn't belong in iced tea at all. He had settled for cola since he was too young to sample the fine California Merlot. "Don't be surprised when you first meet them. They look like they got called into the meeting from spring break or something. They're young, hip, don't have a necktie among the whole bunch of them, but they are brilliant. Don't let the way they look or act throw you. They're perfectly capable of making sound business decisions. They know what they're doing."

"I've been looking at their numbers," Billy offered. "They're either very good or very lucky. I just hope they know their way around a business plan."

"Oh, they do. You know as well as I do that some of the guys in the high tech world lucked into a ton of money and got rich despite themselves. But Toby Warren and Martin Flagstone are the real article. I enjoy working with them. And so will you, Billy."

"I hope so, Jim. Remember, we're making as big a decision as they are. Maybe bigger. We can't afford to sign on somebody who may go away on a whim. And with the kind of money these guys swim in, our little sponsorship is small potatoes. They could easily

tell us to take a hike and dare us to sue them if we don't like it."

"If I didn't trust them, I wouldn't have gotten you together with them. I think you will all hit it off just fine," Locklear said with a wave of his wineglass in Billy's then Rob's direction.

Billy suspected that first impressions would go a long way toward landing Ensoft's sponsorship money. All the market research, demographics, and facts and figures would have little impact if the principals didn't connect on a personal level. Sponsoring a race team was a different proposition than buying ads in magazines or running commercials on television. To do it properly, they all had to connect. That was the primary reason Rob was along on the very first trip. Billy was sure his driver's easy manner, youth, and good looks would do as much for closing the deal as his driving ability and star potential would.

Once he had gotten over not finding hushpuppies or french fries on the menu, Rob sat quietly, actually enjoying the fancy meal, and listened in fascination to what Billy and Jim were saying. He had never given much thought to the business side of racing. An auto parts store back in Hazel Green had given them a break on the price of parts in exchange for its name being painted on the side of the red Pontiac. Otherwise, he and his buddies had been the "sponsors" of the "Rob Wilder Racing Team." Now, he was shocked by the dollar figures that were being casually tossed back and forth across the table.

Rob had already made up his mind to try to learn more about the business, whether it be driving, working on the car, or how the team's finances were run. He wanted to better understand why Billy and Will made some of the decisions they did, and he was convinced that would make him a better racecar driver in the long run. While piloting the car might be his primary focus, he was convinced he could do that job better if he understood the rest of it.

Jim Locklear picked them up in front of the hotel the next morning and drove them down the valley toward the Ensoft.com campus. Even Billy was impressed with the immaculate landscaping and the sprawling cluster of sleek, modernistic buildings as they suddenly sprang up in their windshield.

"All this is Ensoft?" he asked.

"Every nook and cranny."

"Ensoft.com?" Rob read out loud from a marble obelisk that pointed the way to the headquarters building. "I'm not sure I know much about this 'dot com' business."

Jim Locklear chuckled softly.

"You have to be the only teenager in America that's not totally engrossed in the Internet."

Rob was watching out the window as a group of people tossed a Frisbee around outside one of the buildings while others were involved in a softball game on a broad expanse of lawn that sloped up to a huge glass and metal structure capped with the now-familiar Ensoft logo.

"I guess between working and racing and trying to keep . . ." he started, then seemed to think better of what he was about to say. "Is this a school, too? They look like they're having PE or something."

"Naw, they encourage the employees to take breaks and get outside during the day. They'll work until midnight but they'll get outside and play ball or jog or something several times a day."

Locklear slid the car into a visitor's slot at the entrance to the main building.

"Well, gentlemen. Let's go nail down a sponsorship."

Billy turned and glanced at Rob in the car's rear seat.

"You ready, son?"

"Surf's up, boss," Rob said with a practiced wink and sure smile. He handed Billy his briefcase then retrieved the sealed cardboard box from the car's trunk.

As they walked up the steps to the building, Billy admitted that he felt woefully underdressed.

"Jim, I've never called on a potential sponsor, including you, without wearing a suit and tie. You sure we're all right?"

They were all three decked out in the usual red "Winton Racing Team" golf shirts with the car number stitched above the pocket, and each of them wore khaki slacks.

"Will you quit worrying, Bill? We may actually be overdressed!"

The building's reception area was huge, decorated with surrealistic paintings on the walls and statues someone had made by soldering together bits of electronic circuit boards and other gizmos. A pretty receptionist welcomed them with a smile and ushered them directly into a spacious conference room. It was furnished with a massive table with an ornate chandelier hanging above it, and comfortable-looking high-backed executive chairs arranged around it. It was exactly what someone would expect to find in the offices of a successful company, except for a couple of odd additions. A regulation basketball goal was set up on one end of the room and someone had replaced a strip of the finely woven carpet with a different color piece where the free-throw line would be. And the art on the wall in the conference room consisted of concert posters for rock bands that, of the three men, only Rob had even heard of.

As they were finding places to sit, the receptionist returned, pushing a rolling cart filled with soft drinks, bottled water, and a selection of snacks.

"The posse will be right with you," she said. "Make yourselves right at home."

The posse? Billy mouthed to Jim. Locklear gave him the "okay" sign and a broad wink. Rob was strolling around the room, his hands in his pockets, intently studying the posters, eyeing the basketball goal.

Then they could hear the sound of approaching laughter and good-natured banter in the hallway outside. The door to the room burst open and in poured what appeared to be a tour group from a college somewhere who had apparently wandered off course. Or a group of interns who had undoubtedly lost their way while looking for the snack bar. There were four young men and two young women in the motley group and they pretended to actually belong here in this conference room where big deals were struck and a major corporation was run. With a friendly enough greeting to all, they motioned for everyone to stay where they were, then arranged themselves casually around the table, a couple of them even putting their feet up as they freely sampled from the snack cart.

"Jim, good to see you," one of the young men, the one dressed in a saggy sweater and faded jeans, said. "I assume this is Billy here and that must be Rob. I'm Toby Warren. In counterclockwise order, this is Lee Chen, our vice-president of systems engineering and probably our biggest race fan. He especially wanted to meet you, Rob."

"And ask you a whole raft of questions," the young

man chimed in. He wore a T-shirt with a drawing of Albert Einstein on the chest and a pair of cutoffs. "I've always wanted to take a ride in a stock car on a road course."

Rob almost said, "Me, too." But he caught himself. He said, "We can arrange that," instead.

Warren went on with the introductions.

"That's Michelle Fagan, our director of public relations, who thinks we're idiots if we don't sponsor your team, Billy. And that fellow with the eyeglasses that look like the bottoms of Coke bottles is Nick Arzoff, our programming guru. On the other side of the table, that's Martin Flagstone, our so-called president, and Kathy McGinnis, the chief financial officer for Ensoft.com."

Billy simply sat there and tried not to stare. None of these folks could be over thirty, and a couple had to be shy of twenty-five. Toby Warren, the CEO of one of the biggest companies in the high-tech field, had already kicked off his sandals and sat shoeless while he rocked back and forth in the big chair.

"Jim, I appreciate your getting us together," Martin Flagstone said, picking up the conversation seamlessly. It was clear the two men often double-teamed. Billy noticed that Flagstone, at least, wore a shirt with a collar but it was unbuttoned halfway down his chest. "Billy, I know you've done your homework on us and we've checked you folks out, too. Just as some more background, though, Toby actually started this company while we were at Cal Tech. It sounds funny, but it was really a science project gone berserk. I'm not even sure what grade he ended up getting on the project. You remember, Tobe?" Warren only shrugged and crunched down noisily on a potato chip. "Anyhow, next thing we know, we got ourselves a little company, developing software for the Internet, designing search engine logic loops, writing a new programming language for designing databases for access on the World Wide Web, and all that boring technical stuff. Six years ago we were operating out of the spare bedroom in Toby's apartment in Palo Alto and charging computers and office supplies on our Master-Cards. Then Kathy took us public and the Internet went crazy and now we got more people on our payroll than the entire population of the town in Oregon where I was born. Not bragging, but in this room, we've got the combined net worth of some small countries. And, as my hero, Jimmy Buffet, puts it, if we weren't all crazy, we'd all go insane."

Toby leaned forward and picked up the story from there.

"It's true. I don't think our mothers even understand what we do. Just that it has something or other to do with computers and seems to pay better than selling insurance." He paused to take a swig from his bottled water. "Now, as to racing. Most of us here came to the sport a little late, but we all know about the new, young drivers. Jeff Gordon, for sure. Kathy thinks he's cool, don't you, Kath?" She blushed slightly but still smiled. "You'd have to be in Timbuktu to not know who he is. Maybe you could introduce us to him someday. Anyway, we think the demographics of the racing fans nowadays match up pretty well with the people who are potential customers for our new Internet products. Even before we got your information, Billy, we suspected that sponsoring a car would be an excellent vehicle . . . no pun intended . . . to gain product awareness."

Billy agreed with a vigorous shake of his head, and immediately volunteered to make sure they met Gor-

don. Then they were off, talking business, and Billy
Winton understood that subject just as thoroughly as
he did jetting a carburetor or adjusting tire stagger.

As they got down to dollars and cents and contrac-
tual obligations and were poring over the mountain
of charts and graphs Billy had shipped ahead or
brought with him, Michelle motioned for Rob to follow her to the far end of the room.

"Let's let them talk. I wanted to meet you and get
to know you a little better."

She had begun the conversation as if they had just
sat down in a restaurant somewhere and had struck
up a casual chat. Then, without him even realizing
she had done so, she began to make notes on a legal
pad as he talked. But she still laughed with him,
seemed generally interested in what he had to say, and
succeeded in putting him totally at ease, even to the
point where Rob pulled out a chair and went through
the motions of shifting up through the gears and
showing her where everything would be inside the
racecar's cockpit.

Meanwhile, Chen and Arzoff had clearly grown
tired of all the business talk. They began ripping pages
out of their own legal pads and launched into a brisk
game of "Horse" at the basketball goal.

At the same time, Kathy McGinnis stood and began to jog in place, pausing every so often to add a
comment or check her pulse.

Despite all the chaos in the room, the talks were
accomplishing everything Billy had hoped. He had
wondered if these people would be seriously interested
in being his team's major sponsor once they knew the
hefty price tag such a commitment carried. Just when
he thought the atmosphere couldn't get any more dis-
ordered, the receptionist showed up at the door carry-

ing an armful of bags of freshly-popped popcorn.

"Sustenance break!" Toby ordered at once and grabbed one of the bags. So did the others. The two basketball players never wavered from their game, though, and Kathy ate and jogged at the same time.

Billy caught Jim Locklear's big wink and he returned it with a subtle nod of his head. Of all the Fortune 500-size companies he could have landed to sponsor his team, he had to end up with the one that most closely resembled a junior high school at recess.

After the break, though, the discussions with Toby, Martin, and Kathy grew even more serious, dealing with the details of the sponsorship. Billy was duly impressed with the questions these kids asked, with the recall of detail they exhibited. They seemed to know from memory every clause and codicil from the rather involved proposed contract Billy had faxed to them the week before. Their legal department had approved the language with a few changes and Kathy quickly explained the reasoning for each, first for them, then for Billy's attorney on the speaker phone, and they resolved the few remaining issues quickly and effectively.

They were good negotiators, too. They wanted to know precisely what they could expect from the marketing alliance, from how the logos would be displayed on the cars and hauler to the exact amount of time they could expect to have from Rob Wilder.

"The car is one thing," Toby began.

"But the driver is who our youthful clientele will identify with," Kathy said, finishing the thought as if it was a conclusion they had discussed before.

"Hear, hear!" Michelle chimed in. Somehow, she had been listening to their conversation even as she

talked intently with Rob clear across the room, beyond the game of "Horse."

"And so will our distributors and employees," Martin added. "All these folks will share in your success, but they'll mainly be pulling for Mr. Wilder there. If he wins, we all get excited. And so will our customers."

A couple of times, though, the discussion took abrupt turns, and Billy felt his stomach go sour each time. Just when he was certain they had finally sewed up the deal, one of them would take the talks in some bizarre direction. Some of the questions were dagger-sharp, and the trio seemed to be leaning toward some far-out ideas that matched their unorthodox business style. That's where Jim Locklear was able to jump in and explain alternatives and reel them back in to planet Earth. He understood the ends they were trying to achieve and used his real-world familiarity with racing as well as the software business to help get them to where they wanted to be by a more direct route. The fact that Jim had been there, had sponsored a team and had reaped some of the benefits of such a move, seemed to carry great weight with the management team from Ensoft.com.

"Hey, Toby," Nick Arzoff finally yelled from somewhere near the free throw line. "You guys going to talk all day or sign the papers?"

"So, you think we ought to sign?" Toby asked, looking up at Nick lining up another shot.

"I don't know of any other way we'll ever see our logo going two hundred miles an hour," he said, and bounced the wadded-up paper basketball through the rim without touching net.

"And if we don't jump now," Lee Chen added as he lined up his own version of the identical shot, "then

some other major software company is gonna. You
know the boys from Redmond could beat us to it. We
got where we are by being first, not bringing up the
rear."

His shot dropped off the front of the rim and Arzoff
jumped and whooped.

" 'E!' You're a horse!"

"No! That's only 'S'," Chen whined, and the two
faced off and argued like a couple of kids on the play-
ground.

Toby, Martin, and Kathy ignored them and looked
pointedly at each other. Michelle grabbed Rob's arm
and brought him back to where the others sat at the
end of the conference table.

"I agree," Kathy said. "What about the rest of
you?"

"Rob's going to be perfect. I think he matches up
with our target demos," Michelle Fagan said. "The
under-forties will love him. So will the women." Rob
blushed. He wasn't sure what a "demo" was but he
was glad he matched it if it was important to all these
odd folks with the big money. Meanwhile, Michelle
was pointing to the stack of charts and printouts that
rested on the edge of the table. "And we've seen how
well that matches the racing audience these days. I
can't wait to get him in our booth at Comdex. Or
take him on a road show for our distributors!"

"Same here."

"And here."

The rest of them quickly made it unanimous.

"Okay, Billy, it looks like we have a go for launch
from mission control," Martin said, but suddenly his
face went totally serious. He no longer looked like a
kid at all. "I just have one more question and it's the
crucial one and we would all appreciate an honest

answer. Understand that we believe in doing everything the right way with all the necessary resources or
we simply don't do it. If it were not prudent to spend
what it takes to put us in the most positive light, we
would rather not have anything to do with it. If we
don't think we're going to get return on investment
sponsoring this race team, we will take the money and
put it somewhere where we will."

Martin Flagstone stopped talking then and leaned
forward. All of a sudden, the turmoil in the room had
ceased. The rest of the senior management team from
Ensoft had gathered in a group behind their CEO and
were waiting for the question.

Uh-oh, Billy thought. He had been on enough
sponsorship pitches before to know everything could
unravel now, no matter how well it had been going.
This was the point where a dollar figure had been
thrown out, maybe seriously discussed, and where the
eager, panting prospect would usually gulp, blanch,
and back away. Sometimes they would try to haggle
a partial sponsorship deal or, most often, they would
give him a flat "No," or a "Well, we'll have to check
our budgets and get back to you, Billy."

"Okay, Martin. What's the question?" Billy asked.

"Is this enough money to do this thing correctly? I
mean, is it enough for you to field a team that will
win and, at the same time, get us the exposure we
want for our products?" He held up his hand as if
stopping traffic. "Before you answer, let me tell you
what I mean. We don't want to get neck-deep into
this thing with you and then find out that if you had
had another five hundred thousand or a million, you
could have beaten the world. Give us the figure you
think you need, not the one you think we want to
hear to do the deal. If it's too much for us, we'll shake

hands and part friends. If it's not enough to do the job right, we'll inevitably part, but it won't be friendly, I'm afraid. Ensoft has never failed at anything yet. We don't intend to fail here either. We like winning. We don't want any part of anything that doesn't win."

"Well, uh . . ." Billy sputtered, hesitating. He had never had a potential sponsor say such a thing to him before. They usually tap-danced, ducked and dodged around the issues, and they expected him to do the same. He quickly reviewed in his head the numbers he had been running through spreadsheets for the past week. He decided to be totally honest. "I think it's adequate for the time being. We are looking at a three-year plan. The technology of the sport is changing so fast it's hard to predict what will be needed in three years." Everyone in the Ensoft group nodded their heads. They, of all people, understood rapid and unpredictable change. "Next year, we'll run a full schedule in Grand National, then, the following year, we'll move up to run the Cup circuit. We expect Rob to challenge for rookie of the year once we do. I think the amount we've discussed will allow us to be competitive and will assure the kind of exposure you're looking for so long as we . . . Rob, Will Hughes, myself and the rest of the crew . . . do our part. After that, I honestly don't have anything more than an educated guess for you."

Then Billy hushed. He hoped his candor would not put them off. He suspected it would not. Apparently, he was right.

"Good. You have been up front with us all along, Billy. We appreciate that. If you could only imagine how much smoke gets blown our way." The others were nodding again. "Why don't we sign this thing before the cheeseburgers get here?"

Billy had to fish around in his briefcase for a pen for Flagstone to use. The rest of the group crowded around to watch him initial the few changes they had agreed to and put his signature at the end of the lengthy document. Then, when Billy had followed suit, they toasted the signing with sodas and spring water.

Right on cue, a couple of staffers showed up with a cart full of cheeseburgers, french fries, chips, and cookies of all types. As they ate, Rob opened the cardboard box he had brought in and showed them the new team shirts. They were still the same bright red color of the car and had the number over the pocket, but they also proudly carried the Ensoft.com logo.

Billy made a ceremony of presenting the first ones to Toby and Martin and they both, without hesitation, ripped off their own shirts and pulled the sparkling new Ensoft.com Racing Team shirts over their heads. The others cheered, whooped, and hollered, then grabbed their own shirts out of the air as Rob tossed them around the room. Billy had an anxious moment when he was sure the two young women were about to strip off their own tops as the men were doing, but they simply slipped them on over what they were wearing. The receptionist seemed to anticipate a need and appeared with a camera. Everyone put down his burger again to pose for various group photos amid much laughing and kidding.

After lunch, they toured the Ensoft facilities and met many of the employees. They all seemed excited to meet Rob, to learn that a deal had been struck, that he would be carrying the Ensoft colors when he banged fenders with all the young guns in racing. And it was exciting to all of them that many of the people they met seemed to truly be interested in racing, to know some of the drivers, to especially be familiar with the Cup teams. Rob couldn't believe how many hands he was shaking, but Toby explained that they ran a very open company, that they worked hard to make all the employees feel a part of what the company did. And that included sponsoring the next championship team in Grand National racing.

It was amazing to Billy and Rob, too, how young most of the Ensoft staff appeared to be, most of them apparently not much older than Rob himself. That simply drove home the realization that that was one of the reasons the company was interested in sponsoring a car with a young driver like Rob instead of one of the older, more established teams.

Finally, as they strolled through the lobby saying their goodbyes, a staffer rushed up and handed Martin Flagstone an envelope. He took a slip of paper from inside it and scribbled something on it as Billy, Rob, and Jim shook hands with the others. Just as they turned to leave, Martin handed Billy the slip of paper, now folded double.

"It was nice to finally meet you Billy. I know it's going to be a pleasure working with you." He nodded to the paper he had placed in Billy's hand. "This should help us through the rest of the races this year."

Billy smiled politely and slipped the paper into his pocket without looking at it.

"We have some good racecars, a good crew, and . . . well . . . you've met the driver. I don't think you'll be disappointed. Maybe you can all fly out and meet everybody else and watch the race at Charlotte in October. It should be a good one."

"I'll be there. You can count on it."

The others all nodded agreement, too. It appeared to be a date.

They were halfway to the airport before Billy pulled the slip of paper from his pocket. He knew it was a check, but when he unfolded it and tried to take in the numbers, he had trouble comprehending what he was seeing. It was more than enough for them to complete the year and would get them well situated for next season. And it was above and beyond the contract they had just signed.

He shook his head and looked at the check again. For all their sophomoric appearance and oddball way of doing business, it was clear that these guys were serious about helping him produce a winner. His own words came back to him, the statement about how it was up to him and Will and Rob and the rest of them to build a winning team. Money would be no excuse. And, as the grass and eucalyptus groves gave way to the cement and asphalt of the San Jose airport, Billy admitted to himself that the pressure was really on now. And he was as excited as he had ever been in his better than thirty years of racing. Finally, he could put to the test the theories and the ideas he had developed, and see if they were applicable to big-time racing at the end of the century.

The inside of the automobile was quiet as they pulled into the rental car return lot. Likely, all three men held similar thoughts. There was much work to be done. There were racecars to order; parts to machine; equipment to install at the shop; people to find, interview, and hire. They needed to meet with the graphic artist to get a paint scheme finalized quickly, needed to get the final versions of Rob's driver's suit and helmet finished because a photographer would be coming soon to take publicity photos. And they needed to get it all done while running the rest of the Grand National season this year.

February and Daytona were lurking dead ahead, and now, they had no reason not to be ready.

C lara Hughes whistled softly as she ran the
dustmop over the hardwood floors in the up-
stairs bedroom Rob Wilder had been using.
She actually enjoyed having him stay there for a
while. He was such a polite kid, neat, orderly, not like
most teenagers she knew.

He had tried to pay her for washing and ironing
his clothes, for keeping fresh sheets on his bed, for all
her wonderful cooking he gobbled up. But she flatly
refused. It was good to have someone besides Will to
do for.

They had never had children. Clara told Will it was
because he stayed gone to races or the shop so much
she never had a chance to get exposed. And she
wasn't totally kidding.

She smiled and shook her head when she checked
the closet. Rob only had three or four pairs of ragged
jeans hanging there, a few golf shirts, one white shirt

with the collar button missing until she had sewn one on, and a threadbare, out-of-fashion suit. A dresser drawer held a dozen or so T-shirts. That's what he usually wore. A T-shirt, a pair of jeans, and the shabby sneakers that rested now in the floor of the closet. Billy had bought him a couple of pairs of khaki slacks, a shirt, and some dress shoes for their trip to California, and the youngster had looked so handsome when they had left.

She couldn't imagine how Rob's mother or father could have sent him off with no more clothes. And apparently the only money he had was what Billy had advanced him from his driver's share.

Then again, Rob had never mentioned his parents or any brothers or sisters. Clara had promised herself she would ask him soon. She wasn't nosy. No, not at all. Only curious, that's all.

The only personal thing in the room was a small framed photograph of Rob, standing with several other young men in front of a dented, dusty old race car, holding a checkered flag and a small trophy. She picked up the photo and smiled when she saw the wild, excited look on the young man's face.

Clara Hughes knew that look well. She had seen it many times on the faces of her husband, Billy Winton, Jodell Lee, and the others. He had won. And nothing else could light up the countenances of all these men in her life like winning a race. She didn't profess to understand it. She simply knew it when she saw it.

"I better get these linens washed while he's gone," she said out loud as she returned the picture to the nightstand and then quickly shucked the cases off the pillows. But then, when she jerked the sheet from beneath the mattress, something heavy and brown fell at her feet.

It was a scrapbook. An old, tattered scrapbook, and it landed open to what was clearly the last page. There, stuck down at its corners with yellowed Scotch tape, was a browned and torn newspaper article.

Clara Hughes was not nosy. No, not at all.

But the book had landed open, and the newspaper article was right there, and its headline was in big, bold letters she could not have avoided reading even if she had tried. And when she picked it up to slide it back beneath the mattress where Rob had apparently placed it, she couldn't help reading the first few sentences of the article. Then, if she had seen that much, she might just as well read the rest of the story and look at some of the other similar articles taped to the pages in the rest of the book.

When she was finished, she knew this was something she needed to share with her husband.

She hurriedly stripped off the sheets and ran them down the stairs to the washer.

Clara Hughes had just solved part of the puzzle of the mysterious Rob Wilder.

THE CHARLOTTE RACE

Rob Wilder continued to show the promise everyone had seen already through the rest of the races leading up to Charlotte. The open test session at the storied track went well, too. The kid seemed especially suited for the fast speeds and high banks at the Charlotte track, and even more reporters and fans had taken note of the handsome young man with the stylish blond hair and natural driving ability. The news of the new sponsor affiliation and continuing rumors about a future move up to the Cup circuit had the journalists talking, too. Rob seemed to thrive on all the attention but, so far, had demonstrated a knack for taking his growing popularity in stride and concentrating on important things. Things like steering the red Ford around whatever racetrack he was on as fast as he possibly could.

Now, with the race at Charlotte approaching, several representatives from the new sponsor were scheduled to fly in. Even without Billy or Will having to say so, everyone was on notice that a good showing was absolutely necessary. But the confidence of the crew in general, and their driver in particular, was building from week to week.

Will wasted little time ramping up the operation. Within minutes of Billy's call from the Sam Jose airport with the good news, he had been on the phone to a mechanic they had already been talking with, and a machinist was on the payroll before another couple of weeks had passed. It had been an especially exciting day when they had placed the order for five new racecars. The first was to be delivered the very next week.

Billy was pleased to see that the chemistry between Rob and Will had continued to build. The level of communication between them had flourished— partly, Billy suspected, from them actually living together, even though they stayed at the shop most nights past ten o'clock anyway. Still short on crew, they took advantage of Rob's willingness to grab a wrench and help in the shop, with the added advantage of him getting a much better feel for the car and what went into its preparation for racing. He was particularly adept by now at expressing his opinion on what needed to be changed, and what impact those changes had on the car once they were made.

For his part, Will was more than pleased with the kid's progress. And he had to admit that he actually liked the youngster. Several times, he had almost broached the subject of the secret he had learned, but it seemed the time was never exactly right for such a conversation. Maybe after Charlotte. Maybe then there would be a better opportunity. And he had so far not shared it with Billy or anyone else. When the time was right, he would.

So far, Ensoft had not been very demanding of Rob's time. They were still putting the final pieces of the marketing campaign together. Other than a few phone interviews, one appearance at a trade show, and a photo shoot or two, he had concentrated totally on driving and learning all he could about the car. Once it came time to start making preparations for Daytona to begin the new season, the shop time would likely dwindle to little or none so it was good he was blessed with this opportunity. More serious demands on his time were imminent.

Michelle Fagan was bringing a couple of the Ensoft marketing team members in early the week before the Charlotte race to meet everyone and to see the operations. Then they would follow the team over to Charlotte and spend the rest of the week there, learning about the sport, observing how the other sponsors did things. Toby planned to come in on Friday and watch the race on Saturday.

Michelle Fagan assumed she had made a wrong turn somewhere as she followed the faxed directions to the Winton shop. She seemed to have left all civilization behind once she left the Tri-Cities Airport and drove through woods, hills, hollows, and not much else. It was beautiful country but hardly what she had pictured as the home of a big-time race team. And she knew the Cup team of racing legend Jodell Lee was headquartered around here somewhere, too. Still, even though it was pretty country, it looked more like Davey Crockett or Daniel Boone territory to her, hardly the place for speed and loud engines.

Finally, she turned off the two-lane blacktop onto a narrow, tree-lined gravel road that seemed to run straight into the side of a mountain. Then, a half-mile or so up, once they had made a turn past a grove of towering water oaks, there was Billy Winton's low, sprawling log house and the big commercial-sized building in a stand of trees beyond that had to be the racing shop.

Billy was resting in a rocking chair on the wraparound front porch, talking on the phone, when Michelle and her two assistants eased into the parking area in front of the house. He hung up quickly and met them at the steps with a warm welcome, then ushered them right on over toward the shop. He was anxious to get them out there. There was something he was dying to show them.

On the way, though, they met Rob, headed to the house for some fresh ice water for the crew. Michelle hugged him as if they were long, lost friends, and both she and Billy noticed the approving expressions on the assistants' faces when they were introduced to the young driver. They even turned in tandem and watched him walk on to the house before they proceeded, at Billy's urging, to the shop.

After introducing them to the crew, Billy stepped over to the back of the shop area to something big, something vaguely car-shaped, and draped with a form-fitting cover. It was clearly a racecar, and Billy Winton was obviously excited about showing it to Michelle and the others. With a flourish, he and will lifted the cover and revealed the car that waited beneath.

"We just finished painting her late last night. What do you think?" Billy asked.

"Wow!" was all Michelle could manage. Beneath the bright lights of the shop, the car's paint job gleamed and glittered. She sat so low to the ground and her lines were so sleek, she seemed on the verge of taking off all by herself. The Ford was painted a brilliant red but with tiny metallic flecks sparkling subtly in her finish. She had been accented in yellow, and she had a bold 6 painted on her sides and roof. Secondary sponsor decals were lined up on her flanks and rear deck.

The Ensoft logo and name were done in a dark blue with sky blue highlighting and contrasted nicely with the car's primary scarlet scheme. Over the door, written out in bold yellow script, was the signature decal of Rob Wilder.

One of the assistants already had her camera out and was furiously snapping pictures. The flashes made the car almost appear to be in motion already. Michelle walked around the racer slowly, taking it all in, obviously sincerely admiring her.

"The body man took your logo and kind of worked something up as a first shot. I hope you like it."

"Like it? I love it!'

"Good. This will give you some idea of the kinds of things we can do with paint and decals on the cars. Main thing we want the graphic artist to think about is how the paint scheme and colors will show up on TV. You want people to be able to pick our car out of a pack of them without any trouble. We'll change up some along the way, depending on whether it's a day or night race, too."

"I don't think we'll have any trouble seeing this," she said as she gently caressed the smooth polished surface of the car.

"You sure? You think Martin and Toby and the others will like it?"

She looked at Billy and pursed her lips.

"Oh, yeah!"

Billy and Will breathed a collective sigh of relief. The paint scheme and the car's appearance had clearly made a good impression on the first sponsor representatives to see it. Both men could recount horror stories of sponsors who had insisted on horrible, ugly colors or impossible-to-read decals or hideous pictures of their products emblazoned all over the car. Or of well-intentioned designers who ended up with schemes that turned out too gaudy or too bland and then had to go with them when the people who wrote the checks actually professed to like them. Both Billy and Will had loved the way the car had turned out. They had no way of knowing if the sponsor would agree.

Michelle and her assistants kept snapping pictures while Will and the crew resumed loading up the hauler with the car and the rest of the gear. Billy continued as their tour guide, showing them all the equipment, the tools, the parts stockpile, the other cars they were working on, and all the rest of what made up a well-equipped race shop. They seemed duly impressed, even if they were not sure what most of the things were that they were seeing.

That night, Billy took their California visitors to a catfish and shrimp dinner in Johnson City and then escorted them back to their motel. He got back to the shop just in time to oversee the final loading, then the truck and trailer pulled away shortly before 2 A.M. headed for Charlotte. He had told Michelle to leave an early wakeup call because they expected to gather with the balance of the crew and leave the shop themselves around four-thirty in the morning.

When she, along with Wendy and Carol, the two assistants, showed up, they looked as if they had had no sleep at all.

"Just remember, it's one-thirty, California time," she reminded them. Wendy erupted into a huge yawn and Carol feigned a collapse.

"Welcome to the glamorous world of big-time stockcar racing," Will Hughes said without a trace of a grin.

THE LONG, LONG DAY

As usual, Rob Wilder was wide-awake and ready to go, despite the fact that the sun would not peek above the horizon for another hour yet. "The curse of youth," Billy called it. "All that stamina and they waste it on girls and parties and the like."

But Rob was even more excited than usual. He couldn't wait to set sail around the famed Charlotte speedway once again. He knew it was the very track where Buddy Baker, Richard Petty, David Pearson, Cale Yarborough, and the Allison brothers had cut their racing teeth. He distinctly remembered watching on television as Dale Earnhardt dominated races there in the late eighties and early nineties.

He knew, too, that Charlotte was a track where many other young drivers had broken a career wide open after an opportune trip to victory lane. After the test session there several weeks before, he felt confi-

dent that he could go right out there and tame the
fast mile-and-a-half track. Will had promised him an
even faster car than the one they had tested there and
Rob believed him. With the car and the testing experience here, he was convinced they would have the
debut run of a lifetime.

The convoy of cars and the van with the crew inside pulled into the track's entrance at about seven-
thirty in the morning. The crew flashed their
credentials and drove on to where the truck and
hauler was already parked in the garage area. Billy
walked Michelle and her party through the process of
getting their own pit and garage passes, as well as the
credentials for Toby Warren, who would arrive the
next day.

As they went through the process, Michelle gazed
about her, taking in all the bustling activity of the
teams swarming around their tractor-trailer trucks
that had filled the infield, unloading the cars and
equipment. It was clearly some kind of carefully or-
chestrated chaos and she wondered out loud how they
kept from running over each other as they shoved the
cars and tire carts and other equipment about. Then,
as they finally parked and walked toward the Billy
Winton Ensoft Racing Team slot in the garage, they
saw the same chaos swirling around a familiar car.
Will was guiding the bright red Ford out onto the lift
so it could be slowly lowered to the ground and unloaded.

The early morning sun caught the paint job beautifully and it glinted and sparkled as the first rays
struck it. She noticed, then, the ecstatic look on Rob
Wilder's face as he watched the car coming out of the
hauler.

"She is beautiful, isn't she?" Michelle asked.

He didn't take his eyes off the car when he answered.

"About the prettiest thing I've ever seen." Then it occurred to him that she might take that statement the wrong way. Or that Carol or Wendy would. They were all quite attractive and he had definitely noticed. "For an old racecar, that is."

"Aren't you nervous?" she asked him.

"No, not at all. I'm just ready to get out there and see what she can do when we let her have her head."

"Well, I know all this hustle and bustle is making me nervous." She waved an arm around the garage and then had to yell to be heard above a couple of cars that had just cranked up nearby. "How does everybody make any sense out of all this?"

"I guess we all manage to sort it out somehow. We're all racers here. This is what we come here to do, to get the car ready and take her out there and make sure she runs faster and longer than anybody else's car. As soon as we get to the track, I start getting impatient. All I wanna do is get out there and drive."

Carol was staring at the first turn.

"Look how steep it is in those curves!"

"It's called banking," Rob explained patiently but with a smile. "Banking helps us get more speed out of the car. They aren't called 'curves,' either. They're 'turns' or 'corners.' That's turn one and turn two over there."

"I guess we have a lot to learn, don't we?" Michelle said, looking where he was pointing.

"Well, don't worry. A lot of this is still new to me, too. Almost nothing is like it was on the tracks back home. I'm still learning. Hang close to me and we'll learn this stuff together."

"You may wish you hadn't said that. We're your shadow for the rest of this trip."

Rob didn't tell her that Billy had asked him to take the trio from Ensoft under his wing until he had to get into the car. He wanted them to get to know the driver better and he wanted Rob to become comfortable with the PR types from their sponsor. They would be spending plenty of time together for the duration of the sponsorship.

The team got the car unloaded then pushed it over for the initial inspection by the Series officials. Will was already knee-deep in his extensive checklist, making sure everything was ready for the car's first trip out onto the track.

Michelle was impressed by how organized and meticulous they were about every single detail, how everything was checked and re-checked over and over. She compared it to their testing and quality assurance efforts at Ensoft. Rob explained to her how important it was not to overlook even the tiniest glitch. At speeds approaching 200 miles per hour, they could not afford to have anything break if it could be prevented. One bolt on the car left not fully tightened or over-torqued might lead to a part failure and that could put the racecar out of the race or, worse, into the fence. Then you would have broken a hundred-thousand-dollar-plus racecar. And worse, you might have a busted-up driver to boot. And all that from an overlooked slip of a wrench. That's why they continually checked and re-checked every bolt, reading, gauge, and setting on the racecar right up until it pulled out onto the track. Then it would become Rob's job to continue to check the gauges, sounds, feel, and handling of the car, ever on the lookout for something amiss.

Some of the Grand National cars were already out there, zooming around the track. Rob finally jumped in and pulled away, more than ready to begin dialing the car in and get it ready for qualifying. He waved goodbye to the three Ensoft representatives, then once he was out there and up to speed, he concentrated hard on finding a good clean line around the speedway.

The car was fast from the moment he hit speed. It was clear to Rob that they were close already and he hadn't even tried to really push the car yet. He bore down as he steered out of the second corner and headed down the back straightaway, pushing the throttle hard to the floor.

He set the car perfectly going into turn three and felt it start to bite, to find traction even when all logic would have told the average driver that he was going much too fast for such a sharp turn. He held his line on the track, staying down low, near the white line that ran all the way through the corner and marked the inside edge of the paved apron. Any lower and he would have been on the flat of the apron itself. With a quick twist of the wheel, Rob guided the car quickly through the corner, then gave her an even bigger swallow of gasoline as he drove toward the D-shaped front straightaway.

Then, once again, it appeared to those watching that Rob had slipped low enough to actually clip the grass as he cut the shortest path through the center part of the D and crossed the start/finish line. Michelle even gasped as she saw a small cloud of dust kicked up from where he just grazed the dirt. She was certain that he was about to lose control of that beautiful new racecar. He was all the way into the center of the first and second turn before she even dared to breathe again.

How in the world could he do that, taking those curves . . . sorry, 'turns' . . . so fast, dropping so low on the track that he was mowing grass? If it was going to be like this every lap, and even on the very first lap of practice before the actual race even started, and if there were going to be three dozen other madmen out there doing precisely the same thing, then she didn't know if her constitution could survive this racing thing or not. She was not surprised to see the looks on the faces of Carol and Wendy, too.

They all three mouthed a single word: "Wow!" Then, they turned to watch their car and driver do the exact same thing through another lap while Billy and Will and the crew casually looked on as if there was nothing truly amazing going on out there at all.

After Rob had brought the car in a couple of times and allowed the crew to scramble around and make adjustments, Michelle and her crew took Billy's advice and wandered around the garage and pit area. They weren't yet familiar enough with the teams to know who was hot and who wasn't, who to watch and who not. It didn't take long to figure it out, though. The television crews and newspaper beat writers clustered around certain stalls and drivers. Even the Ensoft folks had heard of Dale Earnhardt and his son, Dale Jr. And sure enough, there was plenty of media around the younger Earnhardt's car. Another contingent had zeroed in on Casey Atwood. The youngster was creating plenty of interest already.

They quickly figured out who the teams' sponsor representatives were, too. And they all seemed to be working as hard as their drivers and crews were. Michelle began recording ideas as they came to her, talking into a small recorder while Carol and Wendy made notes on their Palm Pilots. Michelle was determined that they get the most from the investment they were making in the Winton team and Rob Wilder. And to do that, they needed to be able to take advantage of every marketing opportunity they could.

Meanwhile, back in the pits, Will stood on top of the toolbox timing each lap that Rob was running. The stopwatch confirmed what his eyes and instincts were telling him. The racecar was plenty fast right off the truck, before they had even touched her. The motor was pulling plenty of power down the straightways. They were losing a little speed in the corners but he knew that could be easily corrected. He had already told Rob to continue to push the car in the turns and report back what he felt, and Will listened, checked his watch, and continually jotted notes in the margins of the sheets on his clipboard, listing things he wanted to try when they brought him in. Good as the car was, they could always make it better.

Now that they had enough laps and data to establish a baseline to work from, Will wanted to try a few experiments with the shock absorbers. He was thankful that, unlike some of the other teams, they weren't out there chasing the setup all over the track, trying to find some speed, any speed, struggling to make massive adjustments to keep their car from doing a one-eighty when their driver pushed it. There was not enough practice time allotted before the first round of qualifying for any team to be floundering around, trying to make a bum car go fast. That's why they worked so hard back at the shop, so they could show up fast already and then tweak to get even faster.

Rob brought the car in one more time, pulling it straight to the garage, where the crew hustled over at a full run to meet him. Will barked out instructions for the changes that he wanted to make. The crew was slipping the jack under the car the instant it rolled to a stop. Donnie Kline gave the jack two quick pumps, bringing the car's tires up off the cement. One of the others began to slip jack stands under the car, then dashed around to the other side and did the same.

An electric fan was hooked over the front end to blow cool air across the radiator. The crew made a miraculously rapid spring change on the right side of the car while Will went over the lap times with Rob. The driver sat patiently in the car while the crew worked, listening to Will and adding a thought or two along the way.

Meanwhile, Billy Winton lifted the hood and checked the engine for himself. He reached in and removed a spark plug, then held it up to the light like a jeweler inspecting a diamond. It was clean with a nice burn pattern, indicating the engine had the right fuel-to-air mixture. He also quickly looked for fluid leaks, saw none, then made some minor adjustments to the cowling that funneled air into the carburetor.

Like his crew chief, Billy was pleased with this first set of runs, but he also knew they had more work to do if they were going to get a good time in the first-round qualifying. And, that still, even with the good car and off-the-truck times, making the race was not a foregone conclusion. There were plenty of good cars here trying to make the race, and some of them would go home after qualifying had set the field. Everyone didn't make it and some decent rides would leave the dance early.

To make it even more competitive, there was a large contingent of Cup drivers trying to make the field as well. The competition for starting spots was going to be furious. Rob was going to have to make the run of his young career if he intended on being around for the green flag of the actual race.

And Billy had told his young driver as much, not to scare him or make him nervous, but to make sure he understood the importance of a productive practice and a flawless run to qualify if they hoped to be in the biggest race left to run this season. When he explained it all, Rob had simply nodded, looked him squarely in the eye, and set his jaw.

It had not been necessary for the kid to say a word. He understood.

Michelle hustled back to the team's garage stall when she saw Rob pulling in to a stop. The crew was working at such a frantic pace she first thought something must be wrong. A young woman standing in the stall next to her must have deciphered the worried look on Michelle's face.

"It's okay. They're just squeezing out another tenth."

"Huh?"

"Doing what teams do. Getting another ounce of speed out of their machine. Looks like this bunch is going to be okay, though." The woman held out her hand. "I'm Stephanie Howell. I work with the sponsor of these guys over here." She pointed over her shoulder at a bright yellow car that carried the logo of a major grocery store chain.

"I'm Michelle Fagan," she answered, returning the handshake. "We've just signed on as sponsor on the 6 team.'"

"I didn't think I had seen you around before. You've got a good bunch to work with, Michelle. Billy is the greatest and Rob Wilder . . . well, you better get your stick ready."

"Huh?" Michelle asked again.

"The stick to beat off all the girls. He's a honey! He's gonna be dangerous if he ever gets out of or out from under that car long enough. This is your first race, then?"

"Yep."

"I thought so. I hadn't seen the paint job yet. That's a great look you guys came up with for the car. I really do like the colors."

Michelle looked at the woman a bit sideways. Did PR people for rival teams really tell you they liked your paint scheme, or was she being sarcastic? The woman seemed sincere enough, though.

"Well, we can't take much credit for it. Billy and his guys worked this up over at their shop for this race. We're so new we're still trying to decide what kind of paint job we want to go with permanently."

"I don't know what you're looking for but that's gonna be hard to beat. Wait'll you see it out there with the other cars. Yours is gonna shine, I bet."

"Well, thanks. I admit I kinda like it but we'll have to let our boss have a look at it. At least this one looks good."

Stephanie Howell still seemed totally sincere in her praise of the Ford's paint scheme.

"That it does."

Just then, their conversation was wiped out by the high-pitched whine of an air gun as one of the crew removed a set of lug nuts. Will and the gang were still going at a brutal pace, as if the race was on already and they were falling laps behind.

"Why are they in such a hurry?" Michelle asked, nodding at the feverishly working crew. The men working on the car in Stephanie's garage slot next door were doing the same thing.

"Oh, you better get used to it. The practice lasts only a little over an hour. They don't get much track time before they qualify and they don't want to waste a minute of it."

"There's an awful lot more to this than I thought. I had the impression that they showed up, unloaded, and raced."

"There is a lot to racing. It's a big-time professional sport with plenty of money invested, as you well know. There's too much riding on these cars and crews and drivers for them to let anything fall through the cracks. But I'll tell you one thing." She gave Michelle a conspiratorial wink. "Most of these guys have a whale of a good time once the garage closes down for the afternoon. There's a bunch of us going out to-night. If you don't have plans, we'd love to have you come along. It sure beats sitting around the hotel talking about spark plugs and carburetors!"

"I appreciate the invitation, Stephanie. Let me see if Billy has anything planned for us later on."

"Well, it's an open invitation. But if I know Billy Winton and Will Hughes, they'll have y'all changing the oil or stacking tires before the day is over." She laughed heartily. "I'll be around all day and it looks like we're stall mates. Just tell me if you can make it and I'll let you know where we're meeting up."

"Okay, I'll check . . ." Michelle started, but she was quickly drowned out as Rob cranked up the Ford and backed it out of the stall, steering for the track once more.

He had been sitting in the car while the team quickly made the latest changes Will had prescribed. He checked the tire temps on the chart that one of the crew had passed to him. They were running a little hotter than they wanted on the outside edge of the right-side tires. But Rob suspected that the changes Will had ordered made on the car this stop would correct the problem that was causing the higher temperature.

He handed the clipboard back out the window and was still mentally reviewing the laps he had just finished when he felt the car come down off the jack stands, first the right side, then the left. As he made his way back out to the track, Will gave him a quick set of instructions over the radio.

As he rolled out onto the track, the kid thought one more time how privileged he was to be out here, making his way around such a historic track. He loved the way it felt to drive it, the way the car responded to his commands as if he was simply giving an experienced thoroughbred its head on a familiar track and letting it find its own fast way around. Sometimes he felt guilty, because it was so easy when the car was finely tuned and the track so good; but he also knew it was his horse to ride. He had to know when to kick and when to rein in, when to gallop and when to trot, or his mount was likely to stumble.

He kept the car down on the apron as he ran up through the gears, then blended smoothly with traffic as he exited turn two. Will was already back on the toolbox, stopwatch in hand, watching the car rush down into the third turn. When it jetted past his position, likely still not completely up to full speed yet, he clicked the button on the stopwatch.

Rob came out of the D, then charged off down into turn one. The car stuck right down on the white line. He cracked the throttle a smidgen as the car dug down in the corner. This time, she didn't want to push up in the center of the corner at all as she had before. She was a bobsled on a downhill course, hugging the lower part of the track.

Rob smiled to himself as he sailed on through and then departed the second corner. Lord, they had built one sweet machine!

Will clicked the watch again as Rob roared by him. He glanced down at the time displayed there and the digital numbers confirmed what he felt. It had been a very good lap, slightly bettering what they had been running. He followed the car off into turn one, watching to see if the car picked up even more now that it had a good head of steam built up.

The next lap did not disappoint. The car picked up a tenth and that found speed put them in the top ten in relation to the other cars' laps that they had been able to watch and time. That had been the spotter's job, to time as many of the competition as he could, and to eavesdrop on their radio traffic and pick up any other information he could to determine the cars to beat.

Billy had climbed back up to his observation spot atop the truck and watched some of the other cars himself. As the spotter was reporting, Dale Earnhardt, Jr., Matt Kenseth, Elton Sawyer, and Jeff Green, along with a couple of others, were running among the fastest. No surprises.

Billy had his watch on Rob as he came around once more. He clicked his own watch as the bright-red car zoomed past.

The paint scheme certainly did make it easy to follow out on the track. The brilliant red and the blues were easy for the eye to pick up. He watched as the kid cruised down the backstretch, then slid in behind several cars running together and picked up their draft. He bided his time for half a lap, then pulled out of line and easily shot past them.

Billy Winton couldn't help it. He pounded the arm of his director's chair mouthing the word "Yes!" That maneuver had confirmed for him two important points. First, the engine had the horses to get the job done. And second, his driver knew how to handle that awesome power. Now, anything else they could find would have to be with a nudge or two on the handling. Then they would be ready to qualify. Once that had been accomplished, they would go right back and start all over getting the race setup under the car. But that would have to wait.

Out on the track, Rob had joined the draft of another set of cars as they exited the fourth turn. The car was sucked right up onto the back end of the rear car in the pack. A mere foot or so separated the two cars and, for those watching, it appeared they might actually be touching at nearly two hundred miles per hour. Running down the short chute, the scant stretch of track between the turn and the curve of the D, he suddenly pulled down to the inside, pushing the nose of his car up beside the left rear fender of the racer he had been following. As they approached the start/finish line, Rob took the car right down to the grass once again as he made a push to complete the pass.

The car on the outside moved over, giving him plenty of room. It was much too early in the practice to try and contest an issue like that. Instead, the other driver let him go past then tucked right in behind Rob as he went to work on the next car in line, a Chevy whose driver was clearly struggling with an ill-handling race car. The back end seemed to want to skew around and try to pass the front end every time a car got tight up behind it. Rob made quick work and got on past before something happened, then, at the radioed request of Will, brought the car back in to the garage for a final round of minor adjustments.

Michelle, Carol, and Wendy had climbed atop the truck with Billy and he was pointing out things they should look for out on the track.

"If you watch closely, you can tell if a car is getting too loose coming off a turn."

"Loose?"

"That means the rear end is prone to break loose, to lose traction." He pointed to a car just as it seemed to wiggle dangerously in the middle of a turn. They could hear the pitch of the engine change dramatically as the driver completely let off the gas to keep from crashing. " 'Pushing' means the car doesn't want to turn with the corner, the front end wants to go straight for the wall. That's not a good thing either."

"I imagine not," one of the women said, and they all nodded in agreement.

"Watch that blue and white car going right there," Billy said, and pointed toward a car that was about to drive into the first turn. "See how he can put the car right down on the white line when he starts into the corner but he can't hold it down there long. See? Right there. Watch it push up."

Sure enough, the car eased higher on the track as the car made its way through the corner. If there had been traffic next to him, he would have either had to get off the gas or bang into whoever was racing beside him.

"Okay, I see now what you're saying," Michelle agreed. "But what makes it move up like that? Why can't he just turn the steering wheel hard enough and make it stay down there on the line where he wants it?"

"He can. But if he does that, he has to slow down at the same time. He's letting the car drift up so he can keep as much speed as possible going through the turn."

"I guess that makes sense," she said, then caught sight of another car as it slid precariously up into the center of the corner, apparently having the same problem the first driver had been having. She watched how the car drove through the turn and sure enough, it did exactly what Billy had described.

"Now watch that one," Billy said and pointed to a yellow Chevy, the same one Rob had hurried past during his last run. Billy had been watching the car for several laps and knew it was running extremely loose. "See how the back end is wiggling there?"

Michelle and the others watched as the rear of the car began to lose its grip on the track surface. They could see in what was almost slow motion as the driver sawed wildly at the steering wheel and then, suddenly, the rear end kicked around as if some angry giant had brushed it aside. The driver instinctively twisted the wheel the opposite way, trying to regain control of the car before it skidded toward the outside wall. All three of the women put their hands over their mouths in horror as the car did a complete smoking, squealing spin on the track, the back end coming within what appeared to be a few inches of whacking the outside wall. Then, once again headed more or less in the right direction, the vehicle screeched on down the track to the inside of the raceway and finally rolled to a stop.

"Wow!" Michelle yelled. "I can't believe he didn't hit anything."

"He was lucky. Real lucky. He came close to knocking down that wall. Like I was telling you, that car was really loose and when he drove into the turn, it just got away from him. You've heard of centrifugal force? That's what we're all trying to overcome out there. That and a few other laws of physics that don't necessarily like to be broken."

"But it happened so fast! One second he was fine and then he was doing a loop-de-loop!" Michelle was still trying to comprehend how quickly the car had broken loose and put the driver at such awful risk. She could only imagine how hard the car would have slammed into the wall if he had not been able to bring it back around. Even yet, the cloud of blue tire smoke and dust still lingered in the turn, although the driver had come on around and was pulling into the garage already.

Will and the crew had Rob crank off several more laps while they looked for any more speed. All the while, the kid's confidence rose with each tour of the mile-and-a-half circuit. He felt supremely comfortable in the car, with the feel of the track, and loved the fact that he could keep the Ford pinned right down on the white line all the way through both turn one and two.

Will continued to call off his times to him with each lap. They were all beautifully consistent, within five hundreths of a second each time around. A computer could not have been any more unwavering.

Michelle was watching the final runs, then saw the car pushed over for the pre-qualifying inspection. Billy had just patiently explained what that was all about when Stephanie came by and offered to take her and the other women to their company's hospitality tent with her. Not only could they grab a bite to eat while they waited for the start of qualifying, but Michelle could get an idea of what the other sponsors were doing with their presence at the track. She was already asking questions as they cut through the cross-over gate down toward the exit from pit road.

As they walked, Michelle noticed for the first time that there were quite a few spectators in the stands already. It was surprising that so many people had shown up simply to watch practice and qualifying, and she mentioned it to Stephanie Howell.

"Oh, that's nothing. Wait until later in the week when the Cup drivers really get started practicing and qualifying. They'll have twice that many or more just watching the practices."

"Really?"

"Yes ma'am. These folks start showing up in town the weekend before and most of them will stay 'til the Monday after the race."

"What on earth for?"

"The race and everything that goes with it. The race is an event that lasts a lot longer than just the time between green flag and checkered flag. It's for several days, like a rock festival or state fair or something. The race itself is just the culmination of all these other things: practice, qualifying, sponsor appearances, show cars on display, driver events, and all the other sideshows that go on while the race is in town."

"All I know is I turn on the TV and they're all lined up, ready to go. I never thought about all the rest."

"Put it this way. Have your driver show up at a local business, say a local store that sells your product, and you will have a mob of people show up wanting his autograph. Throw in a Cup driver or two and you'll have way yonder more show up. No exaggeration. These guys have a tremendous following."

"That many locals show up?" Michelle asked.

'No, not necessarily. Folks show up from all over the U.S. and Canada. It's like a pilgrimage for them. It's sort of 'build it and they will come,' like in that movie. That's why they're talking about building tracks and having races in Chicago, Kansas City, Denver, and even close to New York City. They're soon gonna have more tracks than they have dates for races."

"I don't understand it, but I guess it makes sense."

"For sure! The loyalty of these people to the sponsors is amazing."

"I sure hope they'll be loyal to our products," Michelle said. They were just then stepping into the area beneath a grandstand that led to a massive hospitality village that had sprung up off to one side in front of the speedway.

"You do computer software, right?" Stephanie asked.

"Yes."

"Well, trust me, if they own a computer and if they don't already have your software, they will go out and buy it as soon as they get back home. Watch your sales numbers closely. You can track them directly to how well Rob and the team does in the races."

"We do them weekly and by region, so that will be something we'll be looking at. We expect to see a little spike in the Southeast maybe, depending on where we finish in the race."

Stephanie grinned knowingly.

"Watch the numbers over the next couple of weeks. After you get all the TV exposure, you may be surprised what happens. Even if you get wrecked early, the cameras and the announcers will get you a good plug. I bet you'll see a measurable sales jump . . . and not just in the South either."

"I hope so. This was sort of my idea to start with, and our company and employees put a lot of faith into this program."

"It'll work. The only sponsors who don't do well are the ones who don't understand racing and how to tie it into their marketing. If you do it right, it's a sure-fire winner," Stephanie said as she led them past a security guard into her company's hospitality tent. "You guys hungry?"

Carol chimed in then.

"We haven't had anything but a cup of coffee and a doughnut at four o'clock this morning! I was about to bite into one of those tires back there!"

Stephanie pointed toward a television monitor along one side of the buffet table.

"Looks like you guys qualify late." The screen held a long list of car numbers and they spotted theirs near the bottom. "Will Hughes will be worrying his tail off!"

All three women looked at her with blank expressions on their faces, so Stephanie explained what she meant as they filled their plates.

Sure enough, back in the garage, Will wore a sour expression on his face. They had a good, fast car, but Will worried about the building heat. As the day got hotter, the track would get more and more slick.

Rob Wilder was used to Will's worrying by now so he didn't pay much attention to the gloomy vibes the crew chief was giving off as he fidgeted about the car.

"We're okay, Will," the kid assured him.

"I just hope we got it set up for 'super slippery,' young 'un, or you'll be like you're on ice skates out there."

Gratefully, it was soon time to roll the car out to the line while the first to qualify were roaring away to take their runs. The lone drone of each car echoed eerily off the grandstands, reverberating across the speedway. It seemed odd to only hear one engine at a time after all the roar of the combined motors during the practice.

The several thousand fans grouped together near the start/finish line cheered lustily as each car took the checkered flag. Rob and Billy stood there, arms crossed, casually watching as each car attempted to qualify. Sometimes Billy would click his stopwatch and time one of the cars on its lap. Then they would make comments to each other as they waited for the official time to flash up on the huge scoreboard on the side of the Winston trailer.

Even if they had not been watching the scoreboard, they could have told from the big roar from the assembled crowd when a particularly fast speed was posted. As the session wore on, it became evident that this was going to be a fast field of cars that would make up the starting grid.

Will was now fit to be tied. With each posted time, he grew more and more nervous and paced around the car like an expectant father.

Finally, it was time. Michelle and the others walked up just as Rob, Billy and Will ambled slowly out to the pit lane. Michelle marveled one more time at the gleaming paint job on the car. Sitting out on the pit road among all the other cars waiting to take their runs, the car definitely stood out beautifully. One of the assistants was busily snapping photographs of the whole scene.

Rob was quiet now, getting his game face on. He played over and over in his mind like a videotape the run he would make, mentally touring every foot of the racetrack. Deep in thought, he absentmindedly joined in and helped the crew push the car on up the line. Billy didn't bother telling him again that he didn't have to do that at this level. He just smiled and let him push away.

Once they reached their spot in line, Rob grabbed the railing along the roof and swung his long legs through the open window, then settled into the seat, shifting his body around as the crew pushed the car up another spot in line. He reached for the shoulder belts, fastened them loosely, and put the earplugs for the radio in each ear, securing each one in place with a strip of tape. Finally, as the crew pushed him ahead another spot, he pulled the helmet on. There were two cars left in front of him on the line and the first one had just cranked up his engine, ready to pull out.

Rob pulled on his driving gloves and cinched the belts up tight. He cleared his mind, focusing on getting the very best run he could. He was determined to make this lap the fastest yet. The car in front of him was waved out onto the track and he felt his own car being shoved up to take its spot.

Will pulled up the window net on the driver's side and fastened it. Rob looked out the windshield at the open track ahead of him and felt his pulse pounding. He was ready.

"Alright, cowboy, he's got one lap left to go," Will said, his voice on the radio almost a whisper. "Wait for me to tell you when to fire her up. Get ready."

"I've *been* ready." Rob answered. He stared straight ahead and focused on becoming one with the car, letting his own body be an extension of the fine-tuned machinery he rode, so he and the vehicle could run that one perfect lap.

Will waited until the very last second to have Rob fire the engine. He wanted the motor to be as cool as possible for the qualifying run. A cool engine produced slightly more horsepower and he knew they needed every single horse they could get to pull this wagon.

"Fire her up," he finally said.

Rob's fingers were already on the starter switch and he flipped it, listening and feeling the engine rumble to life. He didn't say a word. The sound of the engine was all the response Will needed.

The Series official standing in front of the car suddenly stepped aside, emphatically waving Rob out onto the track. The car that was just finished its qualifying lap went sailing past at more than one hundred ninety miles per hour.

Rob revved the engine once, shifted up into gear, then dumped the clutch, rolling the car off the pit road. Once out onto the track proper, he hammered the throttle down, running quickly up through the gears as the car hit the steep banking of the first and second turns. He tried to gain as much speed as he could before the car hit the long back straightaway because he needed to have the car as close to wide open as possible before it hit the third and fourth turns. If he was lacking there, it would be difficult to gain the momentum he needed to hit the start/finish line full bore.

He set the car up going into the corner exactly the way he wanted so he could get a good run off turn four as he raced down to the line to take the green flag. The car flashed beneath the flagstand at full speed as the grandstand's public address system announced the beginning of his run to considerable applause and even a few whoops. Rob Wilder was already developing his own cadre of loyal fans.

Meanwhile, Rob zeroed in on the point down in

the first turn where he wanted to put the car. The power of the engine throbbed under his body, happily responding to the wide open position he was commanding with his right foot. The car wanted to run and he was letting her do just that. Heading into turn one, the wheel responded obediently as he twisted it slightly to set the car up to soar through the pitched banking.

The Ford dug in and held as if she was a roller coaster clinging to a set of rails. Rob pinched her down just off the white line and felt the tingle in his chest when he recognized that she could stick right there. Even through the center of the corner, the car held its line perfectly, resisting the urge to kick up in the middle of the turn as so many of the other cars were doing. With the perfect line, he got a good run coming out of turn two heading down the backstretch toward three.

In the condominium that towered high over turn one, the old racer stood at the open window watching the kid from the very beginning of his biggest qualifying run yet. Absentmindedly, he clicked the ever-present stopwatch as the kid took the green flag to start his hot lap. As the Ford headed low through the first corner, it was clear that Rob could have a very fast lap underway.

Standing here in his own condo on a rare day off, the old driver was enjoying watching these youngsters practice and qualify. But it got the old juices flowing, too. He might have trouble remembering names and events or a telephone number nowadays, but he had no trouble at all remembering the sights, smells, and feelings he had had when he first climbed into a racecar four decades before. And watching these young Turks, seeing the way they hopped about and danced around and pushed their cars, made him long yet again for the chance to be down there on the track among them, mixing it up and banging fenders with them. While his skills may have faded with time, the competitive fires still burned as hot and bright as ever.

He recognized one essential fact, though. Some of those kids down there were likely better drivers than he had been. Maybe more talented in their pure ability than most of his contemporaries had been, too. But were they as hungry? Were they like a mad dog when it came to getting a win? Was first place what they lived for, and everything else merely somewhere back in the pack?

Some were. Maybe the kid, Wilder, was. They would know soon enough. If he wasn't, he might be a driver for awhile, maybe win some races, maybe even a championship if he accumulated enough points with also-rans.

But if he was, if he had the ability and the hunger, who knows how good he could be? How many races and championships he could eventually claim for Billy Winton?

Maybe that's what the old driver had seen in the kid that night. Just as clearly as he had seen the gift of talent, maybe he had sensed that desire to win, too. And maybe that was the like chord he had recognized in the kid.

Maybe that was what had excited the old driver so much that he had rung his old friend out of bed so late one night to tell him about the kid.

They'd know soon enough. The hunger was one thing that could not be faked.

Just then, the kid was sailing past the crossover gate where Jodell Lee had first come to confront the dan-

gerous realities of racing. It had been that awful weekend back in 1964, the horrific crash and fire that had
claimed the life of another great driver, Fireball Roberts.

The kid likely wasn't thinking about history any
more than Jodell had the thousands of times he had
passed that same spot in all the years since the trag-
edy. Rob Wilder took the car briskly through three
and four, holding her down tightly on the white line,
running along the bottom of the track. From his prime
viewing spot, Jodell watched for any slip-up. He saw
none. He smiled broadly as he clicked his stopwatch
when the kid crossed the finish line in a blur. Lee
didn't even have to look at the face of the watch. His
years of experience told him that he had just witnessed
an incredible lap for such an inexperienced young
driver on this tough old mile-and-a-half track.

As he watched the cool-down lap, as the shimmering red racecar slowly coasted off turn four and down
onto the pit road, Jodell knew then what he saw that
stormy night at the small backwoods track had not
been an illusion. The talent was there and the kid had
just demonstrated that he was learning how to use it.

*Now, did he have the hunger? The old driver listened
to the chatter off the scanner on the shelf. He smiled
again. Maybe he did. Maybe he did indeed.*

"Dadgum, Will! I could have set it up better out of
four, I think."

There was a short pause before an answer.

"Looked good from here, cowboy," Will replied,
and he meant it, too, but he wanted to wait for the
official results on the scoreboard.

The roar from the crowd as the speed flashed up

on the scoreboard confirmed Will's suspicion. It was the third fastest time of the day so far. Just a tick over a tenth of a second off the current pole speed. With only thirteen cars to try to qualify behind them, and with only three or four of them real possibilities to better his speed, they had a good shot at a top five starting spot! No matter what the other cars did, Rob would be starting up front. That helped because at Charlotte, accidents tended to happen early in the race and in the middle of the pack.

Rob was almost back to the garage when the radio crackled in his ear again.

"Great run, cowboy."

Rob could hear what sounded like the whooping and hollering of the crew in the background. Why were they so excited? He knew it was a pretty good lap, but it could have been better.

"Nice run, kid," came Billy's voice in the ear pieces.

"So, what exactly was it?" Rob finally asked.

Will and Billy both transmitted at once and he couldn't get anything out of the garble. By then, he was parking the car at the stall anyway so he began unhitching himself from all the belts and tethers and waited until he was outside to get the final verdict. He was greeted with a nest of microphones and pencils and notepads thrust in his face and a barrage of questions.

"Hold it! Hold it! I don't even know where we qualified yet, guys," he pleaded.

"Third fastest," one of the reporters told him.

Rob's eyes widened. That was pretty good and he said so.

"Pretty good? It was great!" Will Hughes crowed and grabbed him around the neck. Rob had never seen the man so animated before.

Through a grin, Rob said, "Well, it could have been better. We could have gotten the pole. That's what I'm supposed to do, you know." Then he remembered all that Billy had taught him. "The Ensoft.com Ford crew did a great job getting the car set up this afternoon and I'm just honored to have such a fine car to drive. It was fast straight off the truck. All I had to do was push the gas and she ran beautifully. We've hardly turned a bolt on her. I'm really excited about our first race here at Charlotte. There are some mighty tough cars and drivers in the Series nowadays and we'll have those Cup drivers to contend with, too, so I just hope we can make a good showing for our new sponsors at Ensoft.com. We want to show Toby Warren and Martin Flagstone at Ensoft that they picked the right team to carry their colors." He paused to let them know the sound bite was complete. "Thanks, fellas."

The print reporters scribbled away while the television crews scrambled off to get video on another driver.

"You through preaching?" Donnie Kline whispered in Rob's ear. " 'Cause if you are, we need to get the car put away for the night."

"I may want to sleep in it," Rob said with a laugh.

"Great lap, Rob." It was Billy Winton, now down from atop the trailer and approaching at a trot, and he was offering his hand in congratulations. Michelle and her assistants from Ensoft were close behind.

Michelle knew they had done something good in qualifying but she was a little perplexed at all the high fives the crew was passing around. She had no concept of how difficult it was to qualify so well with a rookie driver and virtually new car on a fast old track like this one. She was standing back with the others watching the celebration when Stephanie Howell walked up and gave her a high five as well.

"Wasn't that something?" she asked

"Must have been," Michelle said with a shrug.

"Honey, qualifying top five at a place like this with this many of the Cup drivers trying to make the field is something to celebrate. For a young driver like yours, it's almost as good as winning the race."

"Really?" Michelle said, perking up. Maybe Ensoft's first day in the racing game had gone even better than she thought. Everyone else seemed to think so.

"Enjoy it. It won't always be roses," Stephanie advised. "Look, I have to run. We still on for tonight?"

"Sure!"

Michelle walked with the crew back to their van and her rental car. Carol and Wendy had decided to go celebrate with the crew and she headed back to the hotel alone to get ready for her night on the town. She had not realized how tired she was until she kicked off her shoes and fell back on the big king-sized bed in her room. She must have dozed because she didn't remember anything until the phone rang.

She couldn't seem to find the thing for a moment but finally tracked it down and grunted a hello. She fully expected to hear Stephanie Howell's soft Southern twang, but instead, it was a very familiar voice on the other end of the line.

"Awesome! Totally cool, Mish!"

"What?"

It was Toby Warren, and she had not heard him so excited since the Ensoft stock price last doubled.

"We made the local early news out here. They even showed our car! And then ESPN ran a story on qualifying and had the car and an interview with Rob and the whole works. Can you believe that?"

"It's apparently a big deal, Toby. They said the qualifying run that Rob made today was incredible. There were all kinds of people from the different networks interviewing him after it was finished. It was like a mob scene."

"I'll tell you. That car looked beautiful. They talked about the guy who won the pole for a second and then panned over to our car and talked about how unusual it was for such a young rookie to grab a top-five starting spot. Then we even got a mention about us being the new sponsor for the car for the rest of this year and next." Michelle started to interrupt him with an "I told you so," but he was still talking. "And then when they panned in close on the hood and showed the logo, you could hear cheers all over the building. Mish, this was a great move. Congratulations."

"I wish you could have seen the guys on the team after the run. You would have thought they had just won the Rose Bowl or something."

"Well, I'm looking forward to getting out there. I have that meeting tomorrow morning with the interface developers, then I'll be taking the plane and be on the way. I'd love to get there in time to look around and learn a few things, maybe see a practice."

"Wendy'll meet you at the Concord airport. Call me on my cell phone and let me know when you leave and I will make sure she's there."

"Okay, then. See you tomorrow for some real fine racin'." He managed a reasonable Southern accent. "You going out tonight?"

"Yeah, I met another girl doing PR so we're going out. I'm hoping to learn a few things from her."

"Well, take it easy and don't overdo it."

"I won't."

But the instant she hung up the phone, she had her head back on the deep, down pillow and was sleeping soundly again. Stephanie's call was the only thing that saved her from sleeping right through all the qualifying celebrations. She admitted as much to her new friend. And for the second time that long, long day, she heard the almost identical words.

"Welcome to the exciting world of big-time stock car racing, honey."

THE "GETTIN' READY"

The pace was even faster the next day, more frenetic for the crews and everyone around them. With the Winston Cup teams and the Grand National teams splitting time on the track, the garage down time gave them more chance to conjure up ways to find more speed. Some were bordering on the edge of desperation, but in the Ensoft team stall, there was an air of quiet confidence.

Even Rob, who usually remained unfazed by all the activity swirling around him, had caught a little of the fever that the rest of the crew had come down with. He was accustomed to still being able to walk through the garage area without much attention, without many even being able to recognize him, but today it was a different story. Fans and media alike stopped him and wanted to talk about the race, his qualifying run, his future.

Rob was usually confident, too, but now, after the

run the day before, he was even more convinced that he had what it took to race with the best drivers on the circuit, and to do it in their own backyard. Now, he had to be consistent, to show that it was no fluke, that he had every right to be out there among the best in the racing game. This race would be the next step. It would take plenty more like it, but at least he knew in his own heart that he belonged.

Over dinner the night before, Billy had cautioned him that the media would suddenly be as much a nuisance as a help and he should prepare himself for it. He had long been exhorting that Rob should be kind and gracious to everyone, all the time, regardless of how annoying or tiring it might be. The reporters had a job to do and the fans were the ones who bought tickets to see him do something millions of folks would give their eyeteeth to be able to do. There would certainly come a time when he would no longer be of interest to them. His image was valuable, to himself, to the team, to the sponsor, so he needed to make certain that he projected a good one.

They had already made changes to the car when Rob took her out for the first practice session. Will cautioned him to take his time, to feel out the car and the track carefully and not to be too overconfident. The setup they had under the car the day before had been nearly perfect for a single, fast qualifying lap all by himself on the track. Now, it would be different. The race setup was designed to last for much longer and to run in traffic.

They basically started from scratch with the first practice run. "The gettin' ready," as Donnie Kline termed it. Will wanted first to make the car comfortable; then they would work on making it faster. The first couple of runs would be to establish a good baseline setup, then they would start to make broader changes. Will, of course, had a very good idea of the direction he wanted to go with those adjustments.

First, with a few hot laps and some comments from Rob on the radio, they brought him in and adjusted the track bar upward. Then, after a few more laps, they made some changes in the wedge, trying to get the car to feel just right in the corners.

Billy Winton and Jodell Lee stood together alongside the pit wall, timing various cars and talking. Twenty or more racecars were out there at any one time, alternately cutting laps on the track and returning to their pits or garages for more work.

"How's he running this morning?" Jodell asked.

"A couple of tenths off yesterday's time, but we got her in race trim now," Billy replied. At the same time, he clicked the stopwatch as Dale Jr. raced by with a roar. The time was in the range of what his own driver had been running the last time out. That brought a slight smile to his face as he showed the numbers to Jodell. "Looks like Rob is going to be right close to the top of the heat. Have you noticed what Kenseth and Lajoie have been turning?"

"About the same. It'll be all the usual suspects up front. But you'll have your 'suspect' right there in the midst of them."

"That'll give the kid lots of experience running with those guys, if nothing else."

"And you know that's all he's lacking, Billy. If you can keep his nose clean and not let all this go to his head and let him mix it up with the good 'uns for a while, he'll gain a world of experience. And I tell you, sure as I'm standing here, that's all he's lacking right now. Experience. He could be something special."

Billy Winton nodded his agreement. He had already begun missing sleep, worrying about what he might accidentally do to mess up the kid.

Just then, Jodell was suddenly jerked off his feet, wrapped up in a rough bear hug from behind. He recognized the cackling laughter instantly.

"Darn it, D. W.! You sorry rascal! You scared me half to death." Jodell twisted away and turned to face his tormentor. Darrell Waltrip backed away, his hands up in mock fear, as if he fully expected Jodell Lee to throw a punch. "You ought to be over yonder trying to make that old car of yours run instead of tormenting us real racers like that."

"I could say the same thing about you," Waltrip said. "I saw the two of you over here having such a deep conversation and I thought I'd come see if it was about me."

"Hah! Maybe twenty years ago it might have been. Not today. We're just standing here watching these young 'uns out there running circles around the older guys."

"Yeah, where do they find these kids? Seems like they get younger and meaner every year," Waltrip said. He straightened his driving suit and adjusted his trademark sunglasses as he watched a pack of cars zip by out on the track. "I guess it's the money. The sponsors. The girls. The fame and glory, now. Like a lot of the stuff that got you and me in the game, Lee. Like what's kept me in it after you got smart and quit." Rob Wilder's Ford zipped past then and Waltrip watched it until it got into the first turn, hugging the bottom of the track just the way it was supposed to. "That boy you came up with sure is opening some eyes. Where in the world did you find him? And why the heck did you let Billy Winton have first refusal instead of me?"

"Racing late-models at a little track where I do some appearances from time to time," Jodell said, ignoring his second question.

Billy picked up the story.

"Yeah, old Jodell calls me up in the middle of the night and tells me I got to take a look at him. I figure he's pulling my leg or something. But we tested him out at your old stomping grounds, over in Nashville, and I became an instant Rob Wilder fan."

"Lot like Casey Atwood and some of the other young guys. Look how the media and the fans have jumped all over them. That's what your kid has to look forward to, Billy." He watched then as Rob brought the red car past once more and headed for the first turn. "Tell you one thing. He sure is smooth. Look at how he holds her down low in the corners. Got her pasted right down on the white line."

"And he does it the exact same way every time." Jodell observed with a nod in the car's direction. "Lots of the young ones don't have that kind of discipline."

"Sometimes I don't think he even realizes what he's doing, it comes so natural to him. It's almost scary, like it's not even him driving," Billy noted.

"I've noticed it myself," Jodell said quickly. "Don't laugh, but sometimes I'd swear that Little Joe Weatherley was driving that car. The kid just has that fluid style that Little Joe had."

"Well, if the kid starts pulling the stunts Little Joe did, I'll believe it," Waltrip laughed and turned to leave. "And if y'all are gonna tell ghost stories, then I guess I better get on back and get ready to beat your tail Sunday, Lee."

"Just be glad I ain't driving, D. W. It wouldn't be the first time I ran off and left you."

Waltrip waved them off and hustled on his way.

Once he was gone, the two men stood quietly as they waited for Rob to come back around. The mention of ghosts and Little Joe Weatherley had, for some reason, left Jodell unsettled. Weatherley, Curtis Turner, Fireball Roberts, and some of the other legends who had died tragically, had been key early influences in his own career. And they were standing not far from the very spot where Roberts had been horribly burned in a fiery crash that had eventually claimed his life. Jodell had been caught up in that same accident and had struggled to help Roberts out of his blazing racer. Sometimes, even now, when he was at this track he could still smell the hellish smoke and feel the scorching flames of that wreck. It would only be someone's blown engine or the sun suddenly slipping from behind a cloud, but it was just as real to him as it had been that awful day.

And there were times when the wind whistled down the length of this track that he was sure he could still hear Weatherley's laugh or the voice of Fireball Roberts being borne along on the breeze.

Even flying in on the company jet, Toby Warren arrived too late in the day Friday to see any of the practices. He was only able to pick up his credentials and get a quick tour of the garage area before it closed for the day. Michelle had decided to pick him up herself at the airport. That was partially because of the late arrival, but she mostly wanted to see his reaction when he got his first glimpse of the Charlotte track.

They had been easing through the traffic on Highway 29 from Concord toward the speedway when, just after they had passed the entrance to the big tobacco plant, she heard Toby gasp. He had caught the first glimpse of the towering grandstands on the horizon.

"We're still at least a mile away. Wait 'til we get close."

"That is just beautiful. I mean beautiful. I've never seen anything like it."

Toby was marveling at the upreaching grandstands that seemed to have far outgrown the tall trees.

"Wait 'til you get inside. I've never seen a facility that big," Michelle told him as she rounded the last curve before reaching the track.

A sea of campers came into view then as they hit the entrance to the giant parking lots. The long frontstretch grandstands seemed to stretch on forever.

"Michelle, I didn't know there were this many campers at any one time in all of America, much less so many of them in one place. Does this remind you of *Woodstock*, or is it just me?"

"Wait'll you get a look at them. All kinds of folks. They say a lot of them have been here all week and the big race is the better part of three days away yet. They're a loyal bunch for sure."

Michelle eased the car onto the access road leading to the infield tunnel beneath the back straightaway. She remained quiet as she drove through the tunnel, allowing Toby an undistracted view of the inside of the speedway. When they popped out into the late afternoon sunshine on the other side, Warren gasped again at the sight that unfolded before him.

The massive grandstand stretched all the way from the fourth turn to past the condominiums that had risen above the first and second turns. The mammoth stands they had spotted from the highway ran through the second turn and partway down the backstretch. And there, circling them and running directly in front of all the stands, was the asphalt racing surface.

And in the middle of it all was another impromptu campground. There were hundreds of cars, tents, and motor homes packed into the broad infield. The smoke from hundreds of barbecues filled the air and from the gigantic piles of beer cans in front of many of the campsites, it was obvious the assembled fans were enjoying their favorite libation. Toby immediately thought of tailgate parties for football games he had attended, only this was a tailgate party to the nth degree.

There was more, though. Multicolored tractor-trailer rigs lined both the Grand National and Cup garages, and that only added to the brilliance and magnitude of the entire scene.

Toby sat in stunned silence as he took everything in. It was far more than he had imagined. He'd been to the Rose Bowl once when he was a little kid, then again when he and his classmates had done their traditional prank during the game. He assumed he knew what a hundred-thousand-person crowd would look like. But to see the sheer size of the grandstands framing most of the racetrack was almost incomprehensible. He could only imagine what it would look like when more than a hundred sixty thousand people filled them.

"Michelle, I never imagined the scale of this thing. You don't begin to get a feel for it on television."

"I told you about Stephanie? She says the fans will start piling in at dawn and they'll still be coming in when the race starts."

"Any chance we can see the garage area now?" Toby asked. He was clearly excited at the prospect.

Warren had explained to Billy that he was a frustrated muscle-car aficionado. As a child, when most kids his age were locked into Atari games or *Star Wars,* he'd grown to love the sleek, powerful machines he had seen the older kids driving through his neighborhood. When he could afford it, his dad had bought and restored a couple of the classic cars from the fifties. Toby had built plastic models and collected car magazines from the time he learned to read, even as he experimented with the early personal computers and wrote programs for them. One of his earliest projects had been writing a rudimentary racing computer game. He had vowed early on that he would one day have a collection of the powerful cars in his own garage when he grew up. That wish had partially come true. His prospering business gave him the means to afford his love for cars, but had, at the same time, robbed him of the time to do anything serious about it.

At that moment, he had an unrestored 1972 Chevelle sitting in the cavernous garage of his home outside of San Jose. It still rested in the very spot where he had had it dropped off the transport two winters before. Other than taking friends out into the garage to look at his "project," he had not laid a hand on what had once been his dream car. Now, thick dust had accumulated on the car's faded black paint. One day soon, he vowed to himself, he would find time to restore the beauty that had once been.

Toby could not wait to prowl around the powerful machines he knew were sitting in the garage area. Or see them out there circling the track together at speed.

Michelle led the way into the garage area. A few of the teams had already packed it in for the day but many still worked on their cars. And that included their own team. Toby tried to take everything in at once while Michelle worked to keep him moving. He kept sticking his head into different teams' garages and drew some unmistakable looks from some of them.

"Our car is over here, Toby. Some of these guys are a little particular about strangers sticking their heads in their stalls."

"This is so cool!" Toby said, stopping again and watching a crew changing out the rear gearing in a car. "These guys could probably rebuild my Chevelle in about fifteen minutes."

"Come on, now, before you get us beaten up. I want to introduce you to everybody on the team before they finish up. And I want to show you the car. You're going to love it."

"Okay, okay," he said, but stopped again to admire a racing engine hanging from a chain in a stall. "I would die to have that thing bolted into my Chevelle."

Michelle had seen Toby's car several times. And she also knew he would never have the time to play with the thing. But she held her tongue and took his elbow and dragged him along.

"We're just a couple of stalls on down. Billy wants you to meet Will Hughes and then he's going to take you over to the Cup garage and show you around there as well."

"We are going to get in the Cup garage? Fantastic!"

She had never seen the man so excited. His cheeks were red, his eyes glassy, and he looked like a kid in a candy store, not sure which sweet he wanted to try next.

"Jodell Lee got you credentials for over there from his sponsor. There is one thing, though. Over there, you will definitely have to behave. You can't go poking around in everybody's stall."

He nodded, then spied the red Ford.

"Wow! It looks even better than it did on television!" He stepped over to the car, which was resting on jack stands, and softly touched the Ensoft logo on the rear deck. "That's the most beautiful thing I've ever seen."

Michelle followed a couple of steps behind, enjoying Toby's reaction. It was about what she expected but, like a lot of self-made men, he could be opinionated, and especially about something so important in which he'd had little or no input beforehand. But the smile on his face confirmed that Billy's body shop guys had hit a home run.

The crew was busy making still more last-minute changes before the garage area closed. They paid no attention to him, assuming he was another lucky fan who knew someone and had gotten a garage pass. Billy walked up then and spied Toby.

"Welcome to Charlotte!" he called.

"Thanks, Billy." Toby never took his eyes off the car. "Man, this thing turned out beautiful."

"Glad you like it. The guys in the body shop worked it up. They were mostly going for something that would show up pretty good on TV."

"It looks great sitting still in the garage! I like the way the red shows off the blue accents of the logo. I'll confess, I've had our graphics guys working on something, but I think we can call them off. I like this."

Billy breathed a sigh of relief. *Lord knows what a bunch of wireheads might have come up with!* He finally got Toby turned around and he shook hands with him.

"I even went down to the TV truck yesterday and looked at some of the tape they shot of the car," Billy added. "The thing just jumps right out at you. I didn't want to be one of those cars that's so hard to pick out in a pack."

"I saw the stories last night. I can't wait to see it out there on the track. Up front, I hope."

"Wait'll you see and hear and feel all those machines coming at you wide open to take the green flag. There's nothing like it. Nothing on earth," Billy said with a grin. He'd seen the start of a thousand races but that exhilarating moment still brought tears to his eyes.

Just then, farther down the garage, an engine roared to life. The sound was deafening in the enclosed space. Someone was putting the final tune in a motor. It ran up through the RPM ranges, held steady for a moment and then, as quick as passing thunder, someone shut it off and it was quiet again.

Toby Warren had stopped and listened to the clamor of the engine and still grinned broadly, even after it had died away.

"This could get to be a habit," he said, and lovingly touched the logo again.

Soon the officials began to chase everybody out of the Grand National garage. As Will and the crew packed everything away, Rob, Billy, Michelle, and Toby found a quiet corner and talked over some ideas they had about ways for Ensoft to have a presence at some of the final races of the season. And Michelle had some thoughts on getting the image of the car, and especially its young driver, into marketing materials the company would be developing over the next few months, even during the off-season. It was clear she had been doing some planning already. She even had mockups of some packaging and trade advertisements they were considering.

While the rest of the group talked such weighty concepts, Will fretted about the last few laps they had run in the car. She had been very fast in the last practice and the weather forecast was for very similar conditions the next day. That was little solace to Will Hughes. He was paid to make the car perfect. Merely being fast was never good enough. He wanted to be the fastest. Now he knew he was destined to stew over it all night. Was there anything else they could do to give Rob Wilder a better shot at a first place? Had they overlooked anything? Was there something somewhere just waiting to break? Something a few extra minutes with a flashlight or an extra turn of a wrench or an added item on a checklist would have ferreted out before it was too late?

Rob had accepted Billy's invitation to join him, Toby, and Michelle for dinner. Will had been asked to go, too, but he begged off. Rob would actually have preferred spending the evening over sodas and pizza with Will, talking over the next day's race. It had become something of a night-before ritual already. But the kid was learning that the demands of the sponsor came first. And Will had urged him to go on to the fancy restaurant and hobnob with the other half.

"Just try not to eat with your fingers," he had advised. "Watch what they do and you just do the same thing."

Will liked the California bunch just fine. But having them all here for this big race had only made his usual concern for the car that much more intense. He knew how important it was to have a good showing for them. And whose fault it would be if the car broke or they blew a pit stop or ran out of gas.

They were back from dinner before ten o'clock. Rob gracefully declined joining the group for coffee in the hotel lounge, explaining quite truthfully that he needed to get to bed. They would be leaving for the track early, he explained, but he didn't mention that three hundred miles would be the longest race he had ever run.

Sleep was hard to come by, though. He tossed and rolled, and when he dozed, he dreamed he was driving a smoking, rattling old car through quicksand while Adam Petty and some of the others kept lapping him and leaving him in their exhaust smoke. And he kept running into the rear end of another slow car ahead of him that he couldn't seem to get past. It was an old, dilapidated wreck of a car driven by someone he knew he should recognize but he couldn't seem to quite make out who it was that was holding him back.

He finally climbed from the tangled sheets of the bed and tried to watch television, then to read the latest *Winston Cup Scene*, but he was having trouble concentrating. Finally, he pulled the old scrapbook from his suitcase and thumbed through its fragile pages. He still didn't know why he had brought the thing, but maybe a trip through it would calm his nerves, heighten his resolve to succeed at this game as it so often did.

The clippings were mostly short articles topped with only slightly larger headlines, and there were usually lines of small type at the bottoms that were clearly results of races of some kind. On each listing, a single name had been circled or underlined.

But this night, the newspaper articles left him unsettled instead of confident. He slammed the book shut.

"Why?" he asked out loud, staring at the back of the scrapbook. "Why did you waste it all?" Then, he tossed the book aside and stepped to the mirror over the dresser and looked hard into the eyes of the tall, slim, blond-haired young man who stared back at him. "Make the most of what you got, Rob Wilder.

You've got the ability and folks who believe in you. Don't you dare waste this chance. Hear me? Don't waste this chance."

He said the last words deliberately, forcefully, almost with a vengeance, then, without even thinking, he spun, pulled on his jeans, T-shirt, and sneakers, and marched out of the room. He wasn't even sure where he was going until he knocked on the door to Will Hughes' room.

"You asleep?" he asked as the door cracked open.

"Naw, come on in, cowboy. I'm just going over the notes from last year's race over here. Tell you the truth, I could use some help."

"Why, what's wrong? That car feels perfect and you know it."

He eased down in the room's lounge chair. Will had papers and notes strewn all over the place as if a sudden gust of wind had scattered them about at random.

"I know it's good, but I'm worried about how she'll do on the long green-flag runs. All we've seen so far is that we're like a jackrabbit for ten laps or so. I want us to be able to carry that over a forty or fifty lap run between pit stops. If we can, then we just might have us a shot at putting you in Victory Lane. I hate to think we could be so close to a win and not finish it on out."

"Will, you know that if you give me your best setup, I'll do my dangdest to win." He paused for a beat. "I'm not going to blow this chance you and Billy are giving me."

Will couldn't help noticing the hard set of the kid's jaw, the sheer determination that made his blue eyes seem to spark.

"I know that. I'm not worrying about the driver at all."

"Then what's got you so tense?" he asked.

"What I've been sitting here all night wracking my brain over is what I've missed. There's something I just can't put my finger on."

For emphasis, Will held up a sheaf of papers with his hen-scratching and complicated diagrams and formulas all over them. Rob had seen all this before. Will was typically a last-minute worrier, but this race apparently had him spooked even more than usual.

"Well, let me give you a hand. I can't sleep anyway. Between the two of us, we ought to be able to come up with some ideas." He leaned forward in the chair and grabbed a clipboard with one of the checklists attached. "We know it's not the motor. We've got plenty of horsepower. I can pull just about anybody down the straightaways."

And so it went for the next hour or so. They reviewed the notes, the readings, the setup. They hashed over possibilities, and shot down each other's theories until, finally, Will tried to shoo Rob on to his room and to bed. No point in fixing whatever nagging detail it was they were poring over if his driver was half-asleep during the race.

But the kid seemed reluctant to leave.

"Okay, cowboy. Shoot. What's bothering you?"

Rob had been silent for a while. He gazed out the window at the lights of Charlotte stretching out below them.

"Will, do you still miss your dad?"

"Sure I do. Every day."

Rob was silent again, uncertain. It was **an** odd thing to see hesitation in a young man who was usually such a sure, hard charger, so crammed full of confidence.

But Will stayed quiet, pretending to study some charts he held until the kid felt like talking again. He finally did.

"Y'all have taken quite a chance on me, Will. Putting me in that car, letting me have so much say-so in how it gets set up out there, putting me in front of the reporters and the folks from Ensoft. I want you and Billy to know how much I appreciate the confidence you've shown in me."

"Thank Jodell Lee. And once Billy and I saw how you handled a car you'd never been inside of before like you did at Nashville, we knew you deserved an honest shot. You did it. You earned it."

"Do y'all ever wonder why I race? Where that drive to win comes from? What makes me want to do it so bad?"

He paused once more, his voice trailing off.

"If it's about your dad, I think I know about some of that," Will said. The kid spun around quickly to face him. "Clara was cleaning your room and accidentally saw the scrapbook. She didn't mean to. She wasn't snooping."

The scrapbook Clara Hughes had found in Rob's room held faded newspaper clippings that chronicled a good forty or more different races, all run on small dirt tracks in rural north Alabama and middle Tennessee and spanning a ten-year period in the late seventies and early eighties. Every article contained the name "Bill Wilder." Will and Clara assumed it must be the kid's dad. The look on Rob's face now confirmed it.

Wilder wasn't mentioned as the winner very often in the races but he was among the top finishers in every one of them. A couple of the articles mentioned how well Wilder had driven, how he had come from laps down to claim a good finish, or had survived bumping incidents with other drivers to take the good spot.

Rob took a deep breath, as if he was about to try to lift a heavy load, and began.

"My father left home when I was six. From what people tell me, my mother never supported him in his racing. Or in anything else he tried to do for that matter. One day, I guess he just got enough and he never came home again." Will sat and listened, waiting for Rob to finish. If the kid had something he needed to get off his chest now was the time to do it. "I never knew my father was a racer when I was growing up. Mother never went with him or let me go. I didn't even know he raced until after I'd already started driving myself. I was going through some trash my mother was throwing out and I found that old scrapbook. Will, can you imagine what it's like to find out that the one thing you most love doing meant just as much to a father you never really knew? That you have grown up with the same drive and desire to win as he did?" Hughes had to strain to hear the kid's soft words. "I realized then why my mother threw such a fit when I started driving those hobby cars."

"You never had any idea he raced?"

"Never, but when I found the scrapbook it got me wondering about him, so I started asking around the tracks. Nobody had ever figured out that I was Bill Wilder's kid. Everybody said that he had the makings of a good racecar driver. Lots of people have told me that. He just never seemed to have a chance to go on to bigger things. But he was a good racer with what he had. Finally, a few years after he moved out, he just sort of disappeared. Before long, people forgot about him."

"That's tough, kid. You know, I lost my dad when I was young, too."

Will knew even as he spoke the words that it had not been the same thing at all. He had told Rob the story of his own dad's death, how much he had admired his father's desire to win, how devotedly he had pursued the racing career his father had been denied by his early passing. It appeared the kid was motivated by his own father's racing, but in an entirely different way.

Rob suddenly turned and looked at Will.

"Do you believe a man is likely to grow up and be just like his father?"

"Huh?"

"Do you believe some people have a bad seed that gets handed down to their kids, no matter what they do?"

So that was it.

"Cowboy, listen to me. I know you can inherit eyes and body type and a tendency to lose your hair early. Probably some more things, too. But I believe every man can decide for himself what kind of person he's gonna be in this life. If he's descended from meanness, he can steer right away from it like it's a wreck on the track. And there are plenty of no-goods out there that came from good stock, too. You're right. Billy is taking a big chance with you, but he knew before we got too far along what kind of person you were. You show about as much confidence as anybody I've ever seen."

"That's what I think about when I look at that scrapbook. He had the talent but he lacked the confidence to follow through. I think I inherited the driving ability. But I know I can make it all the way to the top. Will, when I get out there, it's like somebody else takes over and drives the car for me and makes sure I do it right. I always believe I can win every race I run."

"And that's exactly why you'll win more than your share of them."

Will said the words emphatically and he liked the look in the kid's eyes when he heard them.

"Does Billy know about my old man?"

"Yeah. I told him what little I knew. But he knows what he sees, too. That's all that matters to him. I don't think there's anybody I know that's a better judge of character than Billy Winton. He talks about Vietnam a lot and he says he learned how to tell when you could count on a man and when you couldn't, just by the look in his eye or the way he held himself when the going got rough. You're his driver, Robbie. And the way you're going, you will be for a fair, long time." He paused for a beat and then winked at the kid. "And as long as you finish top five every damn race."

Rob grinned back weakly.

"I just want to make sure y'all know I'm not like him. I can win. I can finish what I start."

"You wouldn't be driving that red number 6 Ford tomorrow if we didn't know that already."

Rob got up to go then, but he paused at the door.

"Thank you, Will."

"Don't mention it, cowboy" he said with a smile. "Now go get some rest."

The talk with Will worked. It had washed out all Rob's pre-race jitters and, once back in his own bed, he was asleep immediately.

And this time, the quicksand dreams and the stranger in the old car that was blocking his way to the front stayed away.

THE EMPTY CAR

For the Jodell Lee Racing team, this trip to Charlotte had just gone from bad to worse for Sunday's Cup race. At Friday's first practice, Jodell had stood on top of his hauler, timing his race-car.

"Might as well use an hourglass!" he muttered to himself.

The car was bad, just plain awful. They struggled with the setup from the time they had rolled the thing off the trailer earlier in the week and drove out for the opening practice. There was plenty of power in the motor but they just couldn't get a handle on the chassis.

"We might just as well be driving a bread truck," Joe Banker had declared. Banker was Jodell's first cousin as well as the chief engine builder, and he had a knack for summing up a situation with sarcasm.

The car was so loose it was hard to drive and they

hadn't even had enough speed to qualify for the Cup race. They were going to be forced to use a provisional starting position to get into the field and that was particularly humiliating for Jodell and the rest of the crew. He always wanted to qualify on speed, not a special dispensation of the rules.

And besides, they were locked in a tight battle in the Cup points and were trying to break into the top ten in the points with this race. A recent string of top ten finishes was beginning to look like it was in jeopardy as they continued to make the car worse instead of better.

Jodell's team had spent their own sleepless night trying to figure out what they would have to do to resurrect the car in time for Sunday's green flag. The team manager, Bubba Baxter, had been with Jodell from the very first race, back in a converted pasture in east Tennessee. He admitted to anyone who would listen that he was baffled. Bubba's boy, Waylon, was the crew chief and he had never seen such a tough case in all the cars he had brought to Charlotte for Jodell. He was sure, though, that the latest changes they had put under the car would help.

And then, as Jodell had looked on, it appeared they finally had, and not a second too-soon. They were in the last practice on Friday. The dark blue Ford was sticking better in the center of the turns and the watch was finally confirming that they had picked up a couple of tenths of a second. They were finally going in the right direction.

Jodell clicked the watch again as the car came roaring past the start/finish line and aimed for the first turn. This time the driver, Rex Lawford, put her right down on the white line, cutting a perfect arc through the corner. Then Jodell lost sight of the car when it disappeared going through turn two. He was turning back to wait for the car to come out of turn four and to pick up the run back to the start/finish line when he heard the spotter's frantic cry on the radio.

"He's loose! Bad loose! Whoa, look out! Hang on, Rex! Hang on!"

Jodell spun back quickly to the exit of turn two and saw the smoke at the same instant he heard the heavy thump of the impact between car and wall. Then there was more smoke. Black, billowing smoke.

Same spot. Lord. Same spot as Fireball in '64.

The smoke quickly died away, then turned white as the safety crews extinguished whatever fire there had been. Jodell, still numb, listened on the radio as the spotter called out to the driver, asking for a status. There was no answer. Each call grew more frantic. Then Waylon joined in, asking Lawford if he was okay, how the car looked, if the spotter could see the driver moving around inside the car.

Then it seemed everyone in the crew with a radio was chattering away, the channel a mass of confusion. The big, booming voice of Bubba Baxter cut it off quickly, though, ordering a halt to all transmissions, and then he sent the crew scrambling to the garage to await the arrival of the damaged car, just in case they could get it going for more practice on Saturday. Just in case.

"Maybe whatever he hit knocked the thing right," Waylon said jokingly but nobody running along with him laughed.

Back up on top of the truck, when he saw the ambulance quickly leaving pit road with its lights blazing, Jodell felt his stomach fall, his head spin. He knew nothing else to do but scramble down off the truck and head for the infield garage so he could be useful in some way. There was still a trace of a limp as he jogged along, a painful, lingering reminder of his own encounters in the past with racetrack walls. Some he had had to be carried away from on a stretcher. But he had always lived to fight again. He hoped as much for his driver.

Before he even realized it, Bubba Baxter was sprinting along beside him.

"Any word?" Jodell asked.

"None. The impact must have knocked the radio out. The spotter says the car hit real hard on the inside wall. The emergency crews were getting Rex out of the car."

"Was he moving?"

"Said he couldn't really tell."

Jodell peeled off and headed for the infield care center.

The ambulance pulled up and the rescue crew pulled Lawford from inside the emergency and onto a gurney. He was awake, obviously in pain, as they wheeled him in the door. The security guard at the door waved Jodell on inside behind them.

Over at the Lee Racing truck, the crew was already pulling the backup car down out of the top of the hauler even as the wrecker was dragging in the damaged racecar. The spotter had already given them fair warning about the car's condition. It would need a new front clip and a lot of bodywork before it could hope to race again.

One quick inspection of the broken car made the decision easy. The team set about doing all they could do to ready the backup car for practice.

But they knew as they worked that there was no backup driver on the truck. So far, everyone kept that thought to himself.

Jodell Lee finally radioed back from the infield care center with the bad news. They were taking Rex Lawford to the hospital in Charlotte to check him over for some possible broken ribs and a potential fractured left wrist. In addition, he had inhaled a lot of smoke from the brief fire. They expected to keep him there at least overnight. Even then they would not know until sometime the next day if he would even be able to drive the race on Sunday at all.

The scramble was now on to get the backup car ready to race, assuming Rex would be able to go. They would only have the "happy hour" practice after the Grand National race on Saturday to get the car race-ready and dialed in, and that was a tall order. This weekend had just gotten inordinately more complicated.

Everyone pitched in to get going on the backup. They would have the few minutes before the garage closed, then most of the day Saturday to get the car set up as best they could for the short practice session and then the race on Sunday.

And they had no idea who might be behind the wheel when all that happened.

Rob Wilder felt like a million dollars. He had awakened an hour before the wake-up call was due and he felt wonderfully rested and ready. He showered, dressed and headed down to the restaurant for grits, eggs, and sausage, and was working on the big platter when Billy Winton joined him.

"You hear about Jodell and them?" he asked.

Rob shook his head as he chewed. Billy told him about what had happened the previous day. He had been so busy with the Ensoft folks he had not even heard about it until he got back to his room and flipped on "Sports Center" from ESPN. He had promptly called Jodell to get the latest. And it had not been good news.

The crash was the main topic in the garage area, too. The word that Rex Lawford had been kept overnight at the hospital was sobering. What most had assumed was a typical racing accident that was going to cause the team to work extra hard to overcome it, was now looking much worse. If their driver was hurt too badly to drive tomorrow in the 500 then any shot Lee Racing had at a top ten finish in the points would be lost.

The team was bent but not broken. Those were Bubba Baxter's words to the whole bunch when they assembled, all sleepy-eyed, in the garage that morning. They were accustomed to dealing with adversity. That was part of racing. You didn't become one of the top teams on the circuit if you folded under pressure. They were going to be forced to turn things up a notch or two today.

Rob Wilder rode from the hotel to the track with Will Hughes. Despite the news about Jodell and Rex Lawford, a driver he had met a time or two already, he was fired up about his own team's race and their chances to win it. He knew he had a car fully capable of winning and he was determined to remain focused on just that.

He had been pleased to find Will considerably more upbeat than he had been the night before. Will winked at Rob when they gathered in the lobby to put all their bags together to haul back to the track and told him why he was feeling so much better in the light of the new day.

"I think I got it, Rob," he said. He admitted the inspiration had sat him straight up in bed about 3 A.M. "Something you said about how she felt in the short chute and some of the tire temps all suddenly made sense."

"If you're happy, I'm happy," Rob said with a big grin.

The team was already busy when they arrived at the track, finishing up race day preparations. Rob tried to help where he could but mainly stayed out of everyone's way. Toby and Michelle arrived at about ten o'clock and he busied himself by explaining what each crewmember was doing and why.

Toby asked once where Billy Winton was and Rob admitted he didn't know. Billy was usually somewhere close by on race day but he had disappeared shortly after he got to the garage that morning.

At that moment, Jodell Lee, Billy Winton, Bubba Baxter and Joe Banker were all huddled together, deep in conversation in the rear of the Lee Racing truck. Jodell had gotten the word that morning that there was no chance at all of their driver steering a racecar on this day and only a slim chance he could start the race the next day. The orthopedist wanted to go ahead and put a pin in the broken wrist first thing this morning. The anesthesia they would have to use would leave Rex Lawford groggy for the rest of the day and it would likely be too sore to steer for a couple of weeks.

Now Jodell and the team were talking about their options and, as always, Billy's counsel was more than welcomed. In many ways, he was still considered a part of the team and no one thought it odd at all that he was a part of this high-level meeting.

The pool of available substitute drivers was slim. Most of the better Grand National drivers were limited in what other driving they could do by contract or sponsor commitments. No one spending the millions necessary to field a team wanted his driver hurt or worn down moonlighting for someone else. Billy had plenty of experience lining up temporary drivers from all sources before Rob Wilder had come along, so his insight on the available talent was most valuable.

Joe Banker, as always the most bluntly outspoken of the bunch, finally succinctly summed up the options.

"One, we go home. Two, we put some yahoo in the car that'll likely run all over the pace car if he can even make ours go that fast. Or Roman numeral three, we take Jodell's advice and see if Billy can bail us out of this mess."

Billy only thought about it for a moment and then nodded his agreement. He tried not to second-guess himself as he headed back to his own car to get ready to run a race.

The Grand National drivers' meeting came and went as the last minute preparations in the garage continued. The race day checklist was completed and the car cleared the pre-event inspection. The crew pushed it slowly out to its earned spot in the starting grid while Rob relaxed in the back of the team hauler, where the air conditioning helped him save strength and stamina. If the pressures of driving this big race, of having the new sponsors watching in person, of having a car capable of winning if only he was talented enough to bring it home were bothering him, he didn't allow it to show.

Michelle and Toby finally got their tour of the Cup garage from Jim Locklear. There they saw many of the drivers who were familiar to most everyone, race fan or not. These were the drivers whose faces were prominent everywhere from Super Bowl television commercials to the fronts of cereal boxes to late-night talk shows. The grandstands, which had so impressed Toby when they had been empty, were even more amazing as they began to fill with people. The festival-like atmosphere was growing even stronger as the swelling crowd cheered every movement in the pits,

every local celebrity and dignitary that rode around
the track waving and grinning from the back of a
convertible.

It was almost time for the driver introductions and
Will Hughes realized he had not seen his driver in a
while. He checked the drivers' lounge and around the
garage area but he was not to be found. Then he stuck
his head in the hauler and hollered his name.

"Rob! Hey, cowboy, you in here? We got us a race
to run."

No reply. He started to strike off in another direction but then stepped up into the truck instead. That's
where he found his driver, stretched out on the couch
in his driving suit in the front part of the truck, sound
asleep. Will shook his head. How in the world could
the kid be so relaxed at a time like this? He gave him
a shake.

"You gonna sleep right through the green flag?
Come on, get up. We got to go out there and win us
a race."

Rob stretched and yawned and blinked a few times.

"What time is it?" he asked.

"Almost time for drivers' introductions."

"Well, we don't wanna miss that!" Rob said, zip-
ping up his driving suit and rolling off the couch.

As they walked out of the garage and toward pit
road, a fan got in step with them and politely asked
for an autograph. Rob scribbled his name on the program as they kept moving. The fan thanked him and
walked away happy, clearly glad to have the signature
of one of the circuit's new young guns.

"Will, why would somebody want an autograph
from a nobody like me? I just don't understand it."

"When you win this race this afternoon you'll never
be able to go anywhere again without being mobbed,

so you better enjoy your last minutes of being a no-name."

Finally, it was time to go racing. Billy sent Toby, Michelle, Carol, and Wendy up to Jodell's condo overlooking the middle of turn one. From there, they could watch the action all the way around the track. The sound system in the suite was set up to get the team radios along with the television broadcast so they wouldn't miss any of the action.

Several representatives of Jodell's sponsors were in the suite, as were his wife Catherine and their daughter Glynn, who were happily serving as congenial hosts for this gang of mostly strangers. They were accustomed to such duty and actually enjoyed serving up their own Southern hospitality. Although the caterers were busy putting out a huge spread of food and drink, Catherine had made biscuits and fried chicken in the condo kitchen and Glynn had brought several of her homemade pecan pies from her home across town. As she sliced up the pies for all takers, Glynn told everyone who would listen, though, that she would much prefer to be down there in one of those cars on the track.

One of the guests in the suite was the head of sports marketing for Jodell's primary sponsor and he and the Ensoft crowd were immediately talking business. As Toby remarked again about how impressed he was with the size of the crowd for a Grand National race, the sponsor rep assured him this was typical, that the numbers Billy had supplied him about attendance at racing events were right on.

Michelle moved over to the windows that looked out over the track and watched intently as the crews began to assemble along the pit road, getting set for the national anthem. The cars were lined up and some of the drivers were already getting buckled in. The rest of the guests in the suite sensed the beginning of the race was near and gravitated over to the seats that ran along the window, settling in for the start.

Back down in the pits, Rob was standing talking quietly with some of the crew when he noticed Billy, Will, Jodell Lee, and Bubba Baxter huddled up, talking intently about something. He wondered if Jodell was looking for advice on his own problems, or if Will and Billy were getting some last minute ideas from Jodell and Bubba. With all their experience, there were few situations they had not encountered, and especially here at Charlotte. He knew Jodell could likely drive this track at speed blindfolded.

When Will finally left the confab and walked over to pat Rob on the shoulder, he gave no hint of what valuable tips he may have gleaned from the other men.

"Let's load 'em up, partner. We got us a race to win."

"It's about ·time!" Rob paused for a moment then looked Will in the eye. "Thanks again for the talk last night. I really do appreciate it."

"Don't mention it. Now listen, you run this race real smart and we can beat these other ·young 'uns and the Cup boys and wind up in Victory Lane."

As Rob buckled in, Will recounted the planned sequence for the pit stops one more time. After Rob had taped in the radio earplugs, they continued on the voice channel, checking the sound and signal. With a rookie driver, the radio was a valuable piece of racing equipment.

Just then, one of the television network pit reporters walked up and stuck the microphone in through the open window as the following camera zoomed right in behind for a close-up of the driver.

". . . reporting. I'm here with the Ensoft-sponsored Ford, driven today by young phenomenon Rob Wilder, who set the racing world on its ear when he qualified at Indianapolis Raceway Park in his first attempt at getting into a Grand National race a couple of months ago. He has followed that up with an impressive string of starts, along with a top-five starting spot for today's three-hundred-mile race. Rob, how do you feel about your chances?"

"We feel real good. The car was good in practice and we made a few adjustments this morning that we think will really help us."

"So you feel like you have a good shot at that first win today?" the reporter asked, holding the mike at the bottom of the full-faced driver's helmet.

Rob Wilder's answer was a bit muffled but it came through loud and clear on television sets all over the country, as well as on the set in the condominium where his sponsors listened intently. Even through the tinted visor, his eyes were wide with excitement.

"I don't just think we have a good chance, I think the Ensoft Ford is the car to beat today. If I can run a smart race and stay out of trouble then we'll be talking later this afternoon in Victory Lane."

The reporter pulled the microphone back to his own lips as the camera panned up to his face, the car big and bold in the background as he strolled away.

"Very confident words from a kid still in the midst of his first season. And that's especially big talk considering he's running against a field of quality drivers, including several today from Winston Cup competition."

Up in the suite, Michelle was squealing with

delight. The network was interviewing their driver and the Ensoft logo on his helmet had been in clear view the entire time. Now, as the reporter moved away, the logo on the car was gleaming prominently on national television. The sports marketing exec quickly estimated that that much network airtime was in the neighborhood of a hundred thousand dollars' worth of ad time. And they had not even run a lap yet.

Rob Wilder's confidence had also caught the attention of the TBS crew that was announcing the race from the booth. He was definitely a driver to watch, they said, along with Atwood, Dale Jr., and a couple of other young drivers, and they told the audience they would be doing just that all afternoon, keeping cameras on those youngsters and commenting on their performances.

"Gentleman, start your engines," came the call.

Rob flipped the starter switch while Will talked to him on the radio.

"Okay, remember to check those temps carefully as she warms up."

"Got you. Everything is looking good. Real good."

"Okay, kid. Good luck."

The last words were Billy Winton's, getting in the last good wishes as the cars began to roll off pit road.

The radio fell silent then as the field of cars moved off behind the pace car for the start of the parade lap. Rob pulled into his place in line as the field slowly made its way around the track. The better than one hundred thousand fans were all standing on their feet, cheering wildly as the field passed in front of them. They were ready to finally see some racing.

Rob watched the gauges carefully as the temperatures in the engine began to rise, then he swung the car back and forth to keep the tires clean. He did not want to risk tearing off down into the first turn with tires that would not hold traction. That was no place to go skating!

Now, as the field passed along in front of the different sections of the grandstands, the thunder of the forty-plus engines seemed to accumulate and increase accordingly, rumbling, echoing, filling the entire giant speedway with their din.

Then the lights went off on the top of the pace car, signaling one lap to go before the throwing of the green flag. Coming down the backstretch, the cars began to tighten up, running within inches of each other, side by side, nose to tail. The field ran slowly through turns three and four, their drivers straining to try to see the green flag held high in the hand of the starter.

In seconds, the field would be set loose, every man trying to spur his racecar to the front, to claim the glory of the victory at Charlotte. But not a one of them wanted it any worse than the blond-haired kid in the sparkling, bright-red Ford. And not a one of them was any more certain than he that he could take it.

THE RUN

·

Go! Go! Go! Go!" the spotter yelled emphatically

Rob had just stretched his arms one last time before tightening his grip for the start. Now, the words hammering into his ears, he jammed the accelerator down to the floor. He and the cars around him raced off two by two toward the start/finish line, the deafening barrage of over three dozen powerful engines painfully loud.

The thunder gently vibrated the windows of the condominiums that watched over the first turn. Toby Warren sucked in his breath as the cars flashed by that first time and almost forgot to breathe again when they powered off into the second turn and the backstretch. It seemed he could feel the quake all the way down to his very soul, and he knew his heart was pounding, his pulse racing, and he felt tears welling in his eyes. He had never experienced anything like it before. He knew he would have a difficult time explaining it, but he sensed that the sensation he experienced as he was seeing, feeling, smelling, tasting, and hearing the power of those collective beasts down there when they were sprung loose was something basic and primal.

Even though she had watched plenty of practice sessions over the last couple of days, Michelle Fagan was not prepared for the noise and speed of the charge of the entire field into the turn so close to where she stood. She seemed to tingle all over as she stood on the balls of her feet and cheered Rob on as he jockeyed for position down the backstretch and into turn three.

Inside the car, Rob had immediately gone to work, settling his scampering pulse and concentrating on keeping the car down on the inside. He kept his front bumper tucked up tightly on the back bumper of the car directly in front of him. He even gave the Chevrolet a slight nudge in the rear as the car began to set up for the run through turn three. Mostly running side by side, the cars raced for position on the first lap with only the leaders being able to break out into a single-file line.

Rob's car bounced around beneath him, buffeted by the turbulence kicked up by all the others that were racing around him. He wrestled with the steering wheel, stubbornly holding the speeding racecar down close to the white line on the inside of the track.

The field thundered out of turn four, flying past the long front stretch grandstand for the first time at full racing speed. The fans, still on their feet from the start, cheered wildly as the giant pack of cars, seemingly inches apart, raced by as if they were all chained together.

Rob was already taking a look down to the inside of the car in front of him as they approached the start/finish line. The car's driver seemed to sense Rob's interest and slyly moved downward, blocking his path. Rob thought better of trying to push his way past at that very moment. There would be another chance directly.

"Patience. Be smart. You have all afternoon."

Will's words ran through his head as loudly and clearly as the pounding sound of the race engines all around him. He tucked back in behind the car in front of him and used the time to feel out his own car, to see how she rode at this early stage of the race.

Diving through turn one, he could feel the car kick up slightly, almost nudging the side door panel of the car running on his outside. Rob held tightly to the wheel, fighting to keep the racer under him. Just then, the car on the outside bounced down slightly and the two cars rubbed together, their contact signaled by a quick puff of smoke where Rob's right tire left a black mark across the number on the door of the other car.

High on the roof of the grandstand, the spotter saw the cars bump and held his breath, fully expecting the two of them to spin directly in the path of the bulk of the field. But Rob cracked the throttle just a bit to keep control of the car. Then, when he knew he had her gathered up underneath him, he accelerated once again and chased after the leaders. But with even that slightest of slowdowns, two cars behind his were able to slip by low on the inside and get past him.

Rob cursed his carelessness, fighting all the while to maintain his focus. The high speeds, the closeness of the racing, the vibration rolling up his legs from the floorboard all tried to steal away his concentration. He knew that the slightest lapse could instantly send him some place he didn't want to go.

Finally, the field settled down, the laps beginning to roll off, and Rob held on to a spot just outside the top ten. He was disappointed but others were taking notice. Up in the television broadcast booth, the announcer crew had called his name several times already. Then, even as the commentators were talking about him once again, Rob noticed that the car's handling had gotten better with each lap and he dived down low once again, trying to take a run at the tenth-place car.

"This kid out of Alabama is having a phenomenal run here today in the early going," the lead announcer was saying.

"He certainly is. He's showing poise out there you'd only expect to see in one of the far more experienced drivers on the circuit," the commentator echoed. "Looks like he wants back into that top ten again."

Right on cue, Rob easily set up and swept by the tenth-place car. As soon as he had made the pass, he heard Will's measured, reassuring voice on the radio.

"That's the way to make the move. The car's starting to come around just the way we planned. You're running the same speed as the leader. Patience. Remember, we've got all afternoon."

"Ten-four," was all the reply Rob allowed himself as he quickly punched and released the mike button on the edge of the steering wheel.

Next up was a car being driven by one of the Cup drivers interloping in the crowded field. The traffic was beginning to string out now and Rob was able to run his own preferred line as he quickly closed in on the car and set up to take away the position from him.

Toby Warren had not taken a seat yet since the start. He watched intently as each lap played out below him, trying to take in everything happening all at once on the track. It was like watching a three-ring circus without missing a single trick.

Michelle had given up even trying. She focused on the red Ford as Rob Wilder guided it around through the traffic. When he had rubbed shoulders with the other car early in the race, she had closed her eyes, certain he was about to crash, then get hammered by all the other racecars that were charging up behind him. But when she opened them again, the cars were already exiting the corner heading on to the backstretch as if nothing had happened at all.

She glanced over at Toby to see his reaction but he was locked on the track, drinking in the high-speed spectacle, a slight smile on his face and his eyes wide. She looked back to where Rob was already dashing out of the fourth turn, then she crossed her fingers, shifted nervously in the seat, and grinned broadly. Out of the corner of her eye, she caught a glimpse of Catherine Lee, her host. When Michelle looked over at her, she winked and mouthed the words, "You're hooked, honey."

And it was true. This was certainly the most exciting thing she had ever been a part of.

It was only a matter of time before a couple of racers in the back of the field tangled in a smokey crash. Michelle had just watched Rob roar by in front of her a moment before. The wrecked cars bumped together just before both lost it. They then seemed to slide along in slow motion, enjoined tightly, even though all logic told her they had just been traveling at over one hundred eighty miles per hour. It was shocking how hard they slammed into the wall together, then broke away from their firm embrace and spun off in different directions.

The suddenness of the wreck had caught her off guard. A solid, heavy boom echoed across the raceway and up to the open window of the condo when the cars struck the wall, and the squalling of their tires sounded like a prolonged scream. Then, as they pirouetted back off the wall, several more trailing cars found themselves caught up in the melee despite their best efforts. Parts, pieces, and showers of sparks flew from the spinning fray as smoke shrouded the whole scene, even as more cars piled into the cloud of white tire smoke. Then the breeze pushed away enough of the dust and smoke so other cars in the back of the field could slow and thread their way through the junkyard that had once been a perfectly good track full of racecars, then make their way on to the start/finish line to take the caution flag.

"Cool!" Toby exclaimed as the first of the damaged cars that were able to move began to limp away from the wreck scene. "That was totally awesome!"

Of course, he knew Rob had been well in front of the wreck, and that allowed him to watch the excitement without worrying about his driver. And it was clear, too, that he had no idea of the danger inherent in such high-speed crashes.

"I hope nobody is hurt," Michelle said, straining in her seat to try to get a better view of the wrecked cars. A bright tongue of flame licked out from beneath the crumpled front end of one of the cars.

"He's on fire!" she blurted, a hint of panic in her voice. She watched then as the driver came scrambling out the window and ran away from the car.

"Honey, he's okay," Catherine Lee told her and put a hand on her shoulder. "If they can get out and scramble like that, they're usually fine. It's when they don't get out or drop the window net . . ." She left the rest unsaid.

"I didn't realize things happened that fast or that bad. You see them on television and everything seems so slow, like a fender-bender on the freeway."

"It happens a couple of times a race. That's what a lot of these fans come to watch. If they don't see a good wreck or two then they don't think they got their money's worth."

"But someone could get hurt and they're all cheering. That seems a little like the Christians and the lions to me," Michelle remarked. And sure enough, many in the big crowd were still standing, cheering wildly as the rest of the drivers slowly crawled from their damaged machines and surveyed the mayhem they had been a part of.

"Oh, they're cheering for the right reason now, because the drivers are getting out of their cars and it looks like everybody is alright. That's their way of showing their appreciation that everybody came out okay."

The caution flag had come at an especially opportune time for the Winton team. With the longer run, the handling on the car had continued to improve; but even so, Will wanted to make an air pressure adjustment on the tires to try and free up the car just a tad more in the corners. Rob had a solid top-ten run going already. Will knew that with a little luck and the right tweaking on the car they could likely drive right up there to the front and contend for the win.

"Okay guys, we're taking a pound of air pressure out of the right side and adding a half round of wedge in the rear. Four tires and gas. Got it?" Will barked the orders over the radio to the rest of the crew as they lined the wall, poised, waiting for the cars to come around the track once more behind the flashing lights of the pace car. He repeated the key point for Rob's benefit. "Cowboy, we're taking on four tires and gas. Watch for the signboard coming in and don't overshoot the pit, whatever you do."

"Ten-four."

Rob held his hand out the edge of the window netting, trying to direct some fresh air into the overheated cockpit of the racecar.

"Be easy now, watch your pit speed," Will advised.

Up in the condo, some of the more experienced in the assembly explained to Toby and the rest of the Ensoft people what the radio transmissions meant, and that there was actually a speed limit for the cars once they entered the pit road. There was a tough penalty for speeding, claimed in the form of track position, not as a traffic ticket.

Then the cars came off the banking and onto the stretch of asphalt transitioning down onto the pit lane. Since the cars had no speedometers, the drivers had to use the tachometer to gauge how fast they were going, matching the RPMs to the known speeds they had set on their tachometers in the warm-up laps behind the pace car at the start.

Rob Wilder shifted up into third gear and followed the cars in front of him down pit road. The long line of waving, wiggling signboards that swam in front of him made it almost impossible for him to pick out his own little sliver of pit real estate. The voice of the spotter on the radio, watching from his perch on the rooftop high over the speedway, helped him determine where the pit was until he could finally catch a glimpse of the sign with his number on it. He steered the Ford into the space and brought her to a smooth stop with only the trace of a skid.

While he was still two stalls away from turning into his own pit, the crewmembers hopped over the low cement wall and got ready to start working as soon as the car slid to a stop. Donnie Kline shoved the jack beneath the car and gave the handle two hard pumps. The right side of the Ford was immediately lifted high in the air, ready for the tires to be removed and replaced. The front and rear tire changers were veterans of Jodell Lee's crew who had volunteered to help them out. With a shrill whir from their air guns, they attacked the lug nuts that held on the wheels, loosening them even before the wheels had been lifted off the pavement. The spinning lug nuts flew off in every direction, flying away like a swarm of angry bees. The worn tires were tossed out of the way and the fresh new tires, their paper stickers still stuck on their surface, were hoisted up on the lug bolts and held in place by the tire carriers. In rapid sequence, the lugs were tightened down and Donnie dropped the jack so the new rubber was on the ground. In one smooth motion, he slung the jack around to the left side of the car, the changers right with him, and they repeated the whole fast-motion waltz on that side.

The gasman was already finished with the first can of gas he had been emptying into the spout at the left rear of the car. Next, he heaved the second eleven-gallon can up to the filler spout and held it in place. The fuel rushed into the tank in seconds, splashing out the overflow where a man holding a small container, the catch-can man, signaled that the tank was full.

Just then, the tire changers were finishing up with the lug nuts on the left side of the car. Rob sat there, patiently waiting for the crew to finish the stop, taking deep swigs of water from the drink bottle that had been handed through the window to him on the end of a long pole. Just in front of his face, another long pole with a squeegee on the end was being used to reach from across the pit wall and clean the windshield. There were limits on the number of crewmen who could cross the wall and nobody wanted to waste a body on windshield cleaning or drink delivery.

Rob tossed the water bottle out the open window to the ground just as he felt the car drop on the jack. He already had the car in first gear, his foot on the clutch and gas pedal, ready to take off the instant the servicing was finished.

"Go! Go! Go!" came the cry of Will Hughes over the radio.

But Rob hardly needed the prompting. He was already taking off, all the while being careful to remember his pre-race instructions to take it easy on the clutch as he left the stall, trying not to spin the tires and risk breaking an axle or ripping the clutch out of the car. Overeagerness leaving the pits had ended the day for many a good driver.

The nineteen-second pit stop hardly gave Rob time to catch his breath, let alone collect his thoughts. Only as he blended back into the line of racecars on the track did he allow his brain to slip out of gear, to try to bring everything back into focus. But he also noticed that it was powerfully hot inside the car. His body was bathed in sweat and his muscles now ached where he was bound by the contour of the seat and the tight safety belts. He stretched his arms and twisted his neck, trying to work out some of the stiffness. The stench of burned oil, fresh paint, and hot rubber filled the cockpit of the racecar. He never noticed that, either, during the height of battle. Only in the few down moments was he aware of the discomforts, the powerful smells, how loud all the engines were around him.

He exited the pits in thirteenth position, two spots back from where he had been when the caution flag came out. A couple of cars had decided they only needed to put on two tires so they had made it out of the pits ahead of him. But Rob was confident he could get those spots back. And more, too. Should they get a long, green-flag run to the end of the race, he was confident they would be there, ready to make a run for the win. More wrecks could scramble the field, though, and make it difficult to gain ground. But even as hot and uncomfortable as he was, Rob grinned behind the helmet's tinted visor. To be this far into the race and still have the leaders clearly in sight was a truly wonderful feeling. And it made the temperature and fatigue easy to dismiss.

"One more to go before the restart. Green the next time around. Remember what we talked about. Pick 'em off one at a time and use your head. You got the car to get you there so no cause to try to win the race in the next few laps."

Rob knew what he had to do without Will having to tell him. And Will knew he knew. But both men felt better if the reminders were passed along anyway.

"Ten-four. Just give me the interval times and the lap times occasionally so I'll know where we stand."

"No problem. Now show those cats up front what you can do."

They were set now, still in contention to win this race. There should be more than enough time for the car's handling to once again come to them. And if the changes they had made during the stop worked, then those Cup boys up front had better keep checking their mirrors—Rob Wilder would be coming, and coming in one big hurry.

In the television booth, the announcers were still telling their audience about the kid and his remarkable staying power. He had been in or near the top ten all day long. To have such a good race here at Charlotte, a track he had never raced before, and to remain in contention in such a competitive field made up of both Winston Cup and veteran Grand National regulars was even more impressive.

"This Wilder kid is doing a superb job today. This run will definitely make people sit up and take notice of this youngster out of Huntsville, Alabama."

"You're right there. If Wilder can hang on and get a top-ten finish then it could really make him another one of the young guns to watch. And attract a lot of attention in the Cup garage from owners and crew chiefs alike."

"Well, I know you've heard the rumors running around the garage that have Ensoft coming on board as the sponsor for the full season next year. And if that's true, this team would likely be planning on running the entire circuit."

"If they do, this team, with its crew chief, Will Hughes, and this talented new driver . . . well, they could be a real force to be reckoned with."

"Well, even with the impressive run so far for Wilder, the kid is still going to have to hang on and out-drive some very tough competition to get himself a top-ten finish here today."

Billy Winton and Jodell Lee stood together behind the pit wall, watching the kid run. With the caution flag, they watched the stop then walked over and climbed to the top of the Lee team hauler. Bubba Baxter and Joe Banker were there already, watching the kid but also seeing how most all the cars handled out on the track. They had their own race to try to run the next day. Joe timed the laps Wilder was running while Bubba used his practiced eye to study the kid's moves.

"Well, whattaya think?" Jodell asked as he reached the top of the platform.

Joe consulted his clipboard for a second before he answered.

"When he's racing on his own, running in clean air away from traffic, he drives about as consistent a lap as I've ever seen here."

"Shoot, he looks exactly like you did, Joe Dee," Bubba Baxter added. He wasn't necessarily extending a compliment. He was simply stating the truth as he saw it.

"He's good but he's also smart," Jodell said. "Lots of folks can drive fast but he knows his equipment and knows how to take care of it. That's precisely the kind of driving we need tomorrow."

Down on the track, Rob was closing in on one of the cars that had gotten ahead of him with the shorter pit stop. He was already lining up for the pass.

Banker did some quick calculations on his clipboard and consulted the stopwatch on the next lap.

"He's gaining but I don't know if there's enough laps left. A lot depends on how he catches the traffic. If the leader falls off a little bit more, it could get interesting."

Rob had already claimed eighth position as they talked about him, but he was only a couple of car lengths off the rear of the sixth- and seventh-place cars, which where racing for position in front of him.

Unbeknownst to them, the television camera panning the speedway had zeroed in on the four men standing on top of the truck. It zoomed in closer and the color commentator told the viewers who they were watching.

"Folks, you are looking at the brain trust behind one of the top teams in racing back in the seventies and early eighties. You don't catch them all together like that much anymore. But that quartet right there has more wins under their belts than any team in racing history after the Pettys, the Wood Brothers, and Junior Johnson."

The announcer picked right up on the thought.

"That is quite a collection of racing knowledge, alright. You have to wonder what they're having such an intense discussion about, though. Billy Winton and his phenomenal young driver, Rob Wilder, who's putting on a show for us today? Or maybe what they're gonna do tomorrow with the Lee Racing car since they have themselves an injured driver."

"It's a crucial decision Lee and his team has to make. With the tight battle for the last couple of top-ten spots in the points you know there has to be a lot of concern up on top of that truck."

"I would say so. The word is they'll be lucky if Rex Lawford can even start the race. Any word on who they might be looking to use as a relief driver?"

"We've heard the names of some of the workhorses . . . guys like Dick Trickle or Morgan Shepherd. Or maybe one of these Grand National drivers . . . Lajoie, Sawyer, or Bodine . . . one of the guys who's driven a good bit in Winston Cup. You wonder why it's so important for Jodell Lee to get a good finish tomorrow? Tenth place in the points means a spot on the stage in New York City for the championship banquet in December, and it's been a long time since Jodell or one of his drivers wasn't up there."

The lead announcer shuffled his script, ready to throw the cue for a commercial break.

"Well, that's a story we'll continue to watch for you . . ."

But then the color commentator had a sudden thought. He interrupted the cue to express it.

"Well, I'll tell you what. For my money, the way this Wilder kid has been running around this place today, I'd be hustling him over to the Cup garage as soon as this race is over and getting him ready for the happy hour practice."

The announcer shot him a sideways glance, a questioning look, then realized the man was onto something.

"I believe that might not be a bad idea at all," he said. "Not a bad idea at all. Now, let's take this break with our leader . . ."

The sixth-place car was being driven by a veteran Cup driver and he was getting all he wanted from another one of the up-and-coming Grand National stars. The Ford running in seventh had managed to pull alongside him several times but could not complete the pass. Meanwhile, the Cup driver was using a considerable horsepower advantage in his motor to hold off the better-handling car that would put him down a spot if he only could.

Rob drove his own Ford right up on the back end of the two cars in front of him just as the challenger put a fender alongside the sixth-place car coming off of turn two. Rob tucked in tight and tried to help push the other Ford on past the sixth place white car but they couldn't seem to get enough extra speed to complete the pass. There was nowhere for Rob to go. He was forced to be patient, to content himself with riding along behind the other two cars until he got an opening to pass.

The next time around, the Ford in front of Rob got another good run in the corner and actually pulled up beside the white car as they exited the fourth corner. For a fleeting moment, Rob looked to the inside of both of them, wondering if he could make it three wide down the front stretch. But then he thought better of it. Patience! He could almost feel Will's words rattling around inside his helmet.

Up on the truck Joe Banker could see what was happening with his stopwatch as well as he could with his eyes. The two slower cars racing side by side were blocking the kid, holding him back. With the laps winding down, Wilder needed to get by quickly or any shot at a victory would soon vanish. The kid clearly had the faster car but he needed to make his move or that wouldn't matter at all.

In the pits, Will had come to the same conclusion. There were not enough laps left for his driver to stay mired down behind these two cars. They had the fastest car on the track by now, but they would soon run out of laps to take advantage of it. He hesitated for only an instant before he pulled the microphone closer to his lips.

"Cowboy, it's time to throw caution out the window. You've got the fastest car on the track. I reckon it's time to use it," Will radioed.

Rob heard the words crackle in his ears but he didn't respond. He had his hands full of jerking steering wheel as he concentrated hard on the two cars in front of him. With the slightest bobble by either driver he was ready to pounce. The time had come for him to show them all that he had what it took to be a winner.

"Fifteen to go!"

The call came from the spotter as Rob crossed the stripe at the start/finish line. Fifteen laps. That's all he had left to work with.

Looking all the way through the windshield of the car in front of him he could see the leader just entering the center of turn one. Right then, it might as well have been ten miles ahead.

He maneuvered the nose of his racer until he was able to get a fender up alongside the inside car, making them three wide down the short chute on the front stretch, heading toward turn one. Rob almost willed the car forward, trying to push his foot clean through the floorboard and on into the engine compartment beyond.

The three cars thundered toward turn one, each of them knowing no more than two could come out the other side in tandem. Rob edged ahead of the car in the middle by a nose but the car on the outside stayed even with him. There was nowhere near enough room for three-wide racing.

Something, somebody, was going to have to give. But none of the three drivers seemed willing to lift off his throttle and allow the other two to gain the advantage.

Rob gritted his teeth and stiffened his grip on the wheel as the steep banking of the corner rushed toward them at over a hundred eighty miles an hour. He and the other Ford touched briefly, each rear end wiggled dangerously, a tire spinning against sheet metal, sending up a tell-tale puff of smoke as they bounced around heading into the corner. They were both on the ragged edge, each in real danger of breaking loose and scattering all over the track.

At the last instant, even as a crash seemed inevi-

table, the driver in the middle finally broke and
backed out, leaving Rob and the Cup driver still racing for the position all the way through the turn.

Michelle sat watching the duel, her hands covering
her mouth to suppress an inevitable scream. By now,
she had picked up enough from the others in the suite
to know that Rob was having a super race but that
he needed to get by the other two cars to have any
chance at a better finish. As they came off the turn,
she watched in disbelief as he dove down to the inside
of the other cars, almost putting the car in the grass
as he tried to power his way past them.

But anyone could see that there wasn't enough
room for all three of them to stay side by side at that
speed once they got to the steep-banked turn directly
below where she sat. They were obviously heading for
a gigantic accident, one much worse than the one they
had already witnessed, and it was going to play out
so close she almost felt she could reach out and touch
it.

She could hear Toby pleading for Rob to pull on
ahead and pass the cars, yelling as if he could actually
hear him out there. Out of the corner of her eye she
could see him, standing, dancing, pumping his fist,
cheering Rob on, but she didn't dare take her eyes
off the three-way battle going on out there.

Then the center car backed out slightly, allowing
Rob to pull out ahead of the Ford and claim the spot.

Having the preferred line down the inside of the
track allowed Rob to clear the other white car completely going through turn two. As he exited the corner, Rob pushed out to the wall, completing the pass.
He quickly pulled away down the back straightaway,
putting the surprised Cup driver behind him, and set
his sights on the next car, the driver running in fifth

place. That racer sat twenty or so car lengths in front of him, but now, with nothing but clear track between them, he closed fast.

He had no trouble taking that car, making the pass as he whipped down the front straightway, then crossed the line as the flagman showed him there were ten laps to go. Now, he could see up ahead that the second-, third-, and fourth-place cars were battling for position while the leader ran on ahead, at least a second and a half ahead of the pack.

Rob forced himself to forget about him for the time being. He concentrated on running as smoothly as he could, to try everything he could do to catch the next pack of cars.

Back in the pits, Will finally admitted to himself that time was running out on them. It would take a mammoth effort for them to catch the pack that was running behind the leader, and even if Rob could manage that, then there was no way they could hope to run down the leader. That would take a miracle.

Oh well. At least they had a shot at improving their finish, at maybe making top three, and that would be quite an accomplishment for this team, for his driver.

Will counted down the laps for Rob. He hesitated doing it because he didn't want to distract his young driver, but he knew he needed Rob pedaling as hard as he could if he had any hope of catching and getting around those next three cars. The red Ford was plenty fast enough and Rob had already shown he had the talent to get it up there, but it appeared the race was going to be a few laps too short for them. A maddening few laps too short.

But then, the crowd suddenly stood and gave a huge, mass groan. Diving into the first turn with only seven laps remaining, the leader had suddenly slowed noticeably and veered down to the low part of the track. The back end of the car wobbled noticeably. Will's eyes darted to the television set that rested on top of one of the toolboxes. The close-up of the leader was already up and he could see that the right rear tire on the car was flat.

And then the TV showed a picture of the three-car pack blowing past the fallen leader on the outside. Then there, almost a part of that bunch already, was his car. Will Hughes felt a tidal wave of emotion sweep over him. Instead of racing for second, they were now, suddenly, racing for the win. All eyes at the speedway were looked on the four-car battle for the victory. .

Rob had not noticed the leader slowing, nor did Will or the spotter call his attention to it. They wanted his eyes on the single-file line of cars with which he was now racing. The second car in line quickly decided to make his move coming out of turn four. Approaching the stripe, the Chevrolet had pulled down to the inside to make the pass. The third place car behind him looked as if he was going to follow but suddenly changed his mind and tucked back in tightly on the rear bumper of the car in front of him.

Then Rob sensed a sliver of an opening and he pounced on it, pulling down to the inside of the indecisive driver and right up on the rear bumper of the Chevrolet as its driver tried to ease past the new leader. He managed to get out ahead by a nose at the stripe.

Rob Wilder knew his car was faster and, for an instant, he debated jumping on down to the inside of the Chevrolet, making it three wide. But before Will could even caution him on the radio, he thought better of it and stayed put, directly behind.

The four cars raced two by two down into turn one. The crowd in the grandstands was in a frenzy. Everyone was standing, cheering, waiting to see who would pull out the victory over these final frantic laps. Everyone in Jodell Lee's condo was on his or her feet, too, hoarse but screaming anyway.

Still in double file, the cars came off turn two and on to the backstretch. Rob went to his horsepower, trying to use the power in his engine to try to dart down to the inside. The Chevrolet sidled downward to effectively block him, though. That forced Rob to back off and pull back in line behind him.

"A Slick Wilson move, huh?" Rob whispered. He had seen it many times back home when he had held together long enough to actually challenge the local hotshot. And now, Rob Wilder grinned as he remembered how he had once overcome the blocking move when it was used against him back there on that small track.

Would it work here? Did he have the guts to try it?

As Rob pulled back in line, he gave the Chevy a slight tap in the rear end to let him know he was still there and that he didn't appreciate being cut off. The Cup driver at the wheel of that car didn't even seem to notice the touch.

As the cars went through turns three and four again, Rob once more moved down to the inside just as he had done before. And once more, the Chevy mirrored him, blocking him again from making it three wide.

But as the Chevy tried to stay in front of Rob, it allowed the Ford running on the outside to pull ahead by almost a full car length. Next, Rob swung high, this time sending a clear message that he was now going to try to pass on the outside. The Chevy, the driver's eyes squinting in the rearview mirror, kicked back up to keep that from happening.

But suddenly, Rob yanked the wheel to the left and used his momentum to get a good jump to the inside. He sailed right on past the surprised Chevy driver, almost clearing him completely as they raced down toward turn one. But snookered or not, the Cup driver was too savvy to give up that easily. None of the four drivers offered to give an inch as they raced into the first turn. In fact, the Ford, running on the outside, found enough extra momentum to push past and take the lead.

Rob tried to pull even with him as he finally cleared the Chevy. They sailed through turn two but he could only get the nose of the car even with the rear fender. And all along, he knew any bobble might take all four of them out of the race and give it to someone so far back they weren't even in the race at the moment. Or at the very least, it would give the other two drivers an opening to get back ahead of him.

For the first time in Rob's young Grand National career, he could see nothing but open track in front of him. He simply had to get past the Ford that was still running a half car length ahead on the outside and the lead would be totally his.

Rob tried to stay in the gas a bit longer, driving the car deeper into the corner. As he did, the other car ran high, up toward the wall, and that gave Rob plenty of room to go ahead and take the lead all for himself.

But then, with a plunge in his stomach, he realized that he had pushed the car a bit too deep and he felt the back end start to wiggle slightly. He backed off only slightly but it was enough to allow the other two cars to pull right back up on his rear end. And the Ford he'd been racing with, that he had been trying to get ahead of, now had a car length's lead on him.

Rob cursed his rookie mistake but he kept driving. He pulled downward again, trying to get a run on the leader as they came down to the stripe again.

Two laps to go.

Rob closed right back up on the Ford going into turn one. The wheel jerked wildly in his hands as he tried to hold the car down as close to the white line as physically possible. He got back into the throttle, trying to use the draft off the leader's car to help propel him past as they headed down the straightaway.

Rob swung wide as the car hit the flat of the straight stretch of track, then he was able to pull even midway through, lining up beside the Ford as both cars raced hard for the turn. Finally, he pushed the nose out in front, and he was actually leading a Grand National race. But he hardly had time to enjoy the moment. He was still racing with the other driver into turn three and had no firm hold on the position at all.

Then Rob pulled cleanly into the lead as the cars hit the corner. But in the process, his momentum carried him high as they barreled into the center of the turn. And the Ford he had just passed seized the opportunity, diving down low, duplicating a move all but patented by Dale Earnhardt over the years.

The Ford shot back around Rob as if he was backing up.

Will sat on top of the toolbox watching the TV monitor. When he saw Rob pull down to the inside to make his move, he felt sure that he could take the other Ford this time. But whether he could hold him off for another lap and a half or not would be another story.

Will could feel his heart racing as, sure enough, Rob took over the lead. He pumped his fist in the air and allowed a quick whoop to escape his lips as he saw his car power out front. But his joy was short-lived. He saw it coming when their red Ensoft Ford pushed up in the center of the corner. And his fears were confirmed as the car they had just passed quickly dived low, driving underneath Rob and retaking the lead.

Will settled back and watched Rob pull back in behind the leader. But he knew the race was over unless the leader made a big mistake or his car broke. Neither was very likely over the final white-flag lap.

High in the suite, the group that had been watching the race below was gripped with excitement. The tight battle for the lead over the last several laps left all of them breathless, nerves on edge. When Rob made the move, with a few laps to go, to run side by side for the lead, a huge cheer erupted throughout the suite.

Michelle was now unashamedly chewing nervously on her nails as she watched the finish unfold. Watching a big-time stock car race was exactly like riding a roller coaster over and over and over. Only far noisier. And clearly, way more dangerous.

Rob chased hard, desperately, after the leader. He ached all over, he wanted so badly to somehow push the car past its limits and retake the lead. The tiny taste of leading he had experienced had only left him hungry for more. Once he had been up front with a real shot at winning, it was not something he would give up easily.

But he shoved those thoughts aside and drove,

somehow managing to close the gap back to the leader yet again.

The kid made a split-second decision to make one last try down the backstretch. But he knew, too, that he had to protect his second place position as much as he possibly could. They had put together too great a day to put the car into the fence on the last turn of the last lap, a phenomenal finish all but guaranteed.

But he was a racer. He would give it his best shot and see what unfolded.

The two went through turns one and two for the last time with Rob glued right on the back bumper of the leader. He tracked the car through the corner, but, with tires worn and the track slick, he had to use every bit of strength he could still muster. He cut down to the inside trying to get a run down the back straightaway, but once more the leader moved over to block him. Rob anticipated the move and cut sharply to the outside.

He hoped he had enough horses left in the engine to pull even, enough tread on the tires so they would stick to the track until he could get this afternoon's race won. Down the backstretch they went with Rob able to once more get a fender up alongside the leader. Going into the turn, Rob was able to use the banking to his advantage and pull up beside the door of the leader running on the inside. There was clear track in front of them as they raced through the corner for the final time and headed down to take the checkered flag.

Rob tried to use the steep banking to keep his RPMs up and once again eased up beside the other Ford, but the car that rode along below him on the track was following the preferred line. The driver politely took that advantage and used his years of experience to hold onto the lead, easily pulling back in front of him as the cars exited the last corner.

Rob dove down off the banking, trying to use the extra momentum to push by on the outside. The cars raced for the finish line with Rob trying desperately to find that last ounce of speed in the car, any kind of extra surge that would propel him back ahead if only for the instant when they passed the line. Like a frantic jockey whipping his horse to the finish, Rob urged the car on.

But even as he gave it all he had, he knew it was futile.

The fans in the stands had not come to that conclusion yet. They still thought the kid had a chance to pull past the veteran driver with a last-second burst of speed. And they had loved every second of these last few laps' pyrotechnics. This was precisely what they had paid their money to witness. And they would be talking about what they had seen for a long time to come.

Only when all four of the cars had flashed beneath the checkered flag did they get out of the gas. Rob gave the winner a wave, a salute for running a good, clean race to the checkers. The veteran returned the signal and gave the kid a hearty thumbs-up. But all the while, Rob Wilder was cursing himself under his breath, still mad at himself for the basic mistake back in turn three that had likely cost him the win.

Second was okay, but not quite as good when you knew you should have won the race.

Rob was still brooding as Will directed him to take the car to the gas pumps for a final check by race officials. As Rob pulled the racecar to a stop, he pounded his fist on the dash. Will pulled the window netting down.

"Whoa, cowboy. Take it easy on my cockpit."

Rob hit the release on the belts, unhooked all the tethers that had tied him to the racecar, and dragged his tired body out the window. He ripped off the driving gloves and disgustedly threw them back inside onto the seat.

"Man, I can't believe how I got suckered out there!"

"Hey, we got second place. We'll take that any day in this league. That was a heck of a run you made out there today."

"A heck of a way to lose," Rob said, shaking his head sadly. "Second place doesn't get a trophy, Will."

He nodded toward victory lane where the winner was standing on the roof of his car accepting the cheers of the crowd that had gathered as he sprayed them all with a shower of shaken-up soda pop.

"You tired?" Will asked.

"Tired? Shoot, I could go another three hundred miles right now I am so frustrated with myself."

"Don't be so hard on yourself. It was a darn good race for us today. You can bet they'll know who we are the next time we get to the track."

"I guess you're right," Rob finally said with a slight smile. "We did put on one whale of a show, didn't we?"

As the crew was pushing the car toward the truck, Billy, Jodell, Bubba, and Joe came walking up.

"Fine job, kid!" Billy shouted with a hearty slap on the back.

"Thanks, Billy. I just wish . . ." he began, but then one of the reporters for the racing radio network stepped in to interview him, and a camera crew or two shoved their way in while several newspaper reporters jockeyed for an opening so they could try to crowbar in a question or two.

Jodell stood there and observed how poised and natural the kid was during the interviews. He, of all people, knew how bittersweet the finish must be for the youngster. A second place at this point in his career was unheard of, an amazing feat. He had accomplished something plenty of drivers on all levels would have given their gas pedal foot for. But it was still second. And in some racer's minds, anything but first place is a loss. No glory in being an also-ran.

The reporters stepped over to interview the proud car owner and get his thoughts. For a rare moment Rob found himself standing there alone with Jodell Lee while Will and the crew were busy packing up. Most everyone else had gone on to find a spot to watch or prepare for the final practice for the Winston Cup cars.

The old driver tossed the youngster a cold, wet towel and then handed him an icy bottle of water.

"You showed them a thing or two today, son. But, unfortunately, you've removed the element of surprise from your arsenal. Won't anybody underestimate you anymore," he said. Jodell had a look on his face like a proud father might wear.

"Thanks, Mr. Lee. But I did remind myself of one thing today."

"What's that?"

"How much I hate anything that does not involve winning." Jodell nodded as the kid took a deep draw on the water, then turned to look at him. "Mr. Lee, I do want to thank you for the confidence you showed in me and for talking with Billy about putting me in his car. I hope I haven't disappointed you. And I don't think there is ever going to be any way I could repay you."

"Not hardly. If you didn't do anything else today, you showed us all that you belong in this car." Jodell Lee stepped closer then and put his hand on the young man's shoulder. He almost whispered the next words. "But now that you mention it, I do need a couple of favors out of you."

"What? Anything! You name it, Mr. Lee. Hand me a wrench!"

"Naw. First, I want you to call me 'Jodell,' not 'Mr. Lee.' "

"Okay . . . Jodell."

"Second thing: What I really need now is for you to practice my car here in happy hour."

A look of disbelief crossed the boy's face. It was as if he was waiting for the punch line of a bad joke.

"What? You serious, Mr. . . . uh, Jodell?"

"I need you to help Bubba and Waylon get the car set up to race. You know it's an untested car and we've got a lot of work to do in a very short time."

"Well, absolutely. Absolutely. I would be honored."

"Good. And there's one more thing I am going to need, kid."

"Shoot."

"If you don't have other plans, I need you to hang around until tomorrow and do a little relief driving for me in the 500. My driver's beat up pretty bad. He's in no shape to do anything but start the car."

Billy Winton had finished the interview and moved back over to join them. He enjoyed immensely the look on the kid's face. He was speechless but the question he was trying to ask was obvious in his eyes when he turned toward Billy.

"Yeah, Robbie, it's okay with me. If you want to, that is," he said.

"I'll be glad to be your relief driver," the kid finally said, his voice surprisingly even and controlled.

"Great! It's settled, then. You better grab your helmet and gloves. They're already pushing the car out to the line."

Rob ran down the 6 car and retrieved his stuff from the seat then took off at a trot for the spot on pit road where Jodell Lee's backup Winston Cup car sat gleaming, ready to take out and test for the big race the next day. But he stopped in the middle of the garage and yelled back to them.

"Thanks for the opportunity, Jodell. You too, Billy. Y'all won't regret it."

Moments later, the television cameras zoomed in on Rob Wilder as he climbed through the window of the Lee Racing Ford. The commentators, near the end of their race wrap-up, paused to take note of the significance of the picture the viewers were seeing on their home screens.

"Looks like our new young gun is going to be doing a little double duty this weekend after all," the announcer said.

"Like we suggested earlier during the race, with the connections between these two teams and the terrific run by this Wilder kid here today, this does not surprise me at all. It'll be very interesting to see how he measures up tomorrow if he actually gets in the car against the best in the business," the color commentator added as the theme music rolled up beneath his voice.

"My bet, after watching him today, is that he'll do just fine."

"I wouldn't bet against him either. That's for sure.

This kid is special. And I suspect we'll be watching him running circles in this game for a long time to come."

The theme music swelled as the camera closely followed Rob Wilder, guiding the Jodell Lee Ford out onto the Charlotte Speedway, already pushing the racecar up through the gears, eagerly seeking speed.

THE OLD DRIVER

*H*e sat in his usual spot, in the director's chair high atop the hauler, watching his crew get the car ready for the 500, a radio headset loosely clinging to his graying head so he could hear the chatter. But this Sunday, he was mostly watching the young driver standing on the edge of the pit wall. The kid was ready to climb into the racecar after his busted-up driver had run the first lap.

The youngster danced from one foot to the other, clearly eager as the field took the green and circled the track that first time. Now, here came the whole pack of cars out of turn four finishing lap one. Then, as planned, the blue Lee Racing Ford peeled off from its spot at the tail end of the field and rolled down pit road toward their stall. With the distinctive signboard marking the spot, the car rolled to a stop with the window net already down. The driver inside flipped the release on the belts and was carefully helped out of the car.

He was clearly in considerable pain but he tried not to limp as he made his way to the shade of one of the toolboxes to rest.

As soon as the hurting driver had cleared the window, Rob Wilder climbed in to take his place. A crewman dived into the passenger-side window to help him hook the belts up and get the radio plugged in. When that was accomplished, another member of the crew bolted the right side window back into place. Waylon Baxter tugged on the belts one last time to make sure they were secure, then he pulled up the window net. Even as he snapped it into place, he was yelling over the radio for the kid to goose it, to go back out there and rejoin the fray.

No one mentioned to the kid that he was already at a distinct disadvantage. The field was now coming off turn four, about to put the car down a second lap as they went roaring past him with a sound akin to a sonic boom.

But Rob Wilder didn't even seem to notice as he concentrated on bringing the car up to speed. He ran up through the gears, steering the car around the apron in the corner, waiting to blend smoothly into the racing groove down the back straightaway. He knew his assignment, to drive intelligently, to finish the car somewhere in the middle of the pack to collect enough points to earn this team a spot on the stage at the Waldorf Astoria in December. All he really had to do was stay out of trouble, steer clear of wrecks, and he would have accomplished his mission.

But as he hit the backstretch and accelerated hard, it finally struck him full force that he had finally arrived, that he was out here on a legendary stretch of track, driving one of the most powerful racing machines on earth, in the middle of some of the most talented racers to inhabit the planet. It would be a strain for him not to push it today, not to race for position when the opportunity ultimately presented itself.

But he wouldn't do that. There would be other days. He now knew there would be plenty of other races, lots of other chances to dive for daylight and steer for the front and claim the victory that was rightfully his, because he had earned it with his skill and strength and perseverance.

And atop the hauler in the Charlotte infield, the old driver settled back in his director's chair and smiled.

He knew exactly what the kid out there in his racecar was thinking.